SHIFTING TIDES

SHIFTING TIDES

DANIELLE FORREST

The Eternal Scribe Publishing
Indianapolis, IN

PRONUNCIATIONS

- Kou - Coo
- Surg - Surge
- Diehli - Day-lee
- Ateles - Ah-tell-ease
- Taln - Talon
- Eirse - Air-see
- Danaus - Duh-nos
- Delyn - Dell-in
- Tesa - Tessa
- Faelee - Fay-lee
- Kaea - Kay-ah
- Mae - May
- Aesa - Ay-sah
- Aella - Ella
- Wesa - Wee-sah
- Tui-tui - too-ee too-ee (Note: tui should be pronounced as one syllable)
- Uso - oo-so
- Usan - yoo-san

DEFINITIONS

- Dicero(s) - about 2 minutes
- Horo(s) - 50 diceros or 1 hour 40 minutes
- Erno(s) - 15 horos or 25 hours
- Morgo(s) - 25 ernos or just over 26 days
- Oxna - work animal on Wesa
- Parush - a communal space, often left empty for flexibility of use.

Jessie smiled at the finished painting on the easel. It was a commission, and it was finally dry enough to deliver. This was always a bittersweet moment, that moment when she gave her art over to someone else. It felt like a part of her was leaving, and while she'd never had the abandonment issues her sister had, it was still a hard thing to do.

"Just think of the look on their faces when you hand it over it," she told herself. "This is joy delivered." She smiled and picked it up. The rough texture of the canvas brushed against her fingertips as she placed it in a bag for transport.

Hefting it over her shoulder, she made for the door and pushed out into the early morning sunlight. It was dimmer than on other worlds she'd been to, and the city cast shadows against the mostly empty walkways. Most people hadn't left work yet, but that was convenient, allowing her to smoothly make her way across the city.

The air had a slight bite to it, just cool enough to send goosebumps prickling across her skin. That, too, was a welcomed experience. It made the morning feel fresh and new, like it was somehow cleaner, clearer, more open to possibilities.

She passed by curved green roofs and brown walls, some with obvious windows, others with windows that blended in, given away only by a shine from the early morning light. As she left the residential area around her apartment, more and more people spilled out onto the walkways between buildings. Soon, it was quite crowded, with voices calling out to each other in a chaotic din that was impossible to understand. English was her first language, Uso her second. Kou had taught her the language of the Ateles, but she would never say she was fluent and picking up words in this crowd would need skills far greater than her own.

Jessie didn't mind, though. She liked just experiencing the sound. It made her feel like she was part of a greater canvas of reality, like she was in the middle of something bigger than herself.

But as much as she liked to revel in the canvas of life, that would have to wait. She spotted the street she was looking for. The street's name was etched onto the side of a building in Usan script. Not the easiest to read, but at least it wasn't in the Ateles language. She hadn't gotten around to learning their writing yet. Uso, on the other hand, was a universal language. It came from some goodie-two-shoes species that had served as ambassador between planets for far longer than humans had been in space.

Having a universal language certainly made things easier for her and other spacefaring individuals.

Jessie turned, slipping onto a far less crowded residential street. She counted off the doors until she spotted the one she was looking for. With a bounce in her step, she knocked.

Someone called out from inside, their voice muffled by the material separating them. Moments later, the door opened to a short Ateles woman with vibrant hair dyed red and a matching dress that flowed around her knees. "Oh, is it here?" she said, clasping her hands together in excitement. Behind her, her tail flicked back and forth, causing her skirt to shift.

"Right here," Jessie said, lifting the bag off her shoulder.

"Oh, come in, come in."

She entered and was hit by a wave of floral scent, both powerful and hard to identify. She couldn't decide if she liked it or not, but she took in a deep breath as she crossed to a table against the right wall, laying the bag out. Opening it, she slid the painting carefully out, laying it overtop the bag.

"Oh my, it's beautiful." The woman looked over at Jessie. "You're so talented. I can't even imagine doing something like this. I think the blank canvas would simply overwhelm me. I just can't see things like this in my head."

"Thank you. And we all have talents. This is just mine." She looked back down at the painting, that hesitancy to leave it behind hitting her once again. "I hope you love it. It's really hard to part with."

"Oh, I'll treasure it." Her client picked up the painting, being careful with what she touched, and held it out at arm's length. "Amazing."

"Well, I should be going."

The woman turned around, lowering the painting to her side. "Yes, thank you. Again."

Jessie nodded and saw herself out.

"Jessie!" an angry voice yelled from down the street.

She flinched. Looking around her for an escape, she found nothing but a mostly empty space with no alleys or crossroads to get lost down. She didn't see a way to avoid this confrontation. She turned her gaze to where Rae was stomping toward her, an exceptionally dark expression on his face.

"You blew me off!" he yelled as he approached.

"I didn't want to talk to you." She shrugged, but somewhere deep, alarm bells were ringing out, screaming at her to get away. There was something crazy going on in his eyes, and she didn't like it.

"So you just turn tail and run in the middle of the market? You made me look bad."

No, you made yourself look bad.

She chose not to say anything.

"And what about that second date you promised me?"

She shook her head. "I never promised you a second date."

"Yes, you did. Don't lie to me."

Jessie rolled her eyes, but anger sparked across his face, causing her to tense and still. "I *didn't* promise you a second date. I didn't say anything. You assumed."

He tensed, like pressure was building within his body and soon he would erupt. Then his gaze lifted up to the door she'd just left.

He exploded. "And who the fuck is this? You slinking back home in the morning like you don't belong with me? You think I'm not going to do something about that?"

"What are you talking about? Are you fucking nuts?" She shook her head and waved her hands. "Forget this. I'm out of here. I can't deal with you right now." She moved to walk around him, having every intention of taking the long way around so she could lose him, when he grabbed her by the arm. His fingers dug in, the claws at his fingertips pricking through her sleeve. She glared at him. "Let. Go."

"Don't think you can just walk away from this, you bitch."

She pointed a finger in his face, channeling her sister. "I will break every finger in that hand. Let go."

His grip lessened but didn't release. Then his demeanor changed, like a curtain dropping over a stage. "Come on now, baby. Don't be like that." His thumb rubbed against her throbbing arm.

"Please, let go." She stared him down, determined to win this contest of wills. She had to.

He released his grip, shifting to rubbing the outsides of her arms. "Come on, Jessie, let's just go somewhere. We could have a nice dinner, maybe some dancing? What do you say?"

How did she attract this nut job? She stood there dumbfounded as he switched from angry to jealous to dangerous to cajoling. She couldn't keep up with his mood swings, and she didn't know what to do. What did you say to a clearly unhinged man who wanted you to follow him to a secondary location?

On the one hand, any woman from Earth knew you never let a guy take you to a secondary location. On the other hand, she was already in a pretty isolated space. She discretely looked around her, but no one had stepped out onto the street since he'd shown up. It was deserted, a perfect place for a kidnapping or murder.

Wonderful.

"Come on," she said, deciding on a plan of action. "I have a place in mind."

"That's my girl."

She walked with him behind her, trying to keep her shoulders relaxed and her breathing calm. She needed to get somewhere that contained people, somewhere she could lose him like she did at the market the other day.

Unfortunately, it was late in the day for the Ateles, and even the market would be winding down by now. But if she could get there soon, there just might be enough people to disappear among.

Hopefully.

She was short, which worked to her advantage, but she was also another species, so she tended to stick out like a sore thumb.

When they reached the market, she let out a sigh of relief. It was still crowded. There were fewer patrons than at the peak of the day, but still enough to bump elbows with. She slipped into the crowd, using her small size to her advantage. With quick movements, she advanced across the market.

Behind her, Rae spoke up. "Hey, slow down."

She ignored him, looking for an out.

"Jessie, are you all right?"

She looked up, spotting the produce vendor, who had an alarmed expression on her face. She rushed up to her. "I need to hide."

The other woman nodded and ushered her behind the table and through a door. "Just stay here. What do I need to look out for?"

"A tall man with a rakish haircut."

She nodded and closed the door behind her.

Jessie leaned against the wall and sagged to the floor with a sigh.

How did I get into this mess?

CHAPTER ONE

The not so distant past...

Jessie had a small apartment and studio on the edge of the city looking out over the wilderness. The trees created an almost impenetrable wall around the city, an evergreen bastion to the prowess of nature. She had an easel set out next to a floor-to-ceiling window so she could paint when she felt inclined. Sometimes, she even packed up some supplies and trekked out into the woods.

It was beautiful and inspiring.

Since the Ateles were nocturnal, in the evenings, she could hear the comings and goings of the locals as they set out to start their day. She would sometimes watch from the window on the opposite side of the apartment as children were ushered off to school and adults moved swiftly to their places of employment.

In moments like that, she often felt separate, detached and alone, even though the people here had been extremely welcoming. They smiled at her as she walked through the streets, greeting her with hearty gestures and calling out her name if they knew her. They respected her talents, and she'd even received a few commissions, supplementing her savings. She could really see herself making a life here.

And that was the goal… to finally start her life. She'd been living on her sister's ship, the *Trojan*, for much of her teenage years, but it had slowly become stifling. Things had always been a bit rough, seeing as her sister had no problem flaunting her sexual escapades, but once Kou had come onto the scene, it became impossible.

Kou was perfect for Cass, the very thing she'd needed to get over the betrayal of their parents abandoning them. But his arrival had also left Jessie feeling like a third wheel, like a constant voyeur to their great romance and adventures.

Turning eighteen and becoming an adult was the final straw, the ultimate reminder that she didn't belong there anymore. She wasn't a kid staying with her guardian. She was an adult, but her sister still saw her as the little girl she'd been and would probably always be in her eyes. Jessie couldn't grow like that. She couldn't come into her own, find her own love and purpose. She needed to find her own place in the universe.

Which was how she'd ended up here a few months back, tearfully hugging her sister and Kou, saying goodbye, and promising to call *every* day. She'd started exploring, experimenting, experiencing. Dating, painting, drawing, or just people watching, she ate it all up, loving every minute of it.

And yet not everything had been so rosy. Most people here were Ateles. They slept by day, and she slept by night. They had family and friends, and she was alone. They blended in, and she felt like an eyesore, a constant physical reminder that she didn't belong. Again.

Did she belong anywhere? Would she ever get everything she truly wanted?

Based on the dating market here, she suspected the answer would be a emphatic no. She'd dated a few men since moving here, but she was never more than a novelty, a fascinating specimen only good enough for a few dates before the male moved on to greener pastures. Each was exotic to her eyes, as striking as Kou in their own ways, but they never saw the same in her. They always seemed to move on without a backward glance.

She sighed and sat down at her window, staring out at the life below, a deep unsettled feeling dragging her down.

Jessie was in a better mood the next morning when she went out to run some errands. She always enjoyed getting out on the streets and among the people, and the market was her favorite place to do so. It was a sea of bodies and movement and color. A cacophony of voices and shuffling feet. Savory scents taunted her nostrils while tantalizing perfumes drifted on the winds. It was sensory overload and ecstasy at once.

She smiled as she entered the mass of people. Victoria would hate this, and her sister would probably act like the space was filled with pickpockets or something. But it was manna to Jessie. It gave her a feeling of connection with the universe. She stepped into the crowd as people jostled her back and forth.

Jessie moved along the edge of the market, close to the shops and stalls. She liked to run a wide circuit and often bought snacks or trinkets along the way, little things that teased her senses, making her smile. She stopped at a food vendor. "One, please," she said, indicating a kebab of meat roasting on the grill.

"Yes, ma'am. Coming right up," the vendor said with a playful flair.

She smiled, both pleased with being called ma'am and with his good-hearted nature, which always made her day. She almost always stopped at his stall, the aroma of his wares drawing her in from all the way down the street. But it was his attitude that ensured she always came back for more.

"Here you go," he said with a smile, handing her the stick.

"Thank you." She took a bite, the juicy, perfectly seasoned meat causing her mouth to water and a moan to escape her lips.

Behind her, he laughed, and she chuckled herself before swallowing and stuffing another bite in her mouth as she moved on. Next, she stopped at a produce vendor. The array of things she didn't recognize never ceased to amaze her.

"Good morning, Jessie," the woman behind the table said. "How can I help you today?"

She pointed out some fruits and vegetables she'd come to enjoy during her stay here, then pointed at an oval purple item she hadn't seen before. "What's that?"

The woman smiled. "I knew you'd ask. It's tui-tui fruit. Just came in season. It's sweet and tart with a juicy center. What do you say? Wanna try?"

"Okay, I'll get it, too."

"That's my girl."

Jessie laughed and handed over her tote so the woman could bag up the purchase.

"Here you go," she said as she carefully ushered the bag over the laden table. "Enjoy!"

"Thanks."

The morning continued on like that until she'd purchased everything she needed, and she moved on to simply wandering and people watching. Small children often cried at the late hour while parents cooed and ushered them into their arms, soothing them into an exhausted sleep against their shoulders. Others yawned, their necks leaning back impossibly far as they stretched, trying to get just a little more energy out of their tired bodies after a long day. For most Ateles, a dark-skinned and dark-furred species adapted heavily for night, an hour approaching midday was exceptionally late, like staying up half the night for a human.

The market had thinned as the sun grew higher in the sky, making it a little too bright for the Ateles' sensitive eyes. With stores closing down and everyone going home to their beds, Jessie stopped at a community bulletin board. There were flyers asking for tutors and laborers. There were swap ads and ads for services. There was an announcement about a community meeting later that week.

Her gaze stopped on a flyer requesting a surrogate. It was such a strange request, one she'd never seen before. It seemed so out of place on the board, and she wondered about its origins. Who had put it there? Was it a member of the community, someone desperate for a family? Maybe they had a birth defect or had suffered an illness or injury. Maybe they were a gay couple hoping to start a family. Her mind whirred with possibilities as she let fancy get the better of her.

"Jessie!" a familiar voice barked behind her.

She immediately tensed, a part of her wanting to run, or maybe to pretend he didn't exist. While everyone had been welcoming, Rae had taken it to a new level. They'd gone on a single date, but she'd immediately known something was off about him. He'd asked her on another date at the end of the first, but she'd hemmed and hawed, slipping out without giving him an answer. She'd been a little afraid of telling him no. Some part of her had *known* he wouldn't take it well.

And though she was a shifter, had been raised a pirate, and could take care of herself, she was also lanky and scrawny, something no amount of shifting could compensate for. And he was big, really big. Maybe not Kou-big, but he was certainly drastically larger than herself. She was afraid of getting in a fight with him.

Jessie turned, spotting his rakish hair above the dwindling crowd. She remembered thinking that hairdo was handsome when they first met. Now it sent her into a panic, and she turned into the nearest alley, not caring or noticing where it might lead.

"Hey, I was talking to you!" he yelled, causing a commotion behind her.

Jessie didn't care. She didn't turn back. She just needed to get home.

And make sure he didn't follow her.

Jessie's heart was pounding when she arrived home, her hands sweaty as she dropped the bag of groceries on the floor and collapsed into the overstuffed purple chair in the corner. She leaned back, her hand on her head as she breathed slowly in and out.

"It's fine. He doesn't know I'm here. He doesn't know where I live."

After several minutes of controlled breathing, she felt more steady, and got up to put her purchases away. She enjoyed the feel of each exotic item as she settled it in the refrigeration unit, something both familiar and alien to her. So many things had been new to her when she moved here. Not only was she not Ateles, but she'd spent a significant part of her formative years on a spaceship, rarely planetside. When she'd arrived, she hadn't even known how to cook. On the ship, she'd relied on the cooking robot, which could make anything it was programmed to, but it also meant she'd never developed that essential life skill.

Fortunately, the universe was filled with resources, and she was never without recipes and how-to articles and videos. Sometimes, she felt like she'd learned more in the past few months than she had her entire time living with her sister.

Not that she blamed Cass.

Which reminded her. She needed to call her.

Jessie crossed the room and got comfortable in her chair, took a deep breath, and tapped her wrist communicator, selecting Cass's name from the contact list.

"Connecting," Angus said, the voice thick with a Scottish brogue. A screen powered up on the wall across from her, and she sat up straighter.

Then the screen came alive, her sister's spiky purple hair the first thing she saw. "Hi, sis," she said, waving her hand.

"Hey, Jess." Cass turned around in her seat and yelled down the hallway behind her. "Kou! Get in here! Jess is on the comm!"

Jessie winced at the nickname, but tried to keep a smile on her face.

Jessie hated to admit it, but she did actually miss them, even with the daily calls. She'd been living with her sister her entire life, and it felt weird living alone. Too quiet. She liked her peace, her space, the people, but sometimes she missed the action and excitement.

And then there was Rae to remind her why sometimes excitement could be a bad thing.

On-screen, Kou's bulk came into view, filling the background. "Hello, Jess."

"Hi, Kou. Do anything fun lately?" *And please don't say sex…*

"We've got a new job from Varn."

"Well, that's exciting." Varn worked for Cass's employer, Inia Intergalactic. A series of unfortunate events had resulted in Cass accepting a position there as a privateer, with the goal of combating the underhanded tactics of the company's leading rival, Diehli. Diehli being the same company that later kidnapped their friend, Victoria, so it wasn't really a hardship to go after those scumbags.

Inia's owner, Surg, who had actually hire Cass, was a good guy. He was in a relationship now with Victoria, and it was pretty easy to see how great they were together. Varn, on the other hand, she'd never been able to get a good read on, something she usually had no trouble with. He was very business-minded, bordering on obsessed with maintaining and growing the company his brother founded. And that could be a good thing (or not), so she was still withholding judgment.

"The little bastards hijacked a shipment of goods destined for Inia headquarters." Cass rubbed her hands together, licking her lips like a cat anticipating prey. "We're gonna get it back."

Jessie smiled. "Of course you are."

"What about you? What's been happening on your end?"

"I went to the market today. Had some really good meat on a stick."

"What else is new?"

Jessie shrugged. When you called each other every day, it wasn't that common to have noteworthy updates to give. She doubted her sister was interested in hearing about when she slept in late… or the times she would sit in front of her easel for hours trying to get inspiration.

The only eventful things in her life right now were Rae and her failed love life, neither of which she had *any* interest in sharing with her sister. And after excluding *those* details, it was a pretty peaceful life, but it also didn't offer much fodder for storytelling.

Not like her sister's life. Cass's days were full of adventure and intrigue.

You didn't want that life, remember?

Sometimes, it was hard to remember why she'd left. She missed her sister something terrible, having lived with her consistently her whole life. The daily calls helped, even though she would never admit it to anyone, let alone her sister. One word of dissatisfaction, and Cass would be turning the *Trojan* around and hightailing it back here, job be damned.

"Any guys I should know about?" Cass wiggled her eyebrows, a shit-eating grin on her face.

Jessie rolled her eyes. "Gross, Cass. You may live your romantic life on page one, but I am not telling my sister that stuff. I'm scarred enough as it is."

Cass gave her a lopsided grin. "Oh Jessie, chill out. It's a part of life. The sooner you accept that, the better off you'll be."

Jessie bristled, feeling defensive. "Our parents abandoned us when I was two," she snapped. "I think I know what life is."

The grin dropped from Cass's face, and Jessie immediately regretted her words. She didn't even remember her parents. Cass had been a teenager at the time, and she'd only recently gotten over the mind fuck it had done to her. Poking at that old wound was really stupid.

"Cass, I'm sorry."

Her sister waved her off, looking away. "It's fine. I gotta go." Cass disconnected the call.

Damn.

CHAPTER TWO

Back to the present...

Jessie sighed as she stepped into her apartment, rubbing her arm where Rae had grabbed her. She could already feel the ache where he had dug his fingers and nails into her arm.

How did this happen?

She wasn't stupid. She knew men could be dangerous. Any woman from Earth would know that. Today's encounter had just made it all the more real. Until now, she'd underestimated him, thinking him a whiny, angry guy who just didn't take rejection well.

Now, she knew better.

He was an abuser.

"And they don't stop."

The way he'd switched gears like that, going from clenching her arm so hard it hurt while yelling in her face in a jealous rage to cajoling and promising a good time, had been the nail in the coffin. She now knew she was in over her head.

She was just lucky there'd still been a crowd in the market, and that the vendor lady, Kaea, had been willing to hide her and tell her when Rae was gone. By the time she'd exited the stall, the crowd had dwindled to almost nothing. Kaea had looked at her with this truly heartbroken, worried expression that Jessie couldn't quite handle, and she'd vowed silently to buy something truly extravagant from her later to thank her. Or maybe buy her a gift, though she didn't know what the woman would like.

Looking around her home, it felt confining, claustrophobic. Her body was trembling with the adrenaline high she didn't have the wherewithal to control, even with her shifter abilities. She needed to unwind, and she knew just the place to do so. She grabbed a bag, her drawing tablet, water and snacks, setting them by the door. Moving with purpose to her closet, she quickly changed into her hiking gear. Medium-weight, straight legged pants, a moisture wicking top, and a jacket went on first. Then she grabbed her boots and wool socks and sat on the bed to put them on.

The bed dipped under her as she sat down. The tight, scratchy socks fought her, becoming twisted as she went, but that was easy enough to fix. Next, the boots went on, and she cinched them as tight as she could, like an equestrian putting a saddle on a horse. She didn't want them slipping and sliding on the trail.

Once dressed, she crossed the room and hefted her bag onto her back, the weight resting heavily on her shoulders. When she reached the door, though, she paused, her recent experience holding her back. The outside world didn't feel like a safe place right now. It felt like a threat, and in spite of not wanting to be inside, the outside world was just as daunting.

"You came here to live your own life, Jessie. Just live it."

She pushed through her fear.

The sun was bright, at least by this world's standards, and had burned away some of the morning chill. As she stepped out onto the street, angling toward the path leading out to the woods, she had to admit it was a perfect day for a walk in nature. The sky was a pale, grayish blue and cloudless. It was just warm enough not to be cold, but not so warm that the activity would have her sweating like mad.

She was right on the edge of the city, so after making one quick turn, she was staring at trees. The trees were tall and thin, with thick greenery that reminded her of pine needles. As she approached, she could see the bark, a smooth brown that disappeared into the pale sandy earth. She stepped into the shade of the trees as birds sang around her and small animals rustled in the underbrush, which grew thicker as she went deeper into the woods.

Even with the thicker underbrush, there was still a clear path. The trail was carefully managed by the Ateles colonists, giving them a respite from city life. The path wound back and forth, with roots and rocks disrupting it. And unlike on Earth, they weren't just gray or brown stones, but sometimes quite color-ful. She didn't know anything about rocks, but some were a milky pink, others were purple, blue, or green. They were beautiful and sometimes she found herself staring at the ground beneath her, not just to watch her footing, but also to appreciate the beauty that lay below.

It took about a half hour before she reached her destination. The sound of rushing water came to her first, putting a smile on her face.

Finally.

She picked up her pace, grabbing onto her backpack straps. The trees thinned and a small pool surrounded by sandy beaches and rocks came into view. Once her boots hit the sand, she looked to her right, where a small waterfall filled the view. She crossed the clearing, dropping her bag on a flat rock. She looked around, wondering what would catch her eye today.

Then she closed her eyes, taking several deep, calming breaths. All she could hear was the rushing of water and wind traveling through the trees. There were no people, no troubles, just nature. "Perfect."

She joined her bag on the rock and opened it, pulling out her drawing tablet. Settling her stylus against the screen, she just picked a direction and started drawing, not caring what ended up displayed there. It didn't matter. She just needed to steep herself in beauty after experiencing so much ugliness.

The sun was setting over the buildings by the time she returned home, casting the streets in deep shadow, but she didn't care. Even the chill in the air didn't bother her after the afternoon she'd had. The streets were quiet once more as most Ateles were still in their beds, hopefully dreaming of happy things.

She entered her apartment and collapsed into her chair with a sigh, letting the overstuffed cushions swallow her alive. It felt great on her abused body, which had eventually complained about sitting on a rock for hours on end, her back contorted over her tablet.

Still, she didn't care. It had been a perfect afternoon, filled with creativity, beauty, and life. She couldn't ask for more.

Jessie looked to the side, wondering when she could start people watching. The sun had almost completely set at this point, though it was still bright enough for her human eyes to see by. As she looked out, she saw a solitary figure standing by a building across the street, unmoving. They were cloaked in shadows, but the window next to them gave her an impression of the person being tall. She frowned, wondering why someone would just stand there like that. She was at a loss to explain it, and the mystery intrigued her.

That is, until a door across the way opened, spilling out a family of three and enough light to show the figure's face.

It was Rae…

And he was pissed.

CHAPTER THREE

Jessie paced the room, her feet pounding on the cool stone tiles. "What do I do? What do I do? What do I do?"

Her mind was running in panicked circles, like a pinball machine, making lights and noises but in the end going nowhere.

Jessie shook her head. "How the fuck does he know where I live?" She stopped her pacing, her body practically vibrating with nervous energy. "He was… he wasn't in the market. Kaea assured me of that. I didn't see him. He wasn't there. He couldn't have possibly followed me."

And yet, there he was, standing on the street corner like some ominous sentinel.

She didn't know what to do. She didn't know the laws here that well. Was there recourse for her? Had he done anything wrong? Certainly, Kaea had seen fit to protect her from him, but she hadn't exactly called in law enforcement or any other service.

What could she do? What would *he* do? She knew that after only one (botched) date, he'd become attached to her. Why was it escalating, though? It wasn't like that had been her most recent date. When he'd suddenly called out to her in the market, it had been a week or two since the last time she'd seen him. So why was this happening now?

She didn't know, but in the end, it didn't really matter. She tried to push away horror stories of stalkers and abusers on Earth. Earth was no stranger to masculine entitlement and delusions, but this was another species, and she wasn't sure how far he would go, what she was in danger of.

Jessie thought of calling her sister, but dismissed it almost immediately. First, she needed to solve her own problems, not go crying home to her sister every time things didn't go as planned. Second, Cass would probably freak out, resulting in her being swaddled in cotton batting for the rest of her life. She *definitely* didn't want *that*.

But that meant coming up with a solution herself, and she didn't have the slightest idea where to start. What could she do? She could move, but she liked it here, didn't want to leave it behind. That should be a last resort.

"Okay, what do I do?" Jessie ran her hand through her hair, but felt awkward. She wasn't usually like this. She had always been a happy, bouncy person, always seeing the positive and enjoying life to the fullest. This was a whole new experience for her. She didn't know what to do with herself when she was anxious and afraid.

"So, don't be afraid. I can't control what he does. I can only control what *I* do."

Her pacing changed in character, becoming more intent rather than frantic. "Hm. Step one, be prepared." She looked around herself and realized she was absolutely *not* prepared.

With fresh eyes, she noticed that her apartment only had one exterior door, the windows didn't open, and she had no emergency supplies like flashlights and preserved food.

And while her sister was loaded for bear, her weapons were in a box in the bottom of her closet, which would be utterly useless in an actual fight. She crossed the room, dropping to her knees. She slid a black plastic, contoured boxed from the corner and popped the latches. A sleek black gun sat on a bed of foam, a knife with a four-inch blade was pressed into the foam beneath it, and spare ammunition sat snuggled in the dead space to the right.

She lifted the gun, feeling its heft. It felt heavy and ominous in her grip, leaving her uneasy. She stood up and grabbed the shoulder holster off a hanger, slipping the gun into its cradle. Then she slipped it on, the weight feeling far more reassuring on her shoulders than in her hand. She grabbed the boot sheath for the knife and strapped it around her calf, slipping the knife in place. Cool metal and warm leather settled against her skin.

She smiled. All in total, she now felt like a badass, and the fear that had overwhelmed her only minutes before drifted off into the ether.

Not that her problems were gone, mind you. She still had a somewhat delusional Ateles male with an apparent obsession with her standing outside her apartment. She walked across the room, settling at the frame of the window that overlooked the street, and peeked out. It had grown darker in the time she'd been in her apartment, the street outside busier. Still, she could see that the street corner was no longer occupied by Rae. Either he had somewhere to be, or he'd changed his observation point.

"No time like the present."

Jessie pulled on a jacket, grabbed her market bag, and stepped out into the street, making sure to lock the door behind her. The path was now crowded with people starting their day, and she slipped into the stream of traffic. As she walked, she was forming a shopping list in her head, things she might need in an emergency.

She was also thinking about creating a go bag. If she had to run in a hurry, what did she need to grab? She figured water, light-weight, shelf-stable foods, a change of clothes, her drawing tablet, spare ammunition. The rest of the essentials, she could easily keep on her at all times.

Jessie reached the market while still lost in thought. She loaded her bag down almost on autopilot. She made a point to go to Kaea's stall, exchanging comm info. Finally ready to leave, she found herself pausing at the bulletin board like always, though she probably shouldn't have stopped. Again, she saw the ad asking for a surrogate. It gave her pause. She realized it looked like no one had touched it. It was older than the rest, like it had been rained on, but not so old that it was no longer relevant.

She touched the paper, which was wavy with water damage.

An idea started forming in her head…

Back home, she dropped the ad she'd torn from the bulletin board onto the kitchen counter and started putting together a go bag, though now she wasn't sure she would need it. The ad taunted her from the corner of her eye, making her stomach churn a little.

Would responding to the ad be any sort of solution? Or would it just mean delaying a confrontation? Maybe she just needed to get away for a little while so Rae could figure himself out or, less ideally, glom onto someone else. If it was a similar gestation to humans, that could mean nine months elsewhere.

But did she really want to leave her home? She liked her apartment, liked its location. It was fairly quiet, but still let her people watch. It was also on the edge of the city, so it had easy access to the wilderness, a resource in short supply when she'd lived on the *Trojan*.

But maybe she would find somewhere better next time? Or she could move to another colony, see somewhere new and exciting. She was an artist, after all, and they were often seen as free spirits. Why be confined to one place? She'd practically grown up on a spaceship, so it wasn't like staying put was normal for her.

And she had Kaea's contact information. They could keep in touch remotely, maybe even become friends. She felt like there was something there, something they hadn't had an opportunity to explore yet.

And she could always come back here if she wanted to. There was nothing to say she couldn't. And yet, Jessie didn't know if it would be safe. Jessie didn't know what to think of Rae's actions. She wasn't really that wise or worldly. She was only nineteen, after all, and while her life had taught her to be wary, Cass had done everything in her power to protect her from the worst life had to offer.

Jessie chuckled. She'd grown up on a pirate ship, and yet she was sheltered.

But maybe she was ignoring one of the more important elements here. Did she really want to be a surrogate? She doubted she would have any trouble with carrying a child, even though she was a trans woman. She was a shifter and that changed certain things. What she'd always questioned wasn't whether she could carry a child. She'd never really thought about it. She had wondered, however, if she would ever have children of her own. Shifter women were capable of reproducing with practically any species known to man, but she wasn't a cis woman, she was trans. Cis male shifters could only reproduce with other shifters. What if the same held true of trans women shifters?

Jessie supposed, at the moment, it didn't really matter. She didn't think she was ready for kids. She'd only just set out on her own, hadn't found love or a partner, and wasn't entirely sure what she was looking for on that end, anyway.

Still, she was curious. If she *did* eventually decide to start a family, it would probably involve adoption or step-children. That would be fine, she guessed, but she *was* curious about what it would feel like to carry a child, even if it wasn't hers.

And there shouldn't be any major issues. Shifters had a lot of benefits. Healing was one of them. She should bounce right back. And she'd get to learn first hand about something she'd always been curious about. And without any of the consequences.

Which brought the last concern. Did she really want to end up staying with someone she'd never met? The ad didn't specify who the person was, their sex or gender, or their species. She could end up in a worse situation than she was already in.

Jessie chewed her lip and started pacing again, stopping when she came parallel with the window. She stared out at the street where a woman pulled a child behind her, their little legs speeding along to keep up with the woman's longer strides. She could give someone that. She could give someone a child.

A peace settled over her.

That would be a worthwhile accomplishment.

CHAPTER FOUR

*D*elyn was honestly surprised when he received a response from his ad. He'd placed it in several locations, including some Ateles colony worlds, which he'd suspected were lost causes. What self-respecting Ateles would agree to help a Pardus, a species they saw as little more than slime, a mercenary race they were constantly at odds with?

Not that Delyn was a mercenary. Or even a Fighter. No, the responsibility he'd been given by society was to reproduce. He wasn't big or strong enough to be a Fighter. Nor a Farmer like most of his family. At the age of majority, he'd been a scrawny, lanky boy with barely a speck of stubble and an obsession with subjects that had "no value in reality," as his father always said.

He'd been assigned the role of a Seeder by the local magistrate. It had felt like a slap in the face because the man had looked honestly at a loss as to where to put him. It only grew worse when, after repeated failed attempts to convince females to carry his young and a steadfast refusal to use animals, he'd been sent off-world.

One would think that being offered a ship would be a reward or an honor. Instead, it had felt like they'd given up on him. Which he supposed they had every right to do. He was worthless as a Seeder. He wasn't charismatic, wasn't manipulative.

And now, it seemed, the Magistracy had decided this was his only solution.

He leaned back in his seat and sighed, a part of him wishing he were back home. As a child, he'd never realized being a Seeder could be hard. But with two-thirds of all live births being male, and many of the women in his small community related to him by blood, his options were limited. He'd always found it bizarre, but there was a taboo against planting inside a blood relative. He shook his head. It wasn't as if he'd been raised with most of them, and they certainly didn't need to worry about the genetic issues caused by inbreeding.

He smiled. He'd always been fascinated with genetics, and especially how other species' reproduction compared to their own. With no one to fulfill his role as Seeder with, and nothing else to do, he'd fallen to doing research, even further upsetting his father, who saw him as a drain on the community's resources.

He couldn't disagree.

Still, his father's censure didn't stop his curiosity. He wondered why his people had developed parthenogenesis while every other sentient species had developed sexual reproduction. Considering the ratio of men to women, he didn't think the Pardus way was working very well. Add in their constant fighting with others, and he didn't see his species being long for this universe.

Even so, he had a job to do, and if this message was true, he finally had someone interested. Sure, he would have to pay, which bruised his already abused ego, but what did that matter? He was finally being given the opportunity to be a useful member of society, to live up to the role granted him.

Assuming she agreed. She might back out. Or it might not even be a she. He didn't know every species or their respective biologies. Most likely, since the comm had come from an Ateles colony, it would be an Ateles female, but he couldn't assume.

He settled down in his ship's tiny control room. The space was clearly not a priority in the design, as there was only one seat and a wraparound control console. Also, considering there were no manual controls, he suspected it was assumed no trained pilot would ever man these ships. Besides the control room, the ship contained two bedrooms with attached bathrooms, a medical suite with attached nursery, a kitchen, and an airlock, nothing else. It had been designed for the sole purpose of facilitating a Seeder. Nothing more.

Delyn couldn't even see outside. The ship had no windows, and the cameras were used exclusively for the AI that controlled the ship. Even the ship's maintenance was controlled by automated systems. It was assumed the Seeder would be useless for all these tasks, and he supposed that was true. He'd never been trained in any of those things. Why would he be?

He shook his head, frustrated with his own lot in life once more, and tapped the console screen, bringing up the main menu. A couple more taps on the screen brought him to the comm message from a being with the designation of "Jessie Allen." He couldn't say he recognized the naming structure, but he shrugged it off. So long as the being had an appropriate pouch to gestate his young, it didn't matter.

He wrote his response, pressed send, and backed out of the comm program so he could set a course to meet her.

Jessie was nervous as she stood at the edge of the shipyard where she'd waved her family goodbye only a few months earlier. It felt weird from this direction, like she didn't even recognize it. She remembered standing at the base of the *Trojan's* ramp. Cass had been wearing a kick-ass brown leather jacket, practically squeezing the life out of her with a hug. Her sister had looked like her world was falling apart as they separated. Kou had rested a comforting hand on her sister's shoulder while Cass tearfully said goodbye and demanded daily calls.

Jessie turned around, remembering how she'd looked out over the city from the edge of the shipyard. She remembered her first look at those curving lines, how the colors had blended into the natural environment. In the distance, tall, thin trees had set the city in partial shadow in the low evening light. The light had been warm, a golden orange tinge that had made her want to pull out her drawing tablet.

The lighting was different today, the view different, and she sighed in mild disappointment. Some moments, you could never get back.

Jessie turned away from the view of the colony, beginning her search for the person she was meeting. She knew nothing about them other than their name, Delyn.

She felt nervous the longer she waited. It was only the second time she'd left her apartment since seeing Rae waiting outside like a specter of the deep. Just thinking about him sent her heart racing. She scanned her surroundings, looking for a tall man with rakish hair, but most of those around her looked like harried yard workers or crew-members coming in from long hauls in space, tired and a little grungy. There was a faint layer of dust in the air, and it smelled strongly of exhaust fumes.

Occasionally, an engine would start up, its impressive roar drowning out all else while a sudden burst of blinding light flared and died down.

Delyn had said they would be here any minute now, and she checked her wrist comm to make sure she wasn't too early.

Yep. Any minute now.

Then a tiny ship, larger than a shuttle but smaller than the *Trojan*, started landing in the distance. She couldn't make out any markings on its hull, but it seemed plain, possibly not decorated at all, unlike the other ships in the yard. She'd found that people, regardless of the species, liked to put their own stamps on their property, especially their ships. Sometimes, it consisted of big logos on the sides, other times, racing stripes, and yet others, it would be a special camouflage finish.

As the plain vessel disappeared behind a larger ship, she somehow *knew* that was Delyn. She said she would meet them at the entrance to the shipyard, so she stayed put, waiting semi-impatiently. She bounced up and down, suddenly excited about this new twist in her life. She didn't know what would happen, but at least it wasn't Rae. And she was armed. She hadn't gone anywhere without her gun and knife since spotting Rae outside her apartment.

Slowly, she turned from excited to bored, wondering what was taking so long. How long did it take to land your ship, disembark, and cross the shipyard? It had never felt this long living on the *Trojan*. Then again, she'd never been the one waiting.

Finally, she spotted a figure crossing the yard. They were cast in silhouette by the morning light at their back. Her eyes adjusted well, but still couldn't pierce the shadows consuming their anterior. As they passed by others, they looked shorter, less built. But that wasn't a surprise. There were a lot of big, burly men moving around here.

Still, she couldn't tell if the person was male or female, nor whether it was, in fact, Delyn. They were probably similar in size to her sister, who, admittedly, could intimidate at times. She was a good six feet tall, which was big for a human female.

After several minutes, the person stopped and said, "Jessie Allen?"

"That's me."

Back still to the sun, much of the person was still in shadow, but they did appear male or masculine, albeit not huge like Kou or Rae. Shorter, but still much taller than Jessie, he had more of a swimmer's build, lean but fit. She couldn't tell skin tone, hair color, eye color, even face shape, but he stood with a steady solidity that lacked the brute arrogance of Rae.

"I'm Delyn. Is there somewhere we can go to discuss the particulars?"

"This way." She ushered him out of the shipyard and to a cafe around the corner, bypassing the more frequently used bar. The cafe had a healthy layer of dust on it, the windows not even giving off the telltale sheen. The ships cast dirt in all directions when they took off or landed, making it near impossible to keep any of the surrounding buildings clean.

She pushed the door open and settled at a table in the corner next to a window. It looked out over the street they'd just exited. Delyn sat down slowly, almost cautiously, like he was approaching a feral animal. Jessie tensed a little, her hyperactive instincts saying, "He senses a threat!"

But as he looked around, seeming uncertain and nervous, she calmed down. "Well, uh, do you have any questions?"

Jessie chuckled. "You haven't told me anything."

"Right, sorry. Um, I haven't done this before."

"That's okay. Neither have I."

He looked at her, obviously curious, his head slightly tilted. In the gentler light of the cafe, he was surprisingly human-looking. It was both disconcerting as well as appealing. She'd seen very few shifters or humans since entering space, so seeing someone who looked so similar was just uncanny.

Well, she supposed it might even be close to Uncanny Valley, a concept in robotics where the closer a creator got to making their robot look human, the more it was rejected. It was the little things, really. Like eyes that were just a bit too bright or ears that looked just *slightly* the wrong shape.

Still, she liked the overall package, even if it would take some getting used to. It was aesthetically pleasing, even if a little jarring because of its similarities to humans.

"Why did you decide to answer my ad?"

Jessie paused. Should she tell him about Rae? She was hesitant to do so, so she just shrugged and said, "Needed to get away for a little while."

"And this was your only solution?" He seemed skeptical.

She couldn't blame him.

Jessie shook her head. "No, it wasn't. I could have just as easily called my sister, but I'm not sure my sanity could have survived that choice. And there were some things that appealed to me about this."

"Like?"

"Helping someone have a child, start a family."

Delyn shifted in his seat, looking uncomfortable.

"What? What is it?"

"Um, perhaps there are some things I need to explain about my species."

"Okay."

"I'm a Pardus." He shifted in his seat again, the chair scraping against the stone floor this time. "We have a complex system when it comes to reproduction and child-rearing."

"Okay, go ahead." She leaned her elbows on the table with her chin on her hands.

He relaxed a little. "Our species is divided by roles. Some are Fighters, some are Farmers. I'm a Seeder. Seeders provide the genetic material for each subsequent generation, but that is pretty much the extent of their role. They'll often help care for the Birther after implantation, but take no part after the children's birth."

"Who does?"

"Carers. They are the core of the community, with everyone else working to provide for them to some extent. Farmers feed them and the children. Seeders and Birthers provide the children. Tradespeople provide the objects and buildings they need."

"Do the Carers love the children?"

"I suppose that depends, but tradition dictates that Carers have an open and generous heart, so I believe they do. And children are essential to the prosperity of the community, so I believe everyone loves them in their own particular ways." Then he muttered under his breath, "Though some more than others."

Jessie decided not to comment on that last sentence. She doubted she was supposed to hear it.

Then a man came over with a tablet and a big smile. "How can I serve you today?"

Jessie looked down and realized she hadn't even looked at the menu yet. She picked it up, a thin piece of digital paper that shimmered slightly in her hands. "Let's see." There was an icon in the corner allowing you to change the language. She switched it to Uso, then ran a finger along the surface as she read each meal. "Oh, this sandwich here looks good." A seasoned roasted meat with loads of vegetables on a pan-seared thinbread served with a side of fresh fruit. "I'll have this one," she said, pointing out the entry to the server, "and a glass of water."

"Very well, milady."

She smiled, enjoying the title.

A moment later, the server said, "I'll get it right out to you," and she realized Delyn had ordered without her noticing.

"I guess back to business?"

"Sure," she said with a nod.

"Right. Gestation is just over three morgos."

That would be somewhere around three months Earth time, since Usan days were around twenty-five hours and there were twenty-five days in a Usan month. That wasn't bad, certainly less than she'd expected.

"You'll be staying with me during the gestation, and we'll travel to my homeworld for the birth. There is a medical bay on the ship for emergencies and it can handle any eventuality, but it's best if the Carers are there to take over once the children arrive."

"Makes sense." And she would get to see a new world. That would be nice.

Then the server returned with their food and drinks, settling them on the table with a flare for the dramatic. "I hope you enjoy your fantastic meals."

"Thank you," she said with a smile before picking up a piece of sliced fruit. It was juicy and equal parts sweet and tart as she bit down. Across from her, Delyn used a utensil to dip into what looked like a vegetarian stir fry. It smelled good, almost as good as her own sandwich, which she picked up once she'd swallowed her bite of fruit.

They ate in silence for several minutes. She enjoyed the sandwich, which was spicy, savory, crunchy, and warm. It was a little too big for her mouth, but she devoured it anyway. When she was left with nothing but her fruit, which she picked at slowly, Delyn put down his utensil and continued speaking. "Let's see… what are some things you might wish to know? Um, the young are in soft-shelled eggs which don't require nutrients from the Birther. I know some young create a drain on the Birther, so that might be relevant information. Over twenty-five percent of eggs fail to develop, and a clutch is usually four to six young."

Clutch?

"The young are usually fairly small." He held up his hands, indicating something that looked at most half the size of a human newborn, though she wasn't exactly an expert. "They grow quickly." He tapped his utensil against his bowl a couple times, thinking. "I guess what's left is to discuss the contract, unless you have some questions."

She shook her head. This actually sounded easier than she'd expected, though the four to six young sounded a little daunting.

Delyn pulled out a tablet and powered it on. She waited as he ran his finger over the surface repeatedly until he was satisfied, placing it on the table and sliding it over to her.

She started reading through it, though the language was a bit dense for her, especially in Usan, which was *not* her first language. It mentioned his responsibilities, her responsibilities, expectations upon birth, what would be done in case of certain types of emergencies, and she was happy to see that the contract put priority on the "Birther's" health over the young. Further down, it listed the duration of the contract and the pay. Everything seemed reasonable from what little research she'd managed to do in anticipation of this meeting.

"So I just sign?" A twinge of anxiety spiked in her, making it hard to breathe normally.

I'm really gonna do this.

She tried to calm down, but under the anxiety was a layer of excitement that just made her feel twitchy. She was entering the unknown, doing something she might very well regret, and that terrified her a little, but she was also an unfortunately curious person, and that made her reckless.

He seemed to relax in relief at her words. "Yes, we both sign."

Reckless won out. "Okay, let's get this started."

CHAPTER FIVE

After the meal, where Jessie signed the contract, Delyn followed her to her residence. He'd only been on Ateles worlds a few times, and he always found their architecture a bit surprising. For a species so filled with their own superiority, they tended to develop such humble abodes. He wasn't used to such a monotony of earthy hues. His community was quite agrarian, but even *they* painted their buildings with colors other than brown and green.

And it seemed completely absurd to build structures with curving edges. Wouldn't that make things more complicated? Weren't most building materials flat? He supposed he wasn't exactly the most knowledgeable on this stuff. While there were certainly builders in his community he could have asked, he'd never been really close to them.

They stopped at a building that looked much the same as all the rest, and she unlocked the door and entered. He slipped in behind her and closed the door. The space was not what he would have expected. There was almost no furniture in the room, and it seemed this was all there was to the residence. She had one bed and a kitchen nook to the left and a chair and easel to the right. Next to him, a bag was waiting by the door.

The room wasn't really decorated, just an empty space that didn't seem to fit her. He didn't really know her, but he'd gotten the impression of a warm personality from their brief talks so far. This room did not fit that image of her.

How strange.

"How can I help?"

"Um," she looked around herself. "I've got to do some packing. Why don't you sit in the chair while I'm busy? Shouldn't take long."

He nodded and sat down, the chair engulfing him. It faced a window, and he looked out at the street beyond. Being midday, the people were all in their beds, leaving a street that looked eerily quiet, like an abandoned world.

It felt wrong, like something bad was right around the corner.

"Okay, ready," she said from behind him.

He jerked up and turned around, immediately noticing the small pile of bags of varying shapes and sizes by the door. She'd packed so few that the two of them could easily carry them back to his ship. He looked at her, surprised that this was all she wanted to bring for the several months she would be gone.

It was none of his business, so he just nodded to her, stood up, and crossed the room. "Which would you like me to carry?"

She handed him a couple bags, keeping a backpack and a bulky bag that nearly dragged the ground for herself.

"Okay, let's go." The sun was still high in the sky when they left the building, and the city was deathly quiet. He walked briskly through the paths, making his way back by memory. It was peaceful and almost made him want to linger, but he was also excited, though he was trying not to show it. After all, he would soon be fulfilling his duty to his people for the first time. He would *finally* be valuable to them, even in this small way, instead of constantly being a drain on resources.

He'd felt so bad about it. In fact, he'd even started taking odd jobs so he could pay for his own food and fuel, rather than rely on his people to take care of him. Until today, he'd thought he would always just be a burden to them, a burden they didn't deserve to carry.

But that was about to end. They'd signed a contract. He was about to become a real, contributing member of society.

He was so absorbed in his though that he never saw it coming. Not until a scream and crash came from behind him. Jessie had dropped her big, awkward bag and was struggling with a man much larger than either of them. He'd grabbed her arm and was yelling in her face in a language he suspected neither of them could understand.

"Release her!" he yelled as he dropped his own bags and charged at the other man, his mind and body filled with an odd energy he couldn't explain. Delyn was shorter and scrawnier, but he had momentum on his side, and he used it wisely, aiming low on the other man's body. Bent over, he slammed his shoulder into her attacker's hip, causing him to collapse over Delyn's back. He barreled forward, using his opponent's surprise to his advantage as he plowed them into the wall of the nearest building.

A voice cried out somewhere nearby, but he paid it no mind, instead focusing on soft spots, remembering the training he'd seen for the Fighters. He wailed away at the man's not-quite-soft middle, then a fist came out of nowhere, hitting his face with the force of a spaceship crashing to the earth. Pain radiated from his cheek, and he collapsed to the ground, the scent of blood on the air.

A loud report echoed off the buildings around them, and he looked up, touching his cheek. "Get lost, Rae," Jessie said. She stood in a shooter's stance, a nasty-looking gun in her hand. "I don't care how pointlessly jealous you are. I'm not yours, and I never was. Now get lost." She primed the gun threateningly, making it clear the next round wouldn't miss its mark.

Again, that odd energy rushed around inside him, although this time in an almost sickly way rather than the explosive rush from before. He didn't know what to feel as he saw Jessie standing there with the gun. On the one hand, she looked like a conquering hero or a goddess, powerful and assured. On the other, he had this ridiculous urge to get between her and danger, even though he knew he would be useless. Just look how his one attempt to defend someone went. He ended up collapsed on the ground while the one he was protecting was probably defending *him*.

Delyn didn't like how this made him feel, or what it said about him as a person. Something in his instincts was crying out that this was *wrong*, though he'd never had his instincts speak to him so strongly before. He'd never even realized his species *had* instincts, though he supposed it would make sense if they did. Didn't all living things on some level? Wasn't that intended to protect them or something? He didn't know, and it left him feeling even more uncertain than he already was.

In his peripheral vision, the Ateles male named Rae stepped back from Delyn's prone body. He looked up, catching the pure hatred in the other man's eyes as he looked at Jessie, and a chill ran down his spine. No words were spoken. None were needed.

Rae would not stop.

As they approached, the ship proved to be as small and nondescript as Jessie had thought it was when she saw it landing. Now, though, a new underlying layer of fear and worry colored the experience. Her nerves were shaken, and she was afraid that Rae would somehow follow them. On the way here, she kept checking behind her and scanning her surroundings, looking for him. Her lizard brain seemed to expect him to pop out at any moment.

Jessie took a deep, cleansing breath and shook her head. She hadn't expected Rae to find them like that. He'd seemed to come out of nowhere, spitting anger at her in the Ateles tongue. She hadn't understood a word of it, but she understood the anger full well. When he grabbed her, she screamed, dropping her art bag and beating on him any way she could. She couldn't reach her knife, and at that distance, she'd been afraid to pull her gun, afraid she would simply be arming him.

Then Delyn had come out of nowhere, giving her the space to fight back. And yet, seeing him on the ground like that, it wasn't just about fighting for herself anymore. He'd gotten hurt trying to save her. It made her feel things, though she couldn't say what.

Then Rae had turned to her, spouting jealous tirades, claiming she was running away to be with Delyn, calling him names that didn't much make sense when translated.

When she'd threatened him, told him to leave, the expression on his face had been telling. He'd backed away, never taking his eyes off her, but there'd been a very clear message in his stare. It said things like, "I'm going to get you," and "You're mine," and "This isn't over." Even thinking of that look now sent adrenaline surging through her.

Before her, Delyn waved an arm, causing a ramp to lower. She followed behind him, deep in thought, her small feet pounding beneath her as usual. For a moment, a brief smile crossed her face as she recalled her family and friends commenting on how she was incapable of stealth on ships, always stomping along, her footsteps echoing off the walls.

"Are you okay?" Delyn said.

She looked over at him, seeing the concern there in his pale eyes, and it brought her right back to the moment, the fragile smile fleeing in the face of her current reality. "I'm fine."

"Okay. Well, I'll show you to your room."

The ramp led to a small room that looked like an airlock. That opened into a hallway, and he quickly led her past several doors before stopping and ushering her through. The room was small and plain, with barely enough room to set up her easel. It held nothing but a bed. There were two doors on the left wall. Delyn placed the bags he was holding on the bed, then moved to the doors.

"This one," he said as he opened the first door, "is storage." It was small, just large enough to walk into, with drawers lining every wall inside. "You'll want your personal effects locked down before we launch." He closed the door and moved to the next one. "This is the bathroom. Facilities are similar enough to an Ateles design that you should have no problem with their usage." He closed the door before she could even look inside. He stepped by her, brushing against the bed. "And this," he said, slapping a control panel near her, "is the jump seat." The seat practically fell out of the wall. "Make sure you're strapped in before takeoff." He turned to her. "There's not much else to the ship, but we can go over the rest after takeoff. Any questions?"

"Nope."

"Okay, well, I have to get ready to launch. I'll send a message on the intercom when you need to buckle up."

She nodded and watched as he left, letting the door slip silently closed behind him.

The room was almost eerie without his presence. It felt cold, sterile, dead.

"Welp, no time like the present. Better get these bags unpacked."

Delyn wasn't used to having other people on his ship. Though Jessie had just boarded and hadn't even settled in yet, it still felt different. He walked to the tiny control room and sat down. On the screen, "Pre-Flight Checks" was displayed prominently. He tapped it and the screen changed, saying, "One Moment, Please."

Though he couldn't say why, an urge hit him to look over his shoulder, to look for Jessie. Of course, she wasn't there. She was in her room, probably putting her things away for launch. It was strange, but his entire body seemed to gravitate toward her, like all his senses were now oriented to her as their reference point. He couldn't explain it. He'd never heard of anything like it.

Back home on Wesa, people tended to stay in their own lanes, playing their part in building up the larger community. Some people became friends, often if they worked in the same role, but he'd never heard of someone who almost felt obsessed with another person.

Delyn wasn't obsessed, though. He turned around in his seat, checking the display, which was still cycling through pre-flight checks. Perhaps, he was fascinated. He'd never met someone of her species before. She looked so similar to his own. It was disconcerting. He wanted to ask her what species she was, but suspected it would probably be considered rude.

And why had that man come after them? He had specifically gone after Jessie, not Delyn. Why? He could certainly understand an Ateles going after a Pardus on one of their own worlds. There was prejudice there, possibly more than could ever be eradicated. He didn't understand it, wanted no part in it, but it still existed and knowing about it was an essential survival skill when a Pardus traveled in space.

The screen before him changed to "Ready. Press to Launch."

He instead pressed the intercom button off to the right. "Jessie, we're ready to launch. Strap in."

A moment later, her voice came through, slightly distorted by the speaker design. "Okay. Be ready in a sec."

He wasn't sure what a "sec" was, but he waited, knowing that the control for the jump seat also include an intercom button.

"Okay, ready."

He checked his own harness, the tough material digging into his hands a little, and tapped the screen to launch. The ship came alive. He barely noticed it at first, just a gentle whooshing sound as the atmospherics turned on, no longer using the outer environment. Then the engines started, a massive roar filling his ears to the point of distortion. They twitched slightly, as if annoyed by the noise.

Delyn held onto his harness, taking a deep breath to calm himself. He'd never liked taking off. It was a violent experience that always left him feeling a little shaky afterward. Still, it was a necessary step in getting back to Wesa. And he very much wanted to go home. He missed his family, his community. He missed the sky, the earth, the trees. He missed the smell of home-cooked meals.

Delyn sighed right before the intercom activated with the AI's voice. "Launching in 3… 2… 1…" The engines became deafening, and he was rocked back in his seat. He gripped the armrests, holding on for dear life, as the ship rocketed forward, leaving the world behind. He couldn't breathe as the force of the launch pushed the air from his lungs.

The moment seemed to go on forever, his head pounding as he struggled to stay conscious, smoky blackness playing at the edges of his vision.

Then suddenly, it was over. The force was gone, and a voice, speaking in a language he couldn't translate, said, "Fuck!" at full volume. It echoed off the walls, and he wondered what it meant. Before him, the screen said, "Launch complete. Please input destination." Tapping the screen brought up a list of presets and previous destinations. He selected Wesa, home. The screen changed to "Destination Locked" and a moment later, "Valana, Wesa" and the remaining time until arrival showed up below it.

Delyn released his harness and stood up, leaving the room. When he reached Jessie's door, he knocked, waiting for an answer.

The door slid open almost instantly, and he was surprised to find her practically bouncing with a wide smile on her face. Until now, she had seemed calm and thoughtful, maybe even reserved, but not now. "That was fun. Always loved takeoff."

"So, you've been on a spaceship before?"

"Oh, absolutely. I spent most of my teenage years on my sister's ship. It was fun, but sometimes confining. There is something to be said for some true gravity time. Getting out in nature, seeing a star shining down on ya', feeling a real breeze on your cheeks." She sighed, her smile growing.

"And yet, you're happier here."

"I guess it's somewhat familiar. Also, it doesn't have that asshole, Rae, on it." Her smile dipped slightly, and he felt like the "asshole" now, whatever that was.

"I apologize for bringing it up."

She shook her head, waving off the idea with her hand. "You didn't. I did. Now, moving on. Are you going to show me the rest of the ship?"

"There's not much. It's mostly intended for one person."

She snorted. "Yeah, the *Trojan's* not much either. It was a little tight with two people. Three people was getting to be a bit stifling. I don't know how Ellie does it."

He turned around to face her, having started down the hallway to show her the rest of the rooms. "Who's Ellie?"

"A friend of ours. She has the same ship, although *her* ship is home to an entire Ateles special forces team. I don't know how they fit. The ship's just too small."

He nodded. "Well, this ship definitely can't fit that many. It's designed for at most two adults, plus maybe the young if things don't go to plan."

"Right."

He motioned to the next room on the left, the one right next to Jessie's. "This is the kitchen. I'm afraid the food options leave a lot to be desired." He pointed at the cabinets and refrigeration unit on the left wall. "This is cold storage, dry storage. Everything goes in this device here." Delyn tapped the heating unit. He had no idea how it worked and had no interest in finding out. He couldn't even remember what it was called since they didn't use them back home.

A table with bench seats took up the back wall, and he skipped right over it. It was self-explanatory, after all. He pointed to the wall on the right. "Here, you'll find plates, utensils, and the cleansing unit."

"Makes sense."

He turned to her. "I apologize if the food is not to your liking. Unfortunately, I don't have a lot of options."

"It's fine. I'm not terribly picky." She smiled. "I have my favorites, but I'll eat just about anything."

"Good to know. Shall we continue?"

"We shall."

He could hear her behind him as he left the kitchen. The medical suite was directly across the hall, and he pushed through. This room was clean and sterile, a room he hadn't entered once since coming on board. It, frankly, intimidated him. It held a central bed with a diagnostic robot above it and cabinets and counters along the right and back wall. There was a big sink and emergency shower squeezed in as well. On the left wall was the nursery, which consisted of a series of bassinets.

"The medical suite," she said from behind him. The smile had left her voice.

When he turned around, he found her staring at the bassinets. She seemed withdrawn, thoughtful.

"So, this is where it'll happen."

"Generally, yes."

She nodded absently, and he wondered if she was really ready for this. Seeing this room had changed her mood entirely, and he wondered what he could do to make her feel more comfortable, more ready. He didn't know her or her species, didn't know if there were any personal or cultural misgivings he would have to overcome. She'd volunteered for this, but that didn't mean she was ready to proceed.

He decided he would wait to implant. There was still a while before they would reach his home, plenty of time to make her comfortable with him and the situation.

But how would he do that? He'd never even managed to do so with people in Valana, his home community, people he'd known his entire life. He wasn't suave or sophisticated or charming. How did the other Seeders do it? How did they seem to accomplish their role in life so effortlessly? His father had always looked down on him, seeing him as less, but why? What had he done to inspire those feelings? What did the man see in him that had him drawing that conclusion?

How was he going to do this?

As Delyn took Jessie on a brief tour of his ship, she couldn't help noticing how nervous he seemed. At least, once they reached the medical suite. The room was clearly unused. And considering his discomfort with being in the room, she suspected he'd rarely or never been there before.

She followed him out, taking one last glance at the corner with all the cribs. There were six in total, empty and forlorn. Since the plan wasn't to give birth on the ship, these would likely never be used. It seemed sad, but she tried to push it out of her mind. She didn't know why this room affected her so. There was something almost horror-movie–esque about the exam table in the middle of the room, like you expected to be experimented on by aliens in this room.

Then again, she *was* going to have an alien perform a medical procedure on her in this room, so it wasn't that far off-base. Her smile grew, and she leaned over a little, chuckling into her hand. Delyn didn't turn around, and she straightened up, stopping when he stood in front of the last room.

He looked to his right and pointed. "That's the control room. Please don't enter it."

"Okay."

"This is my room," he said as he opened the door. The room was simultaneously the same as and different from her room. Where hers was barren, his had character. Not much, but some. The reality of living in space was that everything had to be able to handle takeoff and landing. He had pictures of people attached to the walls. No frames, which made sense, just the pictures. It was a little chaotic. The pictures included more people than she could count, and it spoke of a person who had once had a full and rich life. The bedding was green and fluffy, something that made her want to just jump on it.

There still wasn't any other furniture, but it somehow felt fuller in spite of that. "It's nice."

"Thanks."

She paused, unsure where to go from there. She was standing at the boundary of a relative stranger's room, on his ship, with no way to get off without calling her sister for help. Of course, if she did, her sister would drop everything and rescue her.

Why do I keep thinking about that?

It was like it was never far from her mind. Jessie had relied on Cass since she was two, and now she couldn't seem to form a plan that didn't involve her sister coming to the rescue. She was an independent woman, wasn't she? She could take care of herself, couldn't she? So, why did she keep going back to the idea of her sister sweeping in to save the day? Why couldn't she just come up with a plan without her sister popping into her head every time?

It was kind of frustrating.

"Well, thank you for the tour." She pointed down the hall. "Maybe we can sit in the kitchen with a beverage and talk, get to know each other?"

"Sure."

She nodded and bounced down the hallway, feeling a bit better about things. Sure, she was probably in over her head. Maybe she'd made a mistake, and she would regret this, but this was something new, and new, in and of itself, could be fun.

Delyn felt awkward as he followed Jessie to the kitchen, her boots pounding the floor, the sound echoing loudly off the walls. He almost winced, grateful she couldn't see him.

She surged forward and was out of sight within moments as she entered the kitchen. He took his time, trying to compose his thoughts. What should he say to her? How could he make her more comfortable with him and the situation?

She'd suggested a drink and a talk, and he wondered what type of beverage she would like. He personally preferred the bitter flavor of hal, which was usually served hot. He liked the idea of sitting across from her with a hot beverage warming his hands. Hal was a staple on ships because it was lightweight and stored dry, making it very practical. It also had a very high caffeine content, which could come in handy on some types of vessels where sleep was more of a luxury than a necessity. It had become a tradition to always carry it on spaceships.

He'd also grown up on it as they grew it in Valana, even trading it with other communities for staples they didn't produce in enough supply themselves. He'd always been fascinated with the process of drying and preparing the leaves, even watching it being done when he was a child.

Delyn entered the kitchen, moving to dry storage. "Do you have any preferences for a drink?"

"Whatever you have," she said, shaking her head, and he remembered her saying she wasn't a picky eater. It seemed that translated to beverages, too.

He opened the cabinet, staring at the contents. Each type of item was organized in tidy rows, many of the contents color-coded. He hadn't done this. That was how the ships came. The people who did the restocking were trained in a specific way, and food intended for space had color-coded packaging to make their lives easier. He barely read over the contents as he reached in and grabbed a green box, resting it on the counter next to the heating unit. Turning around, he removed two nearly indestructible cups from the cabinet on the opposite wall. Every item was a uniform gray and just as durable. Every item in the cupboard could fall out mid-flight and not a thing would break. He had no idea how they pulled that off.

The cups were cold and smooth in his hands as he walked to the sink and filled them with water. Dropping a bag of leaves in each, he opened the heating unit and selected the appropriate setting. He stood in front of the device, even though he didn't need to. He was nervous, not knowing what to say to Jessie. What would she ask? Delyn had never been in this situation before. He'd lived his life either in solitude or in a community that had known him since birth. He knew nothing else.

The device chirped, and he took the two cups out. Steam rose off the liquid, which was now a color between green and brown. He walked slowly to the table, setting one cup carefully in front of Jessie before taking his seat across from her.

"Smells good," she said, wrapping her hands around the warm surface.

He nodded. "It's a favorite of mine."

She leaned down and took a whiff, seeming to savor the smell, before blowing on it to cool it down.

"So, what did you want to know?" He idly rotated his cup in his hands, the warmth radiating into him.

She sat up and chuckled. "Um, are you usually alone on this ship?"

"Yes."

"Must be lonely."

He paused to think. Was it lonely? He'd never really thought about it. It was his duty to spread his seed. His entire adulthood, he'd failed at that duty. He supposed being alone was a bit of a relief. Here, no one was judging him for his shortcomings, no one was judging him for his failures. He could go about his day, good or bad, without censure or social pressures. "No, I don't think I am."

Jessie looked at him, her gaze intense. "Interesting." She paused, thinking up her next question. "Do you have any friends?"

He paused. When he left, he'd had some. Not many, but some. Would they remember him now? Would they care? Would he be able to pick up where he left off or would he enter Valana like a stranger? He remembered the children he'd played with growing up, some of whom he'd been quite close to. But that had been years ago, and he feared his repeated failures and distance had dissolved any affection they might have felt for him. He shook his head.

She frowned. "What do you like to do?"

"I don't understand."

Jessie tilted her head in an expression he couldn't fathom. "Hobbies?"

He shook his head. He'd never heard the word before.

"You have no hobbies, no special skills? Nothing that makes your heart sing?"

You, some part of him said. Delyn shook off the thought, feeling weirded out by it. He certainly wasn't telling her *that*. He didn't know why he'd become fixated on her or why he felt oddly energized around her, but she certainly didn't need to know it. She was having a hard enough time with what she'd already agreed to. She didn't need to hear that he was having feelings for her that went beyond the parameters of the contract.

"What about you? Do *you* have hobbies?" he asked, hoping to draw the attention from himself and his fixations.

"Yup, I do. I draw and paint. It's kind of like a fusion between a hobby and a career. I've been taking commissions from people in the colony. Not many, just supplementing my savings. Not sure how I feel about it, though. It's weird watching something I created leave my hands. Not sure I like it." A crooked smile stretched her lips. "It's such a personal process, creating. You spend so much time on something that it almost becomes a part of yourself.

"And I guess it is. I mean, it *comes* from my mind." She started gesturing with her hands, speeding up and slowing down depending on her level of excitement. "It's part of me. It *is* my mind. And it feels like giving away a limb."

"I wouldn't know what that's like. If someone asked me to give a limb to help a member of my community, I would do it in a heartbeat."

She scoffed. "I wouldn't." She looked at him like he was a little crazy.

"Why do you have a hard time with that?"

She shook her head and looked away, finally taking a sip of her hal. "Mmm," she said, looking down at her cup. "Not bad."

"Jessie?"

She rolled her eyes. "I know. I guess because people just don't do that. They take what they can and leave the garbage behind. If you don't want to be strip-mined, you do what you can to protect yourself."

"That's a very pessimistic viewpoint."

"Realistic," she said, pointing a finger at him. "I may be more idealistic than my sister, more sheltered, certainly, but I'm not blind. I can believe in the goodness of people. I know there are plenty of people out there who *are* good. In fact, the reality of having bad people means that there will be good people, because bad people don't victimize other bad people. They look for victims, not rivals."

Delyn didn't know what to say. He'd never encountered a mind like hers. He knew the people in Valana were good people, even when they didn't treat him quite kindly. They sacrificed for each other. They worked for each other. There was often no one in the community who didn't have a role, no matter how small. Even the disabled and infirm were given roles they could accomplish, allowing them to feel worthy.

"I'll admit, I've met my share of less than savory people since boarding this ship for the first time, but I've never believed as you do. I've always believed that my community worked together to help each other, to build each other up. I would give a limb for anyone in Valana because I believe with all my heart that any one of them would do the same in kind."

Rae was swirling with a number of emotions. Most of them, he couldn't name at the moment. He pushed them all down. They were a distraction. He needed to focus on getting Jessie back. That was all that mattered.

And the first step was getting to her.

After their last less-than-successful encounter, he'd followed her here to the shipyard. He'd watched her board a small ship and fly away. And after a little more wallowing in self-pity than he was altogether comfortable with at the local dive bar, he'd started to formulate a plan.

Still slightly drunk, he'd bribed the yardmaster to give him the information about the ship. Now, far more sober, he was scanning the yard for the right ship and crew for his purposes. The shipyard didn't operate on the same schedule as the rest of the colony, so even though it was late afternoon, the yard was busy and filled with people. The rest of the world was asleep in their beds, but to look at this scene, you would think it was the middle of the night. Haggard and dirty men rushed about, some excitedly hurrying to the bar he'd left not so long ago while others were moving heavy crates of goods or running errands for their respective captains.

The whole scene was unfamiliar to him, especially since it was the most he'd ever seen of other species here at the colony. While most people living in the colony were Ateles, that wasn't true of the crews coming in from space. He couldn't even name all the species, having lived such a sheltered life here.

He supposed that was the reason he'd taken such a fancy to Jessie. She was different, unique. And seeing the contrast between his dark and her almost white skin was hypnotic. Then, there were her eyes. They were so strange but captivating, a dark center surrounded by the same paleness. But it wasn't just her appearance that he'd immediately found appealing. She was also vivacious. She was passionate in her speech and actions, and even when she was mad at him or rebuffing him, he couldn't deny a part of him still found her captivating.

He *needed* her in his life.

Which was why he was here. He stepped forward, stopping in front of a man of another species who had the look of a captain.

Time to find a ride.

CHAPTER SIX

Jessie was a bit stumped as she wandered off to her room after the conversation with Delyn. She didn't really see the hallway, just stumbled into her room and collapsed onto the bed. It had been a long day, and she stared mindlessly at the plain, white ceiling while the soft bedding engulfed her slightly.

Around her, the ship hummed, reminding her that she was not planetside anymore. She wandered off in her mind, wondering about Delyn's community, Valana. What would it be like to live somewhere like that? Where anyone would do anything for anyone else? Where you didn't worry about someone trying to hurt you? She wasn't usually the worrying type, but she was aware. Aware and cautious. Aware… but hopeful. The situation with Rae had been frustrating because she'd had no control, and there was no way of making that into something more positive than it was. Denial and avoidance were the only strategies that worked with her personality in that situation.

So what *would* a community like that be like? She thought back to the shifter caravan they'd lived in for a spell when she was a kid. She imagined it would be something like that, though she'd always felt like a guest there. The people had embraced them, and she'd had loads of friends. Every day had been fun while she played with the other kids. Victoria had been working on her ship, and Cass had finally let some of her stresses go. She'd no longer needed to work so hard to support them, and that had made a major difference.

Sometimes, she missed that place. There was something almost magical about it, and not just because all of them could change their shape at will. No one was harried or stressed. If someone needed help, people volunteered. If you wanted to make clothes, someone would provide the cloth. If you needed food, there was always a supply in the main tent. More often than not, when people cooked, they cooked for everyone. If a harvest was due, everyone contributed. If you needed someone to watch your kid, there was always someone willing to do so. There were no conventional "single parents" because no one was truly alone.

It was probably the only time in her life that she'd felt a part of something, and it had maybe lasted a couple years before Victoria finished her ships, giving one to Cass. Looking back, Jessie suspected Cass had chafed at being helped by the caravan. She'd done everything herself for so long that getting aid, even well-meaning, was unbearable.

Jessie had never felt that way, though. She hadn't had any sort of community since she was a kid, and she supposed she missed it. Which was probably why she'd chosen to live in the colony, but looking back, she realized it had never really hit the spot. She'd loved her apartment, had been developing a bit of a name for herself with her art, but she was an outsider. Even after several months, she'd only made the earliest of overtures of friendship with one person.

She was the optimistic sort, though, and had enjoyed the beauty of the place and the people, even if she hadn't been a part of them. But now, she realized she wanted more. Jessie would prefer a community like Delyn mentioned. She didn't know where that might be or if it would ever happen, but it could be a fun adventure finding it. She could see lots of new places, meet tons of new people.

Jessie bounced up off the bed, her body overflowing with energy. A smile stretched her face, and she bobbed on her feet. She wanted to run off and tell someone, but who? Cass still thought she was at the colony. Victoria probably wouldn't care and might even get annoyed at being interrupted. And Ellie was probably on some secret mission somewhere. She only ever checked in between missions.

Jessie didn't know much of anyone else. Living on a ship had made meeting people exceedingly hard.

But you do have Kaea's contact information.

She looked down and frowned at her comms device, which said the local time for Kaea was the middle of the day. She would be asleep. "Well, I guess a message will have to do," she said with a small amount of forced cheer. She was determined not to drag down the good mood she'd been in. She typed out a quick message, telling Kaea where she was and that she would be okay.

With that over and done with, she let her bubbly mood return and dashed for the closet, pulling out her easel and setting it up in the corner of her room. It barely fit, and she could practically sit on the corner of the bed while painting, but she didn't care. She had no idea what she was going to paint, but she was excited to find out.

63

The days passed, and Delyn saw Jessie often, partially because the ship was so small and there was so little to do here. She often left her door open while she practiced her art. Sometimes, he would slip in while she was elsewhere and check what she'd been working on. He was always amazed. There was something evocative and emotional in the work she did.

And she was fast. Within a couple days, she'd finished a painting, which she left on the easel to dry. It was an abstract painting, full of color and life. There were emotions imprinted there, but it was so chaotic. He couldn't single any of them out. It made his chest swell with them, though. He could see why she loved art.

"It's beautiful," he said as she exited the bathroom.

"Thanks. I needed to tell someone what I was feeling."

He looked over at her. She'd just bathed, her brown hair wet and slicked to her skull. Her skin glistened in the harsh lighting, and her clothes clung to her still slightly damp skin. He realized she could wear absolutely anything and look like a goddess.

And she smelled lovely, too. Like fruits and something else that was warm and welcoming. He wanted to bathe in her presence, then called himself back, realizing what he was doing. He stood taller, hoping he hadn't made her uncomfortable.

But she had a knowing grin on her face and dropped a hand to her hip without a word.

He turned back to the painting. "What does it say?"

"You can't tell?" She stepped up behind him.

He shook his head. "There's so much here."

"True. But that's life, right? It's the good and the bad at once, order and chaos. And hope."

"Hope?" He turned to her again.

"And fear. Stress. We tend to experience them all at once, not being able to separate one from the other. It all assaults us at the same time, and we are their willing victim, reveling in the chaos."

He looked away. "I don't know that I believe that."

"No?" She paused. "Well, I suppose you do live a very organized, solitary life. There's less opportunity for the chaos life can bring. And from the sound of your community, it's much the same."

He jerked to face her. "Is that such a bad thing?"

"Of course not. It's just an observation."

Jessie had been on the ship for days now. Kaea had sent her a message in response, happy that she was safe. She'd created one painting and started another. She'd made many drawings on her tablet. And she'd also tried her damndest to get to know Delyn. There was something about him and his home that intrigued her.

And so she'd come to practically stalking him. It wasn't hard on such a small ship. She could usually hear when he was moving toward the kitchen, and she would follow him in so they could chat over a meal.

Jessie was growing to like Delyn, but at the same time, she felt sorry for him. She had come to realize that he needed people in his life, people who actually cared for and believed in him. It seemed like his community had given up on him while he simultaneously held them up on a pedestal. Delyn didn't even seem to realize what he was doing. He loved them, and from the way he talked about them, believed they could walk on water. He believed they were perfect.

Jessie had her doubts. More than that, though, she wanted to help him. She wanted to prove all those people in his community wrong. She wanted to show him and everyone he knew that he was worthy.

"So, what's for lunch?" she said as she followed him into the kitchen.

He jerked and spun around. "Why do you always do that?"

She grinned, bouncing on her feet, trying to look innocent. "Do what?"

He scowled at her, but it didn't dissuade her even for a moment.

"Well? Lunch?"

He sighed and turned to the refrigeration unit, opening the door to a lonely light bulb and a rapidly dwindling supply of fresh food. Delyn seemed to rarely pick from the dry goods, and she suspected he did it to please her.

"How's this look?" he said, pulling a mix of fresh veggies and whatnot out.

She didn't recognize any of it. There was an assortment of greens, reds, and oranges. Some spherical foods mixed into a bowl of what looked like some sort of lettuce. Probably a salad. She shrugged. "You know I'm not picky."

He frowned, looking into the fridge one final time like something better would just jump out at him, and sighed. He closed the door and walked the offering to the table.

Jessie grabbed tableware to eat with and joined him. They moved in concert and silence. It was like a dance, each of them knowing the steps and moving around the other with grace in the small space. It felt homey and nice. There was a certain intimacy to the silence, though she wouldn't call it romantic. She didn't know what they were to each other or where this would go, but she *did* want to help him.

Jessie took a bite of the food. A sweet flavor exploded on her tongue as the air filled with the crunching of leaves, and juice from one of the round things filled her mouth. She chewed methodically, watching Delyn the entire time. He played with his food, not looking at her. It was unusually quiet at the table, and she felt compelled to fill it.

"So, when are we doing this implantation thing?" she asked.

And… immediately regretted it.

Delyn coughed and sputtered as the food he'd just put in his mouth flew across the table.

So, *maybe* she could have timed that better.

Delyn recovered quickly from Jessie's blurted question, shaking a little as he took in the mess he'd made and quickly working to clean it up. Greens and fruit were all over the table, and he reached out his hands, rounding them up and dropping them into his bowl. "Sorry about that."

"No problem. I startled you." She shrugged, an amused expression on her face.

He stood with his bowl, the surface smooth against his grimy hands. "So, you're ready?"

She shrugged. "It's what I'm here for."

He nodded and stepped away from the booth, heading to the sink to clean his hands and discard the mess. The sound of running water distracted him as he thought. Was he ready?

He felt so nervous, but he'd waited so long for this moment. Why would he not be ready? Why would he need more time?

He turned around, leaning against the counter. "Do you want to go to the medical suite?"

She shrugged. "Sure."

He nodded and turned toward the door, his mind anxious and filled with amorphous doubts. He walked across the hallway without seeing anything, stepping into the medical suite and freezing.

What do I do?

He'd never reached this point before. He felt locked to the floor with uncertainty. On Wesa, it was a fairly uncomplicated process, usually done in a bedroom or somewhere the Birther felt comfortable, but this wasn't Wesa, and he felt like this wasn't normal. He suspected most Seeders could accomplish their duties without having to resort to begging off of aliens.

He looked back at her as she entered. She seemed a lot more confident than him. And she knew even less about this process than he did.

"Where do you want me?"

"Um, on the table. Your lower half will need to be exposed."

"I figured as much." Her cheeks blushed, and she turned away from him.

He gave her the privacy she craved, turning away himself to do his own stripping. "I should say again that I've never done this before."

"I know."

He placed his clothing neatly on a counter in the daunting room, keeping his back to her. Behind him, he could hear her scrambling onto the bed. His fingers dug into his palms, his hands damp with sweat.

You can do this.

He turned around, facing someone naked for the first time since maturation.

"What the fuck?!"

Jessie stared, her mind going blank as her gaze took in his, admittedly impressive, package. And being a leaner guy, it seemed all the more impressive. She simultaneously thought, "Damn, the girls on his planet must be nuts for passing this up," and, "Why the fuck is he naked?"

She jumped off the table, her feet slapping on the floor tiles, and grabbed for her clothes to cover up.

"What's wrong?" he said, taking a step closer and looking genuinely confused.

How do I manage to get myself in awkward situations like this? First Rae and his stalker tendencies, now Naked Delyn. "Why are you naked?!"

He looked down then back up, seeming confused by her question. "For implantation."

"I thought this was a medical procedure," she said, gripping her clothes tighter to her body.

"No, not really." He seemed increasingly confused and now almost hesitant as he spoke.

"Then why are we in here?" she said, flailing an arm to indicate the room.

He looked around. "I thought this would be neutral ground, that you would see it as less personal here rather than in one of our private spaces."

She ground her teeth, admitting he had a point. There weren't exactly a lot of places to do this on the ship. She bounced on her feet, trying to think. Could she do this? Some sort of medical procedure was one thing. She felt like she could do that, that she was ready for that, but this was too much like sex. Probably, it *was* sex, though maybe not the type of sex her sister liked to have on *every* surface of the *Trojan*.

She shook her head. "I can't do this." She started putting her clothes back on, yanking on the material when her foot got stuck and she nearly fell over.

"Jessie," Delyn said.

She looked up. He was reaching out to her. "No." She pointed at him, desperately needing him to stay back.

Jessie returned to her dressing. It all seemed to take longer than it should have in her rush. With her pants finally on and her shirt twisted around her torso, she picked up her socks and boots, and stormed past Delyn out of the medical suite.

She saw nothing as she headed straight to her room to be alone.

CHAPTER SEVEN

elyn stared after Jessie as she stormed out of the room barefoot. He was shocked, baffled, and feeling stupid and vulnerable now without clothes on.

He looked over to the counter and slowly grabbed an article of clothing and started donning it. It barely registered to him what each item was. He was just going through the motions. When he was finished, it didn't make a difference. He still felt vulnerable, like she'd ripped out a part of him.

He left the suite, staring at his feet as he walked down the hall to his room. Stopping at his door, he turned to Jessie's room, where she'd probably escaped to, but he didn't really see the smooth metal surface. The feeling of being alone that Jessie had often asked about suddenly hit him, nearly driving him into the floor.

Delyn placed a supporting hand on his door, standing there with weak knees, letting the solid, cool strength of the material start to ground him. His breath was ragged as he tried to regain his calm, regain the fortitude and surety of purpose that had driven him forward for all these years.

You have no purpose.

The thought hit him hard, making him gasp. His ragged breathing grew worse, and he scrambled desperately to open his door. He couldn't bear for Jessie to see him like this, this weak, this low.

He fell through the door when it opened, staggering to the bed and collapsing against his hands as the door closed automatically behind him. On some level, he felt like another door was closing on him.

His destiny.

But what could he do now if he couldn't be a Seeder? That was his duty to his people. That was his reason for being, his reason for being born. If not that, then what?

Jessie felt like shit as she sat in her room. She'd been hiding there since the debacle in the medical suite. Now, instead of finding ways to bump into Delyn when she could, she was actively trying to avoid him. She could still remember the look on his face when she'd said no to him. He'd looked like a kicked puppy, and it hadn't changed since. Every time she caught a glimpse of him, he'd been mopey, beaten.

And it's all my fault.

She couldn't forget the fact that, according to what he'd told her about his culture, he had *one* role in life, and she'd just denied him the opportunity to fulfill that role. Sure, there was still the contract. To her knowledge, there wasn't a way out of it. It didn't have a specific end date, but she would need to carry her end of the contract, eventually.

She would just prefer actually *wanting* to have sex with him, even a little, before doing so. He might not see it that way, but she couldn't help how she felt. What he was clearly proposing was a deeply intimate act, something she just couldn't go into lightly.

She wished she felt more for him sexually, but it felt like she'd only met him yesterday. Sure, he was cute, if a little weird, but she could see herself feeling for him, eventually. And he was certainly growing on her. She smiled to herself as she thought of their experiences together so far. There was this awkward adorableness to him that just made her smile and want to support him. She couldn't help it.

Jessie sighed. "Yeah, I could definitely see myself caring about him some day."

Which wasn't helping because now she was imagining what it would be like to have a life with a guy like him. She could see it, imagine it, and she didn't dislike what she saw. She imagined him supporting her art, while she she did the same in kind for him, though she drew a giant blank in her head at what that might be. He seemed to have no interests outside of his role as a Seeder. He seemed to have a bizarrely single-minded idea of purpose, which created a fairly narrow life for himself. She had an impulse to show him the world, to teach him hobbies, to give him meaning beyond what his society dictated to him.

But that wasn't her role here. She'd signed a surrogacy contract, one she'd only recently refused to go through with. The only real role she had in his life she'd just turned down, shunning him. She couldn't imagine he was too happy with her at the moment, certainly not enough to consider what she had to say about expanding his horizons.

So, what could she do? Though he was growing on her as a person, she still wasn't to the point where she wanted to have *sex* with him. Although, that beast between his legs had certainly drawn the eye. It had been both mouthwatering and terrifying. She couldn't honestly understand why the women in his society had turned him down. They must be nuts. Long and thick, it had seemed mostly like a human dick, simple, straightforward, with no weird protuberances or appendages.

Not that she'd studied it or anything. She got up off her bed, shaking her head at her sudden obsession with Delyn's sexual equipment. Though it was something she needed to consider, she didn't need to do so now. Certainly, not in so much detail.

Jessie crossed the room, heading to the closet where all her stuff except her easel was stored. The easel sat forlorn and abandoned in the corner. She hadn't been in the right emotional state for art since that showdown, too angry and confused to be able to express herself in any way that would make sense to the viewer. She'd tried doing a little drawing on her tablet, but it had just been an exercise in futility. One time, she'd screamed under her breath as she'd scratched out everything she'd just drawn before deleting the file entirely.

After that, she'd decided she needed a break from art. That was pretty rare for her. She couldn't remember the last time she'd felt this way, but that didn't change her reality. Opening a drawer, she pulled out her computer. At a glance, it looked like a thin gray piece of metal. She jumped back on the bed, letting the mattress bounce underneath her and trying to regain her normal buoyancy of spirit. She opened the laptop and booted it up, the display filling with the OS loading sequence.

Jessie closed her eyes, groaning at the horses humping each other on-screen. Cass would be Cass. Years ago, her sister had installed a skin to the operating system, which Jessie honestly didn't know how to remove.

She'd tried.

The screen passed and a series of lines of codes flashed on the screen before the computer verified her identity with facial recognition, then proceeded to the welcome screen. "Welcome, Jess," it said, making her frown.

Her sister always called her Jess, even though she didn't like it. It felt too much like a boy's name to her, though she supposed Jessie *did* sound a lot like Jesse, which was her dead name. Still, she'd liked her name, even if it didn't quite fit her as a girl. Which was why she'd picked the name Jessica, and then immediately insisted her sister call her Jessie. It was a logic both comical and typical of a five-year-old.

Leaving the welcome screen behind, she just sort of stared at the desktop for a while, not knowing what to do. Jessie had learned a lot about computers from her sister and the AI her sister had created, Angus. She used to only goof off on the computer when she didn't feel like painting or drawing, but after Kou arrived, she'd found herself on the computer more and more. She'd spent a lot of time learning programming and hacking. Granted, no force in this universe could ever make her as competent as her sister, but she was passable, especially if she could use the programs Cass had made.

She'd never really been any good at hacking on the fly.

Under any other circumstances, she probably would have never even tried to learn hacking, but after Kou entered their lives, she'd felt a little displaced. Sure, she wanted her sister to be happy, and she was genuinely glad that he'd shown up on the scene, but it still left her feeling a little useless. Her main skill was art, which wasn't terribly valuable on a pirate ship. Her sister was an impressive hacker, and Kou was ex-military, a security specialist, and a cyborg. Meanwhile, her sister had rarely ever even allowed her to hold a weapon, let alone go with her on jobs.

Learning to hack and program had at least felt like something productive, even if she could never be as good as her sister. It had kept her distracted as Cass and Kou had humped like bunnies on every surface of the ship. There was not enough eye bleach in the galaxy for the amount of naked times she'd accidentally walked in on since Kou moved in.

Jessie frowned. She didn't consider herself a prude, but there were just some things you didn't want to see in relation to your family members. Anything related to sex was one of them.

Of course, thinking about sex just made her think of Delyn now… and that giant dick. She sighed. "That is gonna be a doozy." She shook her head and returned her attention to the computer, resting her fingers on the keys. She shook her head again and looked away. "What am I doing? This is not solving anything. I'm just hiding in here and delaying the inevitable."

And yet she couldn't seem to get herself to move, to go out there and talk to him. She wasn't ready. She didn't know what to say. Jessie thought about talking to somebody, but couldn't think of who. Cass would be totally enthusiastic, if completely unhelpful. Victoria would probably be the most useful, but Victoria liked socializing on *her* terms. And she didn't know Kaea well enough for this kind of topic.

"Maybe I just need to do some research."

Maybe if she just understood him better, understood his people better, they could have a more meaningful conversation and actually make some progress.

Jessie was avoiding him. Delyn couldn't say he blamed her. Looking back, he realized he'd made some serious mistakes and assumptions, things he should have realized an alien wouldn't understand or know. He should have known she wouldn't know how their breeding process went. He should have explained it to her before she signed that contract.

Now, he felt like he couldn't even hold her to the contract, like he should destroy it or mark it null and void. He'd essentially lied to her by omitting information she clearly needed to make a sound decision, and it didn't sit well with him. He wasn't that type of person.

Standing up, he paced his room, uncertain what he should do. The time was fast approaching when they would reach Wesa. What then? Originally, he'd intended for the implantation process to have already been completed by then. Would he even be welcomed back now?

Or was he overthinking this? Maybe it was perfectly normal for those like him to return home for a spell, even if only to visit. Maybe he could just tell them that Jessie was considering becoming a Birther and that he'd brought her there to help her make her decision. They would probably accept her more than they would Delyn.

With a sigh, he sat back down on his bed, the green material puffing up around him. He stared at the wall across from him, where people he knew, some he saw as family, stared back at him from the pictures there. He felt weird in that moment, like he didn't know what to think of the images before him. They felt different, like the people within them were strangers, even though he'd known them his entire life. Was he a stranger to them now? Did he even belong there anymore?

He looked away and leaned back on the bed, back propped up against the wall, and grabbed his computer from where he'd left it on the bedding. It powered on in a moment, and he started pulling up information on Earth.

Researching Delyn's species had been a bit of a rabbit hole. Or maybe a black hole. She'd started out on easy to access databases, things similar to the internet back home. But so much of the information there seemed incomplete or even propaganda shared by those like the Ateles who didn't really like the Pardus.

That had started her down a path of searching for harder to access databases and networks. She wiggled her fingers in the air over the keyboard, her nerves getting the best of her. Yesterday, she'd found the Pardus government's network. She hadn't tried to access it, feeling a bit too nervous to actually attempt the hack, but today was the day. She cracked her knuckles and tried to emulate her cocky sister.

"You've got this."

She felt a little silly, sitting on her bed with a computer on her lap as she psyched herself up for hacking into a government network. It was stupid. It was insane.

She was doing it.

It was also surprisingly easy once she got started. Like her sister had often commented on, people tended to defend against the threats they expected. Meaning the Pardus would defend against known threats like the Ateles, who hated them. But they had probably never heard of humans, and humans had very different ways of thinking and different approaches than the Ateles. This meant methods that probably shouldn't have worked did, and soon she was in.

It was always a weird feeling when you finally gained access to something by illicit means. Suddenly, the adrenaline of the hack fell away. It was like taking off. There was all that pressure from the launch, then suddenly it was almost as if you were floating as you finally leveled off. For a moment, she just stared at the screen, not sure what to do or where to go.

It was all right there in front of her, every little morsel of information she could possibly desire. At least, she hoped. The screen was filled with little boxes, each with lettering in a language she couldn't understand. She quickly set up a translation program to work, changing everything into English for her.

She read off each box. Laws & Regulations, Departments, Schedule, Members & Hierarchy, Communications Access, Census, Meeting Minutes, Regions & Communities, Historical Texts.

Jessie clicked the first box and hoped she wouldn't fall asleep from boredom.

Jessie had been reading on the Pardus network for days now. She'd only barely glanced over the Laws & Regulation section, feeling like her eyes would bleed if she kept at it for too long. Also, the members, schedule, communities, and census sections were just spitting out information without much context, often lists of names, dates, locations, and demographic information.

Meeting minutes were a little interesting, giving an inside look into what their government and agencies were up to. And the communities section did have a bunch of maps, letting her get an idea of the layout of the planet and what each region was known for. She'd even found a map that showed Valana, Delyn's community. It was a tiny little place in the middle of nowhere, and she'd felt a little thrill at finding it on a map.

But the real pièce de résistance was the Historical Texts. It was a lot of dense, dry information, but it was in story format for the most part. In rare instances, it would document the details of historically significant events in this academic manner that was simultaneously really fascinating and so dry it was hard for her to keep her eyes open. Regardless, it was interesting, and she spent most of her time in that section of the network.

It was there that, after several days, she noticed something peculiar. She had been reading their history in reverse order (that was how it was organized), when it just cut off abruptly. It was telling the story of the end of a civil war and the formation of their consolidated government. But, even though there clearly was history before that, there was no mention of it. It was as if it had never happened. The network didn't say how long the war lasted for, who was involved, how many factions there were, any significant battles of the war, nothing. It was as if the Pardus suddenly began at that point, at least with how the historical texts were written.

It made no sense. She stared at that earliest entry, her vision blurring and spots forming on her eyes from staring at the screen for too long. Lost in thought, she tapped on the surface of the laptop, the smooth metal making a light ting sound with each tap of her thumbnail.

Why did it just end? There should be more, and her insatiable curiosity couldn't handle there not being more, so she started looking for Easter eggs. She slowly and methodically scoured every millimeter of the Historical Texts section, looking for hidden links or maybe an obscure login page. She checked the network directory, going page by page, matching it up to pages she could access through the regular prompts.

Hours passed during her hunt. Soon her eyes were sore and dry, her eyelids heavy, and her entire body was screaming out at her to move. She sighed and stood up, stretching her aching limbs. Her back felt like it had been knotted into a pretzel as she worked out muscles that weren't intended to sit idle for so long.

Jessie crossed to the door and pressed her ear to it, but there was no sound on the other side. She slipped out and jogged to the kitchen, opening the fridge in search of something to eat, suddenly realizing she was starving now that food was nigh. Undecided, she just picked something that didn't require reheating and started shoveling it into her mouth with her fingers. She barely tasted it, just noticing that it was something slightly savory.

She leaned against the counter, bowl in hand, just staring at the wall across from her. The ship was silent other than the gentle hum of the systems that kept it moving and them alive. She could easily forget that she wasn't alone here, that Delyn was right down the hall. Thinking of him made her feel guilty about how she'd reacted, but it had been a surprise. He hadn't mentioned anything about needing to have sex before actually dropping trou. A part of her wanted to be angry at him for leaving out important details, but she also hadn't asked, had she? They'd both made assumptions about the other, and she really couldn't fault him for that. Nobody was perfect.

"Definitely not me."

She stuffed the last bite in her mouth, dropped the bowl in the dishwasher, and brushed her hands together, wiping away any residual food. She hesitated, though, at the thought of returning to her room. It was sort of nice not being confined in those four walls, not that this was much better. It was just different. Until they reached their destination, there would be no escape. Just her and Delyn and a ship that was entirely too small for comfort.

Just how long had he been living on this claustrophobic ship? Jessie suspected she would go crazy after only a few weeks. At least the *Trojan* had some facilities. True, it had the galaxy's smallest kitchen, but it had a weight room (that she almost never used) and that big cargo area. There was space to move.

She had a decent sized room. She could burn off her stir-craziness if they went too long between ports.

This place had nothing and just contemplating it was messing with her head. She rushed back to her room, closing the door behind her with a gentle click. Her computer called to her from the bed, still open and showing the directory for the Pardus government network. She walked to the edge of the bed, staring at the screen, trying to come up with an idea.

Then it hit her… archives.

Jessie sat down and pulled the computer back onto her lap. She didn't know what it would be called. Maybe archives, maybe trash, or something else entirely. The fact that the entire network was being translated for her also created some complications. Native phrases could be mistranslated and misconstrued. Some things might have significance which was heavily tied to culture. Other things might be completely untranslatable.

Still, she searched and quickly found what was probably supposed to be a permanently locked archive vault. Jessie growled under her breath as she worked on the security, frustrated with her skill level. She tried again and again, working the problem from every angle she could think of, but no luck. She grew increasingly convinced that she wasn't smart enough or good enough. It actually took longer to hack this secure digital vault than it had to hack the entire network.

The longer it took, the more excited and frustrated Jessie became. She felt certain she was hacking into the Holy Grail of Pardus secrets. And being denied was making her want to pull her hair out. She was consumed, obsessed. She lost track of everything around her, only barely noticing when her stomach growled or the slight pressure of her bladder.

Then she was in. She shrieked and threw her hands up in the air, nearly tossing her laptop to the floor in her excitement. She caught it real quick and righted it, placing it on the comforter. Her smile was stuck on her face so hard it hurt, but she couldn't stop herself. Her body practically bubbled with excitement, not even caring that the screen just showed another page that looked similar to the Historical Texts section.

Jessie stood and shook out some of the excess energy, bouncing on her feet as she grinned.

Then a knock came at the door.

"Yes?" she said, freezing in place, her grin drooping a little.

"Is everything okay?"

"Peachy!" she said, her voice almost squeaking.

"What?"

She shook her head, realizing what she'd done. *He doesn't know English, stupid.* "Everything's fine."

"Oh, okay." Steps moved away from the door, and she turned back to the computer with renewed interest and a calmer demeanor.

Jessie sat down and pulled the computer back onto her lap, reading the first entry, which continued where the Historical Texts had left off.

"By governing decree, it was decided to continue the drone policy."

"What's a drone policy?"

Captain Narvill paced agitatedly in the small control room of his ship. Worry filled him as he waited for the news that they'd caught up to the ship holding Jessie Allen hostage. The moment couldn't come soon enough.

He shook his head, wondering why he'd let himself get wrapped up in this.

He'd been approached days ago on some backwater Ateles colony he'd stopped at for restocking and maybe some trade. It was always good to stay friendly with the Ateles. They were the single deadliest military power in the parts of space he traveled, and that wasn't something he was willing to cross.

Anyway, the man, Rae, had walked up to him and asked for his help. Narvill had been hesitant at first, but the man had looked desperate. And so, he'd humored him for a while, but when Rae had mentioned his fiance being kidnapped, his stupid heart had betrayed him.

The next thing he knew, he was taking off with a new passenger, following the planned path of a ship that had left less than a day before them. It was nerve-racking, and Rae had been driving his crew nuts ever since.

To a certain extent, he couldn't blame him. Rae had learned the flight plans and origin of the ship from the yardmaster, and it didn't look good. It was a Pardus ship, heading to Wesa, their homeworld. The Pardus were known for two things, really: disliking the Ateles and mercenary work. He suspected this crew had been hired to kidnap her, but he wasn't sure of the motivation yet. Rae had money, had even paid up front to hire his crew, but so far, no ransom had been demanded. Additionally, Jessie wasn't rich or well known, being a young artist just starting to make a name for herself back home.

He sighed and dropped into one of the seats, staring out at the stars on the screen. "Poor thing. She's gotta be terrified." He couldn't imagine what she might be going through. Taken against her will, probably fighting tooth and nail to get away before it was too late. Being thrown on a ship and knowing her chances of escape had just disappeared as the engines came to life around her and the force of launch hit her.

He shuffled in his seat, uncomfortable with the emotions his musings were unearthing. "Enough," he said as he rubbed his hot face. He shifted his gaze to the control screen attached to his chair. The display showed their planned trajectory, time until they reached Wesa, and a line of menu buttons on the right.

"I wish I had a faster ship." Unfortunately, his was a cargo vessel, designed for carrying bulk, not for speed. It saved money on fuel, but in this case, it also meant he might not catch up to them before they reached Wesa. If they were mercenaries, they probably had a much faster ship than him.

Then the screen flashed yellow. Narvill jerked in his seat, startled out of his mood. He tapped the screen, bringing up the sensor readings to find out what it had detected in their path. It wasn't an imminent threat, so after the immediate surprise, he calmly looked through all the data. Within moments, he realized it was a ship. Heat readings, metal detected, rapid movement. That was all consistent with a spaceship.

He looked up at the larger screen. It was still just filled with stars, the other vessel outside of visual range, but could this be it? Had they caught up with the kidnappers?

CHAPTER EIGHT

*A*n obnoxiously loud alarm blared as the steady lights changed to a flashing red. Delyn froze in the middle of preparing a meal, air trapped in his lungs. The alarm sound screamed again, causing him to flinch. He dropped his utensil and rushed out of the room.

"Stay in your room!" he yelled at Jessie as she rushed out into the hall at the same time. She held a knife in her hand, a wicked piece that looked like it was used for gutting people. He pointed at her as he ran down the hallway in her direction. "Just stay there. Lock the door."

"What is that alarm?"

"Don't know. I'll reach you on the intercom."

Still tense, she continued to hover in the doorway as he passed, his focus on getting to the control room. He bounded off the chair as he arrived, his fingers digging into the padding of the backrest. On-screen, the words "Imminent Breach" flashed.

His heart hammered in his chest, and he turned to close the door and lock it. He took several, hopefully, calming breaths and sat down. *Think. Think. Think. What do I do?* He wasn't trained for this. He wasn't a Fighter, didn't know the first thing about what to do in an emergency like this. Probably, telling Jessie to hide in her room and lock the door was a good idea. Limit access. And the ship had to be controlled from this room, so locking the door meant they probably couldn't hijack it.

What else?

He felt like his mind was both racing in all directions at once and running in neutral, not coming up with a single useful idea. "Why can't I think? Come on."

He breathed in and let out several shaky breaths as the alarm on the screen changed from "Imminent Breach" to "Intruders Detected."

His heart froze up in his chest. "What do I do?"

Cameras.

He pulled up all the security cameras on the ship. They populated the large screen with little boxes showing each part of the ship, including private areas. People in dark, unmatched outfits were flooding through the airlock at the back of the ship, filling up the hallway. "This is bad." He and Jessie were excessively outnumbered and outgunned. They couldn't possibly fight back.

Then he watched in cold terror as Jessie opened her bedroom door, slipping out into the hall that was, at that very moment, overrun with intruders.

"No!" he said, jumping from his seat and rushing to the door. It opened far too slowly, and by the time he fell into the hallway, it was already too late. Jessie was surrounded by people so big and tall, he could barely see her.

"Jessie!" he yelled, drawing the attention of every person on the ship.

They all turned to him, some of them looking ready to kill. He forced down his fear and said, "Let her go."

One of the men walked up to him and aimed a gun at his forehead, his gaze daring Delyn to repeat himself.

"I said, 'Let her go.' " He was terrified, and his body was trembling like it was trying to vibrate himself into tiny pieces, but he held firm. For her.

The man shook his head. A moment later, Delyn felt pain, then darkness.

<hr />

Jessie was terrified and pissed. She screamed and kicked and punched as the group of bulky, brainless *morons* pushed and shoved her from Delyn's ship while barely touching her. For not the first time, she really wished she wasn't so fucking tiny. She wanted to beat the living *shit* out of all these idiots, and she steadfastly refused to think about what might be happening right now with Delyn.

He'd been so brave, speaking up and telling them to let her go. He'd had no chance of forcing them to, but he'd said it anyway. And his voice barely shook. He had to have thought he was putting himself in danger, but he did it anyway.

For me.

She didn't feel worthy, and all combined, it had her wanting to fight even harder. She screamed again, the sound filled with all the frustration she was feeling as they herded her onto their ship. When she heard the airlock doors closed, the crowd dispersed into a circle around her, allowing her to see the large, partially filled cargo bay they'd stopped in.

No one was within her reach, so she stopped fighting, just glaring at everyone equally.

A squat man with the most orange skin she'd ever seen approached her cautiously, his hands out in a placating gesture. "It's okay," he said, his voice set in low, deep tones that he probably thought were soothing. "My name is Captain Narvill. We're here to rescue you."

She frowned. "Rescue me?"

He nodded. "Your fiance sent us."

Now, she was really confused. Was this all a misunderstanding? Did they "rescue" the wrong person? She almost laughed, but it really wasn't funny. "I don't have a fiance."

They all froze, looking at each other, probably in confusion.

"But…"

"Sounds like you have the wrong person."

"But you're Jessie Allen, correct?"

Now she frowned even harder. She could *feel* the crease forming between her brows. "I am…"

He nodded in relief. "Then we don't have the wrong person."

"You do," she insisted. "Because I don't have a fiance."

"You don't know someone named Rae?"

"Rae?! My stalker," Jessie said in irritation. She looked away, shaking her head at the absurdity of the situation. *You've gotta be fucking kidding me.* "Listen, he's already attacked me twice. I left the fucking planet because he was stalking me and found out where I lived. He. Is not. My fiance. Clear?"

She was getting increasingly angry the more she talked about it. How could he? What type of psychotic moron did you have to be to lie and tell someone a girl was your fiance, then hire them to kidnap her for you?

"Stalker?"

"Yes! Stalker. I had to threaten him at gunpoint when I left the planet, just to make him walk away."

The skin on the man's face was muddling with color.

"Jessie!" Rae's voice filled the now awkwardly quiet cargo bay.

Jessie spun around, facing the direction it had come from. She wished she still had her knife, but they'd disarmed her shortly after she'd entered the hallway in Delyn's ship. She tensed, ready to fight, her mind running through shifts she could use to get a slight advantage. Since she was so small, the only thing she could think of was spiking her adrenaline.

Too late.

Just hearing his voice had adrenaline surging through her with enthusiasm.

He slipped through the crowd, stepping to the front with a smile on his face and his arms outstretched, as if he expected her to rush into them.

"If I had a gun right now, I'd shoot you." She was pretty sure she could get away with it, too. They were probably in disputed space right now. Because the Pardus and Ateles didn't get along, there was a wide patch of space between their territories that no one controlled. She could probably kill him, and no one could charge her for it.

"Jessie…" he said, using his sweet, cajoling voice. He was playing the loving fiance right now, and it made her want to hit him, because she knew the angry, jealous stalker was right under the surface.

"Don't even start."

Captain Narvill stepped up, the first of the crew to be knocked out of their surprise. "Did you or did you not lie when hiring us?"

Rae's smile faltered for a moment, before returning with even more force. "Lie? About what?"

"You claimed that Ms. Allen here was your fiance and had been kidnapped."

"She is, and she had." He looked just the slightest bit stubborn as he spoke, reminding her a bit of a little boy caught in a lie.

"And yet she claims that she's *not* your fiance, and that she was trying to escape you."

"That's… a lie." He turned to Jessie, a little of that familiar anger creeping into his face, but his voice remained sweet and cajoling. "Come on now, Jessie. Tell the truth."

She shook her head. "You're insane. *That's* the truth. We went on *one* date. I *didn't* promise you a second. I *didn't* ask to be followed or grabbed in the streets or threatened."

The transition from sweet to psycho was instantaneous. "You traitorous bitch." He lunged at her, but got nowhere, the people around him quickly grabbing him and holding him back.

As he continued to yell, throwing insults at her and pulling on his restraints, Captain Narvill ushered her out of the cargo bay. "I'm sorry for all this. I had no idea he wasn't legit."

Jessie shook her head, taking pity on the man. "It's all right. I don't blame you." If she and Cass had been in a similar situation in the *Trojan*, they might have done the same thing. Damsel in distress? Yeah, she could see them wanting to save her. And with their skills with boarding other ships, it would have been easy to organize a rescue mission.

"That's very kind of you," he said, nodding his head, which was actually around the same height as her own. It was a little weird not being shorter than everyone around her. Even Delyn, who wasn't terribly big or bulky, was still taller than her.

"It's really not. You did what you thought was right. I mean, thinking something's right doesn't mean it *is*. We never have *all* the information, but the best we can ever do is what's right based on the information we *do* have."

"That's very wise."

"Well, has to happen every once in a while," she said self-deprecatingly.

He smiled and faced her. "Allow me to take you wherever you wish to go."

Jessie paused, her mind immediately returning to Delyn. Things were weird with him right now, but she wasn't ready to end them. Delyn seemed to be a good guy, so there was nothing to run from other than their awkwardness with each other right now. And that was probably temporary. The simple fact was that Jessie wasn't done with that storyline yet. She wanted to see it through. The nebulousness of their relationship made her uneasy, but she liked him and was looking forward to seeing Wesa.

"Can I go back to Delyn's ship?"

"Yes, of course. Though he'll probably have one ugly headache for a while."

"He's okay though, right?"

"To the best of my knowledge."

She nodded. "Good."

"So, what do you want to do about Rae?"

She shook her head. "I don't know. I thought getting away would be enough. I wasn't even thinking it would be permanent. I thought if I just left and allowed him to move on without me, that everything would be fine. I never expected him to *follow* me." She laughed and shook her head again. "God, even saying that sounds stupid. He's a stalker. He was already following me. Of course, he was gonna follow me. What was I thinking?"

"You were probably reacting instinctually. There are three common responses to a threat in nature: fight, flight, and freeze. You chose flight. You ran. There's nothing wrong with that."

"But what do we do? Isn't he gonna just keep coming?"

"Not necessarily. You said he attacked you? Stalked you?"

She nodded.

"I'm counting nearly half a dozen different charges."

"Charges?"

"Yes. Multiple counts of assault, stalking, verbal threats, attempted kidnapping-special circumstances, fraud."

"Fraud?" Jessie felt like she was missing something in this conversation.

"Yes. He hired our ship under false pretenses. And hiring a crew to commit kidnapping is illegal in Ateles-controlled space, even if the kidnapping doesn't happen in that territory."

"That sounds like a lot."

"It is."

"How do you know all this?"

"I'm routinely in Ateles-controlled space. It's smart to know what I can get myself in trouble over."

"Makes sense." Though now she was wondering what he was doing that he thought he could get in trouble for.

Okay, moving on…

"So, what's gonna happen next? What do I do? Do I have to go back?"

He shook his head. "No. We can record your statement on the ship to hand over to law enforcement."

"And Delyn's. He was also assaulted by Rae."

"And his. Then we'll testify as well. He'll be put on trial, and he'll likely be put in a reform program. If I remember correctly, until he's classified as reformed, all of his movements and actions will be regulated and tightly monitored."

"So, he won't be able to come after me again."

"No, that'll likely be a very specific requirement of his reform."

"Then let's get started."

"Are you sure about this?" Captain Narvill said. He looked over at Jessie with concern.

They were standing in front of the airlock door. His hand hovered over the control panel.

"Yes, I'm sure. Thank you. You've been very understanding and helpful. I don't think I would have been able to figure out what to do with Rae without you."

She still couldn't get over his skin tone or the fact that he was basically the same height as her. He had nowhere near the same body shape, but looking someone in the eye without having to practically crane her neck backward was a novel experience.

Narvill nodded. "Very well." He turned away, working his fingers over the panel. The door hissed as it started to open.

She stepped into the intervening space, then turned to face Narvill. "Goodbye and good luck."

He nodded. "To you as well."

Jessie turned, wondering how she was going to operate the doors, but needn't have worried. The next door hissed open moments later. She looked behind her, seeing Narvill nodding to her through the small circular window in the door separating them.

She saluted and stepped onto Delyn's ship. A feeling like emotional depressurization hit her as she left the airlock behind.

"Jessie!"

She smiled this time as her name was yelled, knowing Delyn's voice immediately. He rushed out of the medical suite and wrapped her in a surprisingly strong hug, then pulled back, his face turning red. "I'm sorry. I should have asked."

"It's fine. I get it. I'm glad you're okay, too." She frowned as she took him in. He had a swelling bruise on his forehead. "Oh… that's what he meant." Her hand hovered over the spot, hesitant to touch it.

Delyn stepped back, looking a bit awkward again. "It's fine. It'll heal."

"Well, I would hope so. How's it feel? Headache?"

"A little. Yeah."

She nodded. "Listen, I'm really sorry about all this."

"What do you mean?"

"You remember the guy? In the street?"

"The guy who attacked you?"

She nodded.

"What about him?"

Jessie looked away, noticing the airlock door was still open. She walked over to the console, trying to puzzle out the controls. She knew she was just stalling, but she was suddenly reluctant to admit that this had all happened because of her. Delyn got hurt because of *her*.

Sure, she knew she wasn't responsible for Rae's actions, but she was the one who had dragged her problems to Delyn's door. He wouldn't have been in the way to be hurt if she hadn't answered that ad, and that was on her. She suspected that if she'd been brave enough to just call her sister, this never would have happened. There was no way Angus or Kou or Cass would have let it. Which meant she'd fucked up.

Delyn crowded in next to her, his hand moving over the console to close the door.

"Thanks."

"No problem. Now, what about him?"

Jessie looked down as she turned to face him. "He was the reason we were boarded. He hired a crew to come 'rescue' me."

"Then why did you say sorry?"

"Because… you wouldn't have been hurt if I wasn't here."

"Jessie, you didn't hurt me. Rae did. He's to blame. He's the one that should be apologizing."

Feeling uncomfortable, she changed subjects. "Right, um, you should go over to the other ship and provide a testimony. The captain is putting together statements to present to law enforcement back on the colony."

Delyn hovered next to her, not saying a word for several beats. "Will you be okay?"

She finally looked up. "Yeah. I'm fine. Go."

He waited for several more beats before nodding his head and reopening the airlock doors. She watched him leave, listened as the doors hissed closed again, thinking how he seemed so much more mature for some reason.

She turned, heading back to her room. When she stepped over the threshold, she saw her computer sitting closed on the bedspread, waiting for her.

That's right.

"The drone policy."

She stepped forward, letting the door close behind her, and sat down. A renewed curiosity, and her propensity for avoiding her problems, persuaded her to open the laptop once more.

The Keeper of Electronic Records raced down the hallway, his mind in a chaotic panic as curse words, which were the only clearly defined thoughts he was capable of at the moment, ran through his head at full speed. He barely noticed the beautifully etched walls around him or the parquet floors under his feet. Mostly, he noticed how hard and slippery the floor was as he tried to make turns at full speed.

Disbelief mingled with panic as he reached the door he was looking for. He collapsed against the wall, not having the ability to stop on his own. With a shaky fist, he rapped on the wooden surface. His forehead rested on the wall next to it as he tried to get his breathing back under control after that mad dash across the building. The surface was cool against his sweaty skin, giving him some measure of comfort and grounding after the panic he was still struggling with.

The door swept open, slamming with a bang against the wall to his left. It was a testament to his fatigue and abused nerves that he barely flinched.

"What's the meaning of this?" an authoritative voice said from the doorway.

He tried to speak, but couldn't get in enough air. His breath wheezed in and out, he gasped, but it still took far longer than he would have liked to speak that first word. He could feel the official next to him getting increasingly irate.

Finally, with breaths punctuating each word, he said, "The Vault… was… hacked." He took in a big breath and let out a sigh, his entire body feeling weak once he'd given the news.

The panic started to recede as well now that the responsibility was on someone else's shoulders, allowing him to think some-what clearly again. He hated this. For any other emergency, he would just activate an automated system, but unauthorized access to the Archive Vault was no ordinary emergency. So few people even knew of its existence that they had no auto-mated systems in place. Automated systems required mainte-nance, they required planning. You couldn't set one up without whole teams of people coordinating on the project.

He was the only person in his department who knew about the Vault. While he hadn't set it up (it was far too old), he had been handed the information from his predecessor. He

managed the Vault, controlled accessed, monitored it, trans-
ferred it to new hardware as needed, but he didn't have access
himself. He didn't know what was on it, only that it contained
state secrets.

"You've got to be kidding me..." the voice said, drawing his
attention. The authoritative tone had left, leaving the voice
sounding tired and almost weak.

He pushed up off the wall, facing the member of the Magistracy responsible for overseeing the Vault. "I'm afraid it's true,
sir."

The man had clearly been roused from his bed, wearing a soft
pair of pants and a silky robe.

"Heavens help us," he said, shaking his head. He looked over
at the Keeper. "We need to find this person and silence them.
No one can know what's inside that vault."

CHAPTER NINE

*J*essie had spent all her time since returning to the ship reading the Archive Vault. It was the perfect distraction, allowing her to avoid talking about the kidnapping or looking at Delyn's bruise, each of which she really wasn't ready to deal with yet. She threw herself headlong into the vault because she didn't want to deal with her problems. She knew that. Jessie was fully aware of how childish she was being. Several times, she'd heard Delyn enter the hallway, hover in the space between their rooms, then move on. She wasn't sure if they were both being childish or if him giving her space was the more mature approach to their relationship.

She didn't focus on it too often at the moment, though. Instead, she set her mind to exploring. And what she found shocked, disturbed, and dismayed her by turns. She frequently had to check the original text and verify the meanings contextually to make sure it wasn't just a translation error.

It wasn't. It was real. The Pardus government had really abused their people this way. Everything Delyn had told her about his people and the structure of their society was a carefully crafted effort by the government to exploit the Pardus people.

The "drone policy" was a policy enacted during the civil war when warriors were dying off like flies. Drones took less gestational time and less time to mature, meaning they could be battle-ready sooner. During the war, that had been useful, essential even. They had used whatever they could to keep their numbers going as tribe battled tribe, seemingly attempting to wipe each other out. They would seed into females of any species, even livestock, if that would keep their tribes alive. It was life or death. It made sense, and she couldn't blame them for doing what they had to in order to survive.

But when the war was over, the consolidated government that formed decided to keep it going. The war had gone on for generations and many of the common folk had forgotten there was ever another way. They'd forgotten there was once a balance between males and females. They'd forgotten it used to take nearly twenty years for their people to mature. They'd forgotten it took the better part of a year to gestate a fetus.

And that wasn't even the worst part. The worst part was that they'd created a societal system that was never questioned, all so they could profit off the extra males in society by using them as mercenaries, as disposable assets.

There was a reason the Ateles didn't like the Pardus. The people leading them were monsters.

"Any updates?" the Magistrate said as he entered the Keeper's office.

He looked up from his computer console, shaking his head at the official. He'd been working non-stop trying to find something, but though they had data, he didn't know what to do with it. They had details on the hardware used for the hack, but couldn't trace it back to any manufacturer on record. And the hack was ongoing. The hacker was treating it like a public access database, going in and out as they pleased.

He'd suggested taking the Archive Vault offline temporarily to stop the hacks, but the Magistrate had refused, saying they would never catch the person if they couldn't trace them back electronically.

He couldn't refute that, unfortunately.

Not knowing what to tell him, he looked around his office, looking for inspiration, but there was none to be had. His normally pristine space was now filled with printouts. They covered every flat surface, and some were even taped to the walls. At times, he stood staring at them, trying to find an insight that would prove fruitful.

The Keeper sighed and looked up at the Magistrate, folding his hands in front of him. He squeezed them tight as he began to speak. "I'm sorry, but no. I've never seen hardware specs like this person is using. It's not from any of the species we routinely work with."

"Not even the Ateles?"

He shook his head. "I checked that first. This is more bare-bones than that. The Ateles would be high end military technology. This," he pointed at the papers in front of him, "is more like someone's personal laptop. I mean, it's high end, but it's nowhere near military-grade. It's powerful, but I can't trace it to any manufacturer. It returns hardware IDs that are formatted unlike any I've ever seen."

"Okay," the Magistrate nodded, not showing his likely disappointment. "What are our next steps?"

He took a deep breath, leaning back in his chair to think. "I can think of two ways to do this. First, the data we have right now is on the actual computer accessing the Vault. The Vault automatically records this information as a way of monitoring usage and alerting of unauthorized access. It's how we knew it was hacked in the first place.

"The Vault doesn't, however, record the *signaling* hardware. It's harder to obtain, and I'm going to have to request some additional resources. It's not cheap, but I can hook that into the Vault hardware, and record information on what signaling hardware they're using and where it is."

"So we'll know where to find them?"

"In theory."

"Do it. I'll authorize any expense. Just get it done."

At first, Jessie didn't know what to do about her discovery. Should she tell Delyn? What would happen if she did?

She ended up pacing her room for hours on end, and continuing to avoid him, but her reasons were changing now. Before, she didn't want to face him because of how awkward they'd both felt after she'd rejected him in the medical suite, an event that felt so long ago now. Jessie had felt uncertain in the aftermath, like she didn't know where she stood with him, maybe even like she'd betrayed him. She'd promised, after all. She'd signed a contract. But then the kidnapping had happened, and Delyn got hurt. She couldn't look at that bruise without thinking of Rae, about all the shit he'd put her through, about how she should have just called her sister to come get her instead.

Jessie still wasn't sure she could face that nasty bruise, but now that concern was overshadowed by something bigger.

The drone policy.

The Pardus government.

The lies.

She didn't want to face him until she knew how to deal with the conspiracy she'd uncovered.

On the one side, she felt like this was something that directly affected Delyn, and it would be wrong to hide it from him. But on the other side, what good would it do if she did? Would it change anything? They were two people. The Pardus government was large, as evidenced by the long list of members in that network she'd just plundered. What could two people do against that?

Nothing. Absolutely nothing. It was a sobering thought, and certainly frustrating, but it was also a little reassuring. She was used to it just being her and Cass against the world. She was used to focusing on her and her family, taking what they needed, and not worrying about anyone else.

Sure, they'd had to think beyond themselves with that weird glowing blue rock that had brought Kou into their lives, but that was different. They'd been thrust into the situation against their will. They did what they had to do, which included giving the rock to someone who wouldn't abuse the power it contained. That was a no-brainer. That was just choosing the best of the options available to them, not trying to wage all-out war on a planetary government.

Doing *that* would be lunacy. Crazy talk. And certainly not in her wheelhouse. For all that she was optimistic, thinking on the positive side, enjoying life to the fullest when she could, she was also fairly practical, too. Do what you can and don't worry about the rest.

What the Pardus were doing was definitely "the rest."

Jessie stopped her pacing and looked at the plain, white door. Beyond it, she could hear Delyn moving around, probably in the kitchen making a meal. She should probably go out and see him now that she'd made up her mind on how to handle the information she'd gleaned.

She wasn't going to tell him. No good could come of it.

But also, she realized as her mind drifted to the original reason they'd been avoiding each other, she couldn't go through with that contract. It just felt wrong to perpetuate the bullshit his government was doing, the abuse they were committing against their own people. She knew there was nothing she could do to stop it. She was only one person, after all, but it was the principle of the thing. Knowing what she knew, how could she possibly participate?

Delyn was eating alone again in the kitchen. Or more accurately, he was pushing his food around his bowl with his utensil while he stared at it morosely. The colors blurred together in an amalgamation of sensory data. His head throbbed with a headache that was slowly going away. Even the lump had gone down, leaving just a yellowing bruise.

When Jessie had returned safely, he'd been so relieved, but his good mood had quickly died. Nothing had changed. He'd gone over to the other ship, given his statement, then returned and detached the two ships. By that point, Jessie had returned to her room.

She'd started avoiding him again.

For a spell, he'd been able to focus on the misery of his pounding head. The medication only really took the edge off, and occasionally, he rubbed at the lump, making it ache anew and distracting him from the constant headache settled deeper in his skull.

But soon enough, the injury wasn't much of a distraction anymore, and his mind returned to his earlier problems, problems that didn't revolve around Rae and kidnappers. With the residual headache, he had trouble focusing and didn't feel like learning about Jessie's people or where she was from, which had been his chosen distraction *before* getting hit.

Instead, he wallowed. He zeroed in on every mistake he'd made since meeting her, on what he could have done differently, sometimes even on what he could do now to fix things. It all seemed so impossible. His first real chance to fulfill his duty to society, and he'd screwed up royally. At this point, he wondered why he was even alive. What was his purpose? To fuck up? To be a drain on society?

Maybe he should just leave his people behind, start somewhere fresh, figure out some way of providing for himself.

Though what that would be, he had no idea. He'd certainly helped out a bit back home, chipping in when he didn't know what his role in society would be, so he'd tried his little hands at everything. It had been fun, but he'd been less than graceful, just a small child trying to help the adults and getting in the way.

Once he'd been given his role, that had become his life. He wasn't allowed to participate in most other activities to support the community. He was to focus on providing them a next generation. Looking back, he realized it was stifling and like a rebuke. He'd felt abandoned, in a way, like they'd washed their hands of him, especially when the females didn't want to help him fulfill his role. He'd questioned why for so long. The question itself had lost its meaning.

Then the door opened, and Jessie stepped in like some celestial being, perfect and bright and sunny. She had a smile on her face that dimmed slightly upon seeing him, and he ducked his head farther toward his bowl.

That's right. She wants nothing to do with you.

As he tried to focus on eating, she shuffled around the kitchen to his right, her steps rhythmic and musical, like a dance. Objects clinked and clicked, cloth brushed against cloth, shoes tapped against the floor. Then finally, a bowl came into his view, and she sat down across from him without digging into the meal she'd prepared.

He looked up, wondering what she was waiting for.

"Hi," she said, a crooked smile on her face.

"Hi," he said back, his voice breathy with lack of use.

"Long time, no see."

"Yes." He nodded and looked down at his food again, which was looking a bit underwhelming now that it had been pulverized into mush. He wasn't sure how long he'd been sitting there, but based on the cold, congealed mess, he would say ernos.

A finger came into his vision, hooked the edge of his bowl, and pulled it out of view.

He looked up.

"That's better," she said, shaking her head. "I think we need to get a few things off our chests. First off, though, how's your head?" She frowned as her gaze traveled to his forehead.

He shrugged. "It's fine."

"I hate that you got hurt because of me."

"We've already been through this. It wasn't your fault."

"I know. It still sucks, though. I just can't change how I feel. I mean, I know, logically, that it's not my fault, but emotionally, I'm still working through that. And all of this Rae drama, it's just getting in the *way*, you know? I mean, we already had issues *before* the ship was boarded." She shook her head. "Issues we haven't addressed. Issues we need to address." She took a deep breath, letting it out in a sigh and sitting up straighter in her seat. "Here goes. I wanted to say I'm sorry for how I reacted in medical. I could have verbalized my feelings better. I'll admit that I didn't like being surprised with that detail. That was something I felt I needed to know to make a decision on being a surrogate, and that contributed to my bad reaction.

"But I also can't blame you entirely. I think we both made assumptions, and I absolutely could have asked more questions, and that's on me."

Delyn blushed, feeling even smaller than before. When sitting with her in that cafe, he hadn't even considered that he should have told her about the details of implantation. It was just something everyone on his planet *knew*, no explanation required, and now he felt like a fool for overlooking it. It was so obvious in retrospect. "You're right. I'm sorry as well. There were so many times for me to clarify things with you, and I didn't consider that we might have different views and assumptions. That is unconscionable of me, and I apologize." He paused, a part of him feeling like he was giving up, like this was it, the end, in more ways than one. As she did moments before, he sat up taller, bracing himself for what he was about to do. He knew he was doing the right thing, but these were the hardest words he'd ever spoken. "I feel it is only right that I let you out of the contract we signed."

She stared at him for a moment before speaking, like she was trying to read his mind. "But don't you need this?"

He wanted to say yes, but he couldn't. It wasn't her responsibility, her duty, and he couldn't force her into something like this just to satisfy his own duty to his people. "It doesn't matter. You didn't go into the contract fully informed. I can't, in good conscience, go through with it under those circumstances." It took everything in him to keep the turbulent emotions he was feeling from showing on his face. He couldn't say what any one of those feelings were, but they left him feeling edgy, stressed, and almost sick to his stomach.

She nodded. "I understand. I really wanted to help you. I like you, and I kept trying to convince myself to do it, but this was an ask I wasn't prepared for." She paused, as if she had something else to say, but she bit her lip, as if to keep the words inside. "Thank you."

He nodded and looked down at his bowl again. It was even less appetizing now, his stomach flipping ominously at the sight.

"So, now what?" she said, drawing his gaze back to her.

Now? "I don't know."

CHAPTER TEN

They ate in silence for a while, and the urge came over Jessie every now and then to tell Delyn what she knew. She didn't know how he would react or if it was the right thing to do. Would it help bolster him out of his sour mood, or would it just add one more complication to his life? She didn't want to complicate his life. Delyn seemed to be struggling, and she didn't want to add to his burdens. He deserved better. He was such a good person, and every experience she'd had with him, except for the episode in the medical suite, had only made her like and respect him more.

Sitting there, eating her food, her mind ran over her recent experiences with Delyn. The moment just now when he let her out of the contract stood side by side with the moment he stood up to the intruders. Both showed his true character in ways that many people probably never got to see. He was fair, responsible, and he stood up for those around him even when he had no hope of winning. It made her think of the moment when Rae showed up, right before they'd left the colony. Delyn had tackled him without thinking. He hadn't even known her back then, but he'd still defended her, fought for her.

Once she finished eating, she picked up her bowl and crossed the room to the dishwasher, Delyn following. They shuffled back and forth as they put their dishes away, then straightened and stared at each other.

Jessie's mind was a blank, unsure what to do or say. She'd known she couldn't go through with the surrogacy, but she hadn't planned beyond asserting that. Growing up, she'd never been the one who needed to make the plans. She only followed them. Her sister was the mastermind, the pirate, the hacker. *She* was the one who picked the targets, evaluating threats and potentials for reward. Jessie was the artist. She went with what felt right, both on the canvas and in her personal life. She rarely planned ahead. Even her decision to leave the *Trojan* had been mostly spurred on by Victoria and had involved no more planning than picking a planet and finding an apartment.

She leaned against the counter, feeling like she needed to do something for Delyn, but she didn't know what. He'd derived so much of his identity from his role that it was sometimes hard to see who he truly was as a person. Sure, she could see his insecurities, the way he *needed* to feel like he contributed and had a purpose. She supposed everyone needed that to some extent, but he seemed almost desperate for it, in spite of having a purpose assigned to him by his people.

Jessie frowned, those thoughts reminding her of what his government had done. The only reason he had such a specific role, a role he didn't get to choose, mind you, was because they wanted to exploit their people. It was hard to see such a system in a good light.

Even so, she hoped the people were good and happy. She knew from experience that some of the most corrupt organizations and governments could have the most kind and benevolent people under their reign. "Will you still take me?" she asked on a whim.

"What?" he said, snapping out of his distraction.

"To Wesa. Will you still take me? I'd like to see it."

"Oh, well, yes, I guess."

He still seemed distracted, or was he concerned? She couldn't tell. "Maybe I could pretend to be considering being a surrogate, if that would make things easier for you?"

He finally seemed to focus in on the conversation, like a cloud had lifted. "Yes, that would be nice. I had actually been thinking along the same lines."

She smiled, glad she'd come up with a solution.

With that settled, she looked over at Delyn consideringly. Jessie hated how he struggled with his role, hated how she couldn't help him. She wanted to help. She wanted Delyn to feel happier, more fulfilled, and then she remembered a conversation she'd had shortly after she'd first arrived on the ship. Her smile grew.

"Now, come on," she said, grabbing his damp hand and dragging him out of the kitchen.

———

Delyn balked as he was dragged by the arm through the ship. Her hand was firm and strong in his, pulling him into her room. The space was as barren as before, just an empty shell waiting for life. Even her easel in the one corner was empty and lifeless.

"Okay," she said, dropping his hand. "I'm going to teach you art."

He lifted his hand, still feeling the echoes of her skin there… and missing it.

In his periphery, she dug in her closet, tossing things onto the bed. Finally, he dropped his hand to his side as she closed the closet door and stood in front of him. "Ready to learn to paint?"

"Why?" He was genuinely perplexed. What had brought this on? And why would she think he would want to learn this? Painting was *her* domain, not his.

She poked his forehead with her index finger. "Because you have no hobbies, stupid. Everyone should have a hobby, even if they're terrible at it."

He rubbed his forehead, staring at her. His chest felt warm, and he dropped his hand there, rubbing it idly as she gathered her supplies around the easel, dropping a fresh canvas on the frame. He stepped forward, coming up next at her shoulder.

She looked at him with a smile that was gentle and real, warming his heart even more. "First things first. There's no wrong way to do this. Whatever you want, whatever you feel, is good and right. If you want to just smack paint on the canvas and call it a day, that's art. If you want to draw in pencil on the canvas to create a framework for the paint, that's art. If you want to paint something real, that's art. If you want to paint fantasy, that's art. It doesn't matter. Just do what feels right and you'll be fine."

"Okay…" Delyn did not feel even the slightest bit artistic. He couldn't even say he had any visual thoughts to speak of. He glanced down at the blank canvas and derived no inspiration to fill it. Jessie might want to find him a hobby, but he was fairly certain this wasn't it. He just wasn't an artist.

"Okay, Delyn," she said, rubbing her hands together. "Pick a color and go to town!"

He looked at her like she was crazy. Just pick a color? And do what? He looked down at the paints she'd laid out and stopped on a blue that reminded him of her eyes. He tapped the edge of it.

"Go ahead," she said, waving at the canvas.

There was a brush in a jar. He picked it up. It had coarse bristles, some that looked like they might be falling out and he was afraid to use it. He was afraid he might damage it, and he couldn't exactly replace it right now. He looked over at her, but she just nodded at him encouragingly.

She'd said there was no wrong way. He looked down and placed it back in the jar, deciding that he would be too self-conscious and awkward to use it. He didn't want to damage her supplies. So instead, he dipped a finger in the paint, closed his eyes, and swiped his paint-covered finger until he felt the rough texture of the canvas slide along under his fingertip.

Jessie laughed, but it was filled with pure joy, and he didn't feel like she was laughing at him, but rather enjoying herself. He smiled and smeared his finger across the canvas some more, making sure not to open his eyes until his fingertip felt dry and in need of more paint.

He was actually enjoying himself.

Well, she didn't think Delyn would ever be an artist, but he'd had fun, and before them was a painting alive with color, even if it was abstract in the extreme. He had a smile on his face. He'd enjoyed himself, and that was all that mattered.

"Not bad, eh?" she said, turning to him He was staring at his accomplishment with a small smile on his face.

"It's awful," he said with a laugh.

"And what did I say earlier?"

"I think I forgot." He turned to her. The smile didn't dim, just as relaxed and warm as before.

"There's no wrong way to paint. Some people do it to create something. Others do it to express themselves. And yet others, they do it just to have fun. If you can have fun just..." she gestured at the painting, "slapping paint on a canvas, that's good. Using your hands, connecting with your senses, that's valid. You clearly had fun."

"I did." He looked down, and his smile grew.

Jessie was glad she'd sacrificed a canvas for this. Her drawing tablet wouldn't have given the same result. He seemed more at ease now.

He looked back up at her. "Thank you. I appreciate this."

She shrugged and turned toward the door, looking back over her shoulder. "Hungry?"

"Starving," he said with a laugh.

She laughed, too, and headed out the door to get something to eat.

The Keeper frowned at his computer screen. He'd expected the hardware to access the Vault at any moment, but there'd been no breaches since he'd put the new equipment in place. He didn't know what to do at first, afraid of what the Magistrate would say once he found out the extra expense had given them nothing.

When nothing came of the endeavor, he expanded the sensing capacities of it, attaching the device to all the Pardus databases, hoping the hacker might access *any* of them. It was a long shot. He had no reason to think they would, and why would they access open databases if they had access to state secrets?

But he was desperate and out of options. He stared at the screen, hoping it would show something before the Magistrate arrived. Nothing showed for hours except a single word.

"Searching…"

He waited, just staring, doing nothing else, until his eyes were dry and bloodshot. He could hear nothing but his own heartbeat as everyone else had left for the day. Light from the windows had darkened, giving a silvery cast to the room.

He hadn't slept well lately, often finding himself dozing off in his chair. Then the computer chirped, and he jerked awake, a trail of drool coming from the corner of his mouth. His neck ached as he checked the screen. "Hardware identified," it said. But it wasn't accessing the Vault. It was accessing the public areas of the government databases.

How strange.

Data started populating automatically, but even at a glance, he began to notice something. Over several diceros of data collection, the hardware stayed the same, but the location data did not.

They're moving.

Finally, it stopped and at the top of the screen, it said, "Connection lost."

He started analyzing the data. The first thing he checked was the signal hardware. The search popped up a result almost immediately. It was a Pardus design, though it couldn't tell him what ship it was installed on. They all used the same equipment.

He leaned back in his seat, a little surprised by this information. Why would a Pardus, someone likely in the employ of the government itself, be using computer hardware he *couldn't* trace from a ship he *could?* Sure, at the moment, he couldn't identify the specific ship, but that was because hardware registration for ships was an entirely different department, one he would have to get authorization to access. After all, there was nothing a government liked more than red tape.

Moving on, he checked the signal location next, mapping it on-screen. He had a lot of data points, and none of them were the same. The pings were spread out over the map, covering a great deal of space. With a quick algorithm, he calculated their speed and trajectory. It wasn't a lot of data, only a few diceros, after all, but one thing was for certain.

Their trajectory would have them reaching Wesa in a matter of ernos.

CHAPTER ELEVEN

For the next few days, Jessie scrambled to come up with things to teach Delyn. She wanted to teach him some hobbies, but she was a bit at a loss for ideas since the ship was essentially void of anything hobby-like. In the end, one of the best options had been writing.

She quickly learned that while he might suck at painting (though he certainly seemed to have had fun doing it), he *loved* writing down his thoughts. Together, they experimented with journal, fiction, and non-fiction writing. He didn't take to fiction, saying he "couldn't see the scenes in his head," but he'd found journaling potentially useful and found researching and writing non-fiction exciting.

It turned out that Delyn loved to learn and writing non-fiction encouraged him to do so. Over the next few days, he would often come to the breakfast table with his computer so he could tell her what he'd learned the night before. Occasionally, he would let her read what he wrote. He had a flair for making even the most boring topics interesting with his passion for them. He seemed especially interested in genetics and biology, coming back to those subjects again and again.

She would smile indulgently every time he rushed in with his computer to show her his next piece. Each one was thoughtful and delightful, and the indulgence never lasted long. Delyn had found his niche, and she loved it. She felt like she was seeing him for the first time now, like he was finally coming alive after a lifetime of being suffocated by his role.

"We should arrive at Wesa today," he said as he sat down. "Not long now." He dropped the laptop-esque computer next to him.

"How long?" she asked, glancing at the computer and wondering what today's topic would entail.

He shrugged. "Couple horos, maybe? I'll have to check."

"It's fine," she said, waving her hand before her. She stood up. "So how about I prepare us some breakfast while you tell me your latest tale of discovery?"

Delyn started animatedly talking about the development of the Ateles eye, which could see in a wide variety of light conditions, but was almost blind in bright light. He seemed to have a fondness for researching the Ateles, maybe as a way of trying to understand the rift between the two species. She couldn't say she was opposed to the interest, as long as it didn't turn dark.

Jessie dove into the fridge as he continued to speak, telling her about the three "light modes" of Ateles eyes. She hadn't even settled on a meal before he was moving on to evolutionary theories for their development and how those modes fit into the environment of their native planet.

She frowned. After weeks on this small ship, nothing in the fridge seemed overly appetizing, even for her, admittedly, less than refined palate. There just wasn't much left in the fridge, seeing as how they'd mostly gone for the food there first.

Feeling uninspired, she just grabbed the first thing that touched her fingers. She had no idea what it was, but she suspected it was getting a little old. She popped it in the warmer for the time listed on the package and stepped back to wait while Delyn continued his lesson on the eye anatomy of the Ateles. The warmer hummed quietly as the turnstile, much like a microwave, rotated the dish to warm on all sides. It finished with a chirp, and she reached in, grabbing the hot dish with hesitant fingers. It smelled good, a little sweet, a little savory. Her stomach growled in response.

"I guess it's time to eat," he said as she sat down.

"Yeah, put away your toys," she responded with a smile.

He laughed and shook his head, snapping his laptop closed. Jessie smiled, enjoying the rare emotion from him. It was a warm sound, deep and resonant. It felt bigger than his body and resonated in her chest.

She wanted to make him laugh again and again for the rest of her life. *That* was how good a sound it was.

Jessie was drawing on her tablet, her easel and supplies put away in anticipation of landing, when Delyn's voice broke out over the intercom. "Okay, we're about to start descent. Please secure yourself."

Jessie stood and powered down the device. She crossed the room, locked it away in a drawer, and closed the closet door. Then, she touched the control panel to release the jump seat and buckled in. With a final test of the harness, she reached over and touched the intercom button. "Locked and loaded."

"What?" he said, clearly perplexed.

She laughed, suddenly remembering she shouldn't use idioms with aliens. You would think she would have learned by now, but she still said them even though they never translated properly to Uso. "I'm secured and ready for landing, Delyn."

"Okay. Commencing with descent."

Jessie held onto the straps as she felt it. There was little or nothing at first, just a thrumming energy of anticipation. Then she started to feel a gentle pressure, like they were accelerating and she was being pressed into her seat a little. Then, it was as if they were going down on a rollercoaster. She had the ridiculous urge to scream, but she laughed instead. The force pressed her into the seat, and she continued to hold on to the straps, a little disconcerted at not being able to see where they were going.

She'd always been in the cockpit on the *Trojan* when they took off or landed. She'd always watched when the ground came up to meet them, when the clouds puffed up around them, maybe even obscuring their vision. It was a visual experience almost as exciting as subspace.

She suddenly had the urge to paint.

But Jessie also wanted to see the planet. She wanted to see what it looked like from space, how the continents were shaped, how much water it had, what colors it was from the sky. She'd seen maps, but it wasn't the same.

As the force of entry continued to press her into her seat, she desperately wished for a window, but all she could do was stare at the wall. It frustrated her that beyond that wall was likely a beautiful vista, but she was stuck looking at plain, boring metal. She sighed. Unfortunately, there was nothing she could do to change that. She was stuck here until they landed.

Jessie grew increasingly antsy as they continued flying through the atmosphere. The descent went on for a long time, though she supposed it always did. She'd never been terribly patient with this part of space travel, always ready and eager to get out and explore, usually while Cass was acting put upon and telling her to calm her shit.

Jessie smiled, thinking of her inappropriate but loving sister. She kind of missed her, though there were certainly some things she *didn't* miss. Like being babied or having no boundaries. Cass was someone to be appreciated in moderation.

Then, finally, the force on her reduced, then stopped. She jerked in her seat slightly as the ship touched down, then Delyn's voice came over the intercom. "Okay, it's safe to get up now."

She popped the buckle, throwing each piece to the side and bounced to her feet. Energy surged through her as she excitedly dashed out of her room. What was it like outside? What would she see? Were the people nice? Where did they land?

Delyn shook his head as he stepped out of the control room. "Come on. The exit's this way."

"I know." Jessie slipped past him. The ship was so small, she was there in a blink, staring at the control console she now realized she didn't know how to use. It was all in his native tongue, a language she didn't even know the characters for. She waited impatiently as Delyn made his way behind her. The seconds felt like an eternity, but before long, he reached out and activated the door. Both doors opened, and a ramp began to descend. Jessie jogged down the ramp, taking in her first view of his homeworld, Wesa.

It was quiet here. They'd landed on a patch of hard-packed earth with long, skinny green vegetation beyond it. The air smelled of wet grass, and she wondering if the vegetation before her was the cause. In the distance, she could see trees, but they were too far away to make out anything but their vaguely green leaves. The sky was a pale bluish-green with white clouds passing slowly overhead.

Just beyond the grass-like vegetation, she could see some colorful buildings, a small collection of them that was probably the community Delyn often talked about. She stepped forward off the ramp on autopilot, her feet wanting to take her farther and farther. There was something simple and quiet and beautiful here. She could just feel it.

She turned around to Delyn, who still hadn't set foot off the ramp. "Shall we go?"

A wistful expression crossed his face as he looked at his home, but he still hadn't stepped off the ramp, his body tense. "I guess we have to."

Jessie frowned as he finally touched a foot onto the ground.

What was that about?

Delyn was hesitant to move forward, but he knew he had to. Standing on the ramp, he'd been hit with a wave of nostalgia. Valana was in the distance, a picturesque symbol of his childhood, and too far away to see the imperfections. At that distance, he could let himself get carried away with the impressions that made him feel at home, like the little details that made Wesa different.

It was often small things, like that exact color of the sky, the shape of the leaves, the smell in the air. He could hear voices in the distance, the cadence unique to his people's language. Everything had just that little bit of nuance that made it perfect.

And yet he knew that perfection couldn't last. Being back only too quickly caused anxiety to lance through him, even before remembering that he hadn't come back victorious. He hadn't found a Birther. He hadn't fulfilled his role. The feeling was nebulous, the thoughts insidious. He pushed them down, refusing to let them gain a stranglehold on him.

Still, that failure made him wonder how he would be received. He wanted to hope for open arms and smiles, but he didn't honestly believe that would happen. His family and community were good people, kind people. They took care of each other, supported each other. Supported *him*. He couldn't speak of them highly enough, but that didn't mean the reverse was true. Would they speak highly of him when he failed again and again and again?

He looked over at Jessie, who was beyond excited. If only some of that energy could rub off on him, but it couldn't. He couldn't steal her mood any more than he could change his father's mind.

His feet felt nailed in place, rooted to the ground like the very strongest tree in the distance.

"Come on," Jessie said, grabbing his wrist and yanking him forward.

He balked as his feet came out from underneath him, stumbling forward as she rushed ahead. He sped up, forcing himself to keep pace with her.

Jessie was practically vibrating with energy.

"Delyn?" a feminine voice said up ahead.

He recognized it immediately as one of his sisters and stopped, looking up. "Tesa," he said with a smile.

Tesa, a tall, thin waif of a girl, rushed forward and hugged him, the power of the hug defying her size. She'd always been like that, small but mighty. "Air," he gasped jokingly.

She pulled back and laughed, pushing a stray bit of red hair behind her ear. It was a common gag between them, one they'd been doing since they were kids. They'd grown up together and were good friends.

Delyn stood up straighter and turned to Jessie. "Jessie, this is my sister, Tesa. Tesa, this is Jessie."

"Hi," Tesa said, seeming a little hesitant.

Delyn wasn't terribly surprised. She was often loving and exuberant with those she knew, but was more reserved with strangers.

"It's very nice to meet you, Tesa," Jessie said, hands clasped behind her back as she rocked on her heels.

The moment dragged on while no one spoke. Tesa eyed Jessie appraisingly, though there was no telling what was going on inside that head of hers.

"Well, shall we go?"

"Yes, let's," Tesa said, smiling at him.

Jessie took the lead while Tesa waited until she could walk next to him. She bumped his shoulder. "So, who is she? Is she a Birther?"

Delyn bristled, feeling defensive about their current situation. He had to remind himself that Tesa didn't care. She would love him no matter what happened. "She's thinking about it," he said, blurting out their cover story without thinking.

"She seems… nice."

He smiled, watching Jessie excitedly take in her surroundings. She seemed enamored of the world around her, able to enjoy it without a care. He wished he was capable of even half of her joy at just being alive. "She is." He thought of her trying to find him hobbies. "And generous."

She was a genuinely good person, and sometimes that made him question his own reality. It made him feel like nothing, like a drawing of a person rather than a fully fledged three dimensional being in the real world.

"You like her," she said, staring at him thoughtfully.

"I do."

Tesa stopped him with a hand on his shoulder. "You know that doesn't work, right?" She paused, seeming to search for the answers on his face. "Have you spent too long among other species? I know some form pair bonds, but we don't."

He looked over at her, a bit surprised. "Who said anything about a pair bond? I just like her as a person."

Tesa shrugged, looking skeptical. "Maybe I'm wrong." She paused, her expression soaked in concern for him. "Just don't get too attached." She picked up her pace, getting ahead of Jessie and disappearing around a corner.

What was that about?

Jessie watched curiously as Delyn's sister, Tesa, rushed off ahead, leaving them behind. Where was she going? How did families work in his society? She knew there were Seeders and Carers, and she supposed Seeders would be like fathers and Carers like mothers. That would probably mean one father and multiple mothers.

But what about siblings? What constituted a sibling? Was it those you were raised with? Those fathered by the same Seeder? She suddenly wanted to meet all his siblings. Were they all like Tesa?

Soon, she was walking into the center of the community, a small square of hard-packed earth with an array of buildings looping it in a circle. The buildings were a lot more like those on Earth. Unlike on the colony, the buildings here had squared off corners and brightly painted facades. It was colorful and lively, speaking of the individual personalities that lived here. There were even little gardens and decorations outside each one, like a testament to the family that lived there (if it was a home).

She wasn't completely sure what types of buildings would exist in a Pardus community. In a human one, there would be residential and commercial districts, each separate and distinct. In the shifter caravan, there were personal and communal spaces, though nowhere near as clearly delineated as in the human world. Looking around her, there was no obvious function to each building. They all just sort of looked like homes to her.

"So, this is the parush," Delyn said from behind.

She turned around, seeing him pointing at where they stood. "What's that mean?"

"It's sort of a communal gathering place?"

"But it's so plain."

"All the better to decorate. It gives it the capacity to adapt to each purpose. There are a variety of holidays that we celebrate here. Sometimes it's used for a play area for the children. Other times, people might use it for preparing products for trade. And, of course, it's used for trade itself."

She nodded, looking back around the circle of buildings. "Are these all people's homes, or do they serve a specific purpose?"

"Both. That big, pink building is the Carers' Lodge. That's where the children live, learn, and grow. That orange one there on the other side is the Seeders' Barracks. That's where I stayed before going out to space. That green one there is for the Farmers. Most of my family lives there."

"So each of these has a specific purpose?"

"Yes."

She looked at him, bereft at the idea of being so distanced from your family by societal design. "So you don't live with your families."

"No, not generally. Sometimes people do, but that's only if those people have the same role as you."

"How sad."

He shook his head. "I don't think it is. All the children grow up together in a loving family. They are encouraged and praised by the entire community. They grow up and are given a role, where they are embraced wholeheartedly, being given every chance at success. They are trained and nurtured in that role until they can be the one training the next generation."

"Except you."

"What?" He jerked his head at her, clearly surprised by her statement.

"Except you." She shook her head. "From what I can gather, you weren't given every chance at success. Either you weren't well suited for the role you were given, or you weren't trained well enough to succeed at it. After all, if either of those things were true, we wouldn't be here, would we?"

Delyn stared at the barracks, not liking what Jessie's words said about his upbringing. Had he been set up to fail? Sure, his father had never really liked him, but he couldn't imagine anyone actually sabotaging someone's life like that.

He looked around him, taking in the unusual silence. It seemed altogether too quiet, like something was about to happen.

Then the double doors to the Carers' Lodge burst open, small children pouring out in a flood. Meanwhile, older children stepped out behind them, herding them into the space in front of the lodge. The Carers' came out last, calling out names to children who were especially precocious.

Delyn recognized each of the Carers immediately. The eldest, Mae, practically creaked as she walked, stopping to rub her knees as she passed through the doorway. Aesa and Aella were herding the little ones, each with an infant on her hip. They were twins and about fifteen years old. He remembered them being about a year older than him growing up.

There were more Carers, but some might be preparing food or taking care of infants inside. Some kids didn't like going outside to play with the others. He remembered the Carers always doing their best to take care of the children's individual needs. He especially remembered Mae growing up. She had been a strong influence on him. Stern but gentle, she had always acted like she wouldn't let you have things, but she was also a push over, always relenting with a smile. Often, he would work to please her, just to see that gentle smile on her face.

"Delyn? Is that you?" Mae said, shading her eyes with her hand. She stood up straight and walked toward them, the smile on her face growing. "It *is* you, you scoundrel. Get over here, boy."

Delyn smiled, but obeyed. "Yes, Mae." When they got close, she wrapped him in a big hug, reminding him that in spite of her steel gray hair, she was still strong as an oxna. "You haven't aged a bit, Mother Mae."

"Oh," she huffed, standing back and swatting at him playfully. "Stop that, boy. You always were trouble." She smirked at the obvious fib, wagging her finger at him good-naturedly, then turned to Jessie. "And who's this stunning young lady?"

Delyn looked over at Jessie, who was smiling and blushing. "Name's Jessie, ma'am. Nice to meet you."

"And respectful, too." She looked over at Delyn. "I like this one."

It was such a strange feeling, like he was being applauded for a good choice in partner. And yet the Pardus didn't partner up like other species did, so his mind ran in circles trying to understand the compliment. Even through the confusion, a place deep inside warmed up at the praise of Jessie. She was indeed someone worth liking.

Jessie watched the interplay between Delyn and Mother Mae. It was clear it was a loving relationship, for which she was glad. Delyn deserved that, and he'd apparently received it in Mae. She was a bit of a firecracker, the type of woman Jessie would want to be at that age. She could just imagine her refusing to take any crap from anyone. Though there was also a soft side to her that told Jessie the woman was probably devoted to her kids.

"Well," Mae said, brushing her palms on her skirt, "I'd best get back to those little hellions before they cause a disaster." She turned around and slowly made her way across the packed dirt.

"She's a sweetheart," Jessie said, smiling as the woman reached a toddler, patting them on their head. The little kid looked up at the older woman with a smile, then showed off their toy.

"Yeah, she is."

"So, that was your mom?"

"Not quite. She was one of the Carers when I was growing up."

"But she was special to you."

He smiled. "Yeah. She was."

As they watched the children play, a door opened behind them with a creak. Jessie turned around as people spilled out of the green Farmers' house.

"I heard the children playing outside," someone said from the middle of the group.

"You and the children," another voice said with amusement. "Every time they're outside, you're always like, 'Let's go.' "

Someone grunted as they were pushed into the doorframe. Jessie smiled at the roughhousing.

"Delyn?" a new voice said. A big man, much larger than Delyn, pushed through the crowd of people, pausing as he got to the front. He was tall, muscular, and tanned, clearly built for hard labor, and in that way was a carbon copy of the rest of the crowd. It was easy to see they were all farmers.

The one who'd called out rushed up and hugged him, literally lifting him off the ground in a bear hug. She smiled. It all felt like a family reunion, something she'd never been a part of since the only family she had was Cass, and Cass was never more than a phone call away.

Granted, there was no telling how Cass would react the next time they met in person. They'd never been parted for so long before, so it could be just as boisterous between them, too.

"Man, what have you been up to? It's been so long." The farmer, who still hadn't been introduced, dropped Delyn to the ground, causing dust to puff up around his shoes.

Delyn shook it off, looking up to meet the man's gaze. "Just searching, Mak. Just searching."

Mak turned his gaze to Jessie. "And I see you've found." He bowed, but his bulk didn't make him much shorter even then. "It's a pleasure."

"Likewise."

"Come on. Let's leave these heathens to play children's games while we catch up."

The rest of the farmers crossed the open space to the kids, while the three of them sat down on a bench in front of the house. It was a nice quiet little spot, in spite of it technically being out in the open.

Mak and Delyn got reacquainted, smiling and joking back and forth, and Jessie could easily see why he spoke so highly of this community. So far, everyone they'd met had been wonderful, and she couldn't imagine wanting to leave. It reminded her of her time with the shifter caravan. Though she'd been young, spending her time running around with the other children, she remembered the sense of community and familiarity between the members. It had felt like one great big family, and she could see the whispers of that same thing here.

Then a dark cloud seemed to go over the small gathering. She didn't even notice the cause at first. She was just watching the two young men talking back and forth, occasionally including her in the conversation by telling her stories of their past antics, which were apparently many.

It was when Delyn got quiet, his eyes rounding slightly and his body going stiff, that she knew something was wrong. Mak narrowed his eyes, almost growling under his breath. Jessie looked up, seeing an older man crossing the space with the orange Seeders' barracks rising up behind him.

At a glance, he seemed like a stern man, certainly someone she would never want to cross. He moved with a determination that spoke of ill intent. She was expecting chills to run down her spine at any moment, and she had the impulse to get in front of Delyn and defend him. Some part of her was certain the man was heading straight toward her new friend.

Time acted strangely, almost distorted, as they watched the man approach.

"That's Delyn's father," Mak said, snapping Jessie out of the weird moment. "Want me to pound him?"

Jessie looked over at Mak, who clearly wasn't joking. He had a stern look on his face that said he meant business. He was absolutely willing to fight and maybe even take a beating for Delyn.

I like this guy.

Jessie looked back at the man who was apparently Delyn's father. She thought it spoke volumes that Mak didn't mention the man by name. Even Mae, who was a like mother to Delyn and could have very easily been introduced as something as simple as "mom," was still introduced by name, but not this man. No, she suspected he wasn't worthy of a name, and the smile she'd had through all the interactions so far disappeared. She tried not to scowl or otherwise give away her emotions, but it was hard. The closer he got, the more her instincts screamed at her.

This man was bad news.

When he finally reached them, he looked down at his son, even though Delyn had risen from the bench as his father approached. "So you've returned. I assume this must mean you've found a Birther willing to have you." He sneered at Delyn, clearly showing how little he thought of him.

Jessie wanted to stand up, to speak up, but she felt planted to the bench. What could she say? They'd planned to say she was considering being a Birther, but she wasn't. She'd eventually turned him down. And lying to this man felt impossible, as if he could see through her like glass.

He didn't even glance her way once as he continued to judge his son and find him wanting.

"Knock it off," Mak said, standing up to the man in a way that neither she nor Delyn could. Mak was the same height as Delyn's father but broader, his muscles more defined.

Even so, Delyn's father managed to look down on Mak, too. "Oh, Mak," he said snidely, shaking his head. "At least you've managed to do your father proud. You are quite the Farmer, aren't you? Last season's harvest was especially fruitful."

Mak growled this time. He actually growled, and Jessie stood up, slightly stunned.

Then Delyn's father turned back to his victim. "You, on the other hand, have never managed to fulfill your duty to this community even once. We've birthed you, clothed you, raised you, trained you, and what have you given us back? Absolutely nothing."

Jessie was shocked. She couldn't imagine any parent saying something like that to their child, and her parents had abandoned her at the tender old age of two. Delyn was looking increasingly agitated, his face turning red and tense.

She wanted to speak up for him, but she didn't know what to say. She didn't know his culture and their beliefs well enough to make a valid argument.

It had been easier before, when it was just the two of them. She could speak up easily when it was just Delyn talking down to himself.

It was something altogether different when the person doing the damage was a parent. She wanted to smack him, to hurt him somehow, but she was behind both Mak and Delyn and couldn't reach around them to get at him.

"Knock it off, Ashe," Mak said, shoving at the offending man's shoulder.

Ashe squared off with Mak. "Do you have any argument to the contrary? He *is* useless," he said, pointing a hand at his son. "The only reason he should ever return here is if he's done his duty, and," he finally took an interest in Jessie, "I very much doubt he has, even with a creature like this."

Out of nowhere, Delyn socked his father in the jaw. Ashe didn't even budge, but a slightly red spot flushed where his knuckles had connected. Ashe looked down at Delyn, a look of profound disappointment on his face, and she could see he'd had enough. He lifted his arm, ready to retaliate

All hell broke loose.

Mak caught Ashe's hand, someone shouted, and the entire area turned to chaos. Children were screaming and cheering in the background, fists were flying, and the commotion started drawing people in droves.

Within moments, big men and women surrounded her on all sides and it seemed everyone wanted a piece of Delyn's father. She suspected most of them didn't even know how the fight had started. All they needed to know was that one of their own was in a fight, and they needed to help.

Jessie didn't know what to do. She'd never been in a fight like this. Usually, she and her sister *avoided* fights. They even coordinated their piracy so all the crew were unconscious when they boarded. She'd only been in real conflicts four times. Once when she was shot in a robbery attempt (that blue glowy rock was worth a fortune), once when some assholes held the medical facility she was a patient of under siege, once when she threatened Rae with a gun, and finally once when Rae hired people to kidnap her. She was useless three of the times, and the remaining one? Well, it mostly succeeded out of luck and sheer surprise.

Now, she could actually *do* something, but she wasn't sure what. There were so many bodies before her, big people with big fists and big attitudes. They yelled, they stomped, they pushed and shoved. There was a smell of sweat and freshly spilled blood on the air. She only occasionally saw the target of everyone's wrath.

Finally, it was over when an authoritative voice said, "Enough!" It was a booming female voice, and everyone around her immediately got sheepish. Jessie looked over and realized immediately it was Mother Mae. She stared everyone down, and as the crowd dispersed, she noticed that not only the farmers had joined in, but those from the Seeders' barracks as well.

Farmers started filing back inside under the stern and watchful eye of the Carer. When it was just Jessie, Mak, and Delyn, Mother Mae shook her head, looking a little sad. "Well, that was inevitable."

CHAPTER TWELVE

After the fight, they moved into the dining room of the Farmers' house. People who'd participated in the fight sat around a large table, many holding ice packs over battle-wounds and smiling like idiots. Mak and Delyn sat down near the end of the table, and she slipped in among them.

No one looked over at them or seemed to blame them. There wasn't any awkward silence, but instead the room was filled with happy chatter, albeit a little fatigued, like after a long, busy day.

Someone came in from an adjoining room and held up another ice pack. "Who still needs one?"

Both Mak and Delyn raised their hands.

She crossed the room, stopping in front of Delyn with a smile. "It's been a while, Delyn. How are you doing?"

"Been better," he said as he accepted the ice pack and applied it to a swelling spot on his cheek.

"Hm… Looks like it," she said. "Was that your father I saw slinking away from the fight?"

Delyn just nodded, leaning into the ice pack.

"Hm… can't say I'm surprised. I honestly don't know what's gotten into that man. He's had a bone to pick with you from the moment you left the Carers' Lodge." She shook her head, lines carving into the corners of her eyes as she frowned. "I don't understand it, but you're welcome to stay here for the time being. I couldn't in good conscience send you over to the Seeders' Barracks when it looked like the whole lot of them got in on that infantile fight out there."

Looking around, it seemed like every face at the table bloomed with embarrassment at the older woman's words.

"But you look like you had the good sense to keep your nose out of it," she said, looking now at Jessie for the first time. "Not a scratch on you."

"Not for lack of trying," she said honestly. "Truth be told, I wanted to sock him something good for what he said, but Mak and Delyn were in the way."

She tilted her head back and laughed. "I like you. You can stay here, too. Name's Faelee."

"Jessie."

Faelee nodded and headed back to the other room.

With her out of sight, Mak leaned in and whispered to them. "You're gonna wanna stay put. Dinner should be coming out soon, and it's always the best."

"He's right," Delyn said, nodding his head in coordination with the hand still clasping the ice pack to his cheek. "The Farmers' house is known for their meals. It's always an honor to be invited to eat with them."

"Yeah, it is!" one of the bruised up farmers said. "Best food in Valana."

People nodded in agreement.

Chatting continued good-naturedly around the table until Faelee came back in and said, "What are you all sitting around for? There's food to prep, a table to set. Get crackin'. I want to see those asses moving!"

All the injured farmers stood up, rushing into the other room. Jessie sat with Delyn, wondering awkwardly if she should get up and help as well. She supposed she was technically a guest, and many cultures wouldn't allow guests to help, but she was also a stranger, not an invited guest, and she felt like she should be contributing somehow. From everything Delyn had told her about this place, it was a place where everyone had a role, and everyone helped out.

And here she was, with no role and not helping. They'd offered her a place to stay while she was here, and presumably, food as well. It didn't seem right to not help while she was sleeping in their beds and eating their food.

When someone came by with a big stack of dishes to set out, she stood up and reached out her hands. "Here, let me."

The woman pulled away. "No. Sit. Food will be out shortly."

Jessie dropped her hands to her sides and sat down.

"Could have told you that would happen," Delyn said.

She looked over at him. He was smiling at her, though now she realized he had a split lip, which seemed to grow a little as his lips stretched wider.

"I suspect a farmer would probably see it as almost an insult. They're strong and hardworking, and unlike a lot of other roles, there isn't a lot of time to be idle. Even the various craftspeople have more opportunity to relax than a farmer. Plants and animals don't wait, so neither do farmers."

"Still, seems to me that would be all the more reason to help."

"I mean, people do help, but there's often a certain generosity to the people chosen to be farmers. It tends to appeal to those who like to give of themselves, to provide for others."

She looked on as more people came in from the other room. Within minutes, there was a steady stream of people loading up the table with food. It smelled wonderful, though like on the ship, she had no idea what most of it was. She recognized a few dishes she'd had for the first time recently, but most of it was a mystery.

Jessie leaned over to whisper at Delyn. "There's so much on the table. I have no idea what I'm gonna pick when it's time to eat."

"Don't worry. I think I have a pretty good idea of what you like by now."

"You do?" she said, looking over at him, surprised. Her sister saw her as a bottomless pit, willing to eat anything in sight. She'd never had *anyone* tell her they knew her preferences before. She wasn't even sure *she* knew her preferences.

"I think I do." He looked over at her and chuckled. "I know. You're not picky. But there are certain things you've gravitated towards."

She did? Jessie wracked her brain, trying to remember when she'd become so predictable. She wasn't sure she liked it.

Then someone at the other end of the table cleared their throat, and the room got quiet. "Better," Faelee said with a smile. "We have a couple guests at our table today." She motioned at the two of them. "Everyone behave." She eyed a couple people meaningfully, and Jessie knew instantly that those were the troublemakers of the group.

When the woman sat down, everyone dived for a dish, and the room erupted into a disharmonious din of clattering tableware. For a spell, no one spoke, just clinking and crunching and chewing reaching her ears.

Delyn loaded her plate up, and he was right. He had been paying attention as she recognized several things she'd eaten before that she remembered especially liking. She started eating as conversation around the table began to pick up.

"You should have seen it," one person said, their eye turning black and swollen from the fight earlier. "It was epic. Everyone piled on top of each other. You could barely see who you were hitting."

"That's not something to be proud of," a woman who looked a lot like the first speaker said, elbowing him playfully.

"Yeah, maybe to you, sis. But to me? Epic."

There was a weird energy in the room as they continued to talk about the fight. She couldn't explain how she was picking up on this, but it was as if they both disliked and felt a begrudging respect for Ashe. He seemed like a villain in their stories, but she learned he was also the head of the Seeders' barracks, which gave him a certain degree of respect in the community. She didn't know what to think about that.

Before long, the conversation moved on to farming, with people talking about what tasks had been done that day, what needed to be done tomorrow, whether anyone needed to cover for someone, when the next harvest should happen.

Jessie felt like she didn't belong, like she should just shyly slink off into the shadows and leave them to their conversation. She looked over at Delyn, who must have been thinking the same thing. He shrugged at her and leaned close to speak. "I haven't heard this much talk about food production since I was a kid. I used to follow the farmers around asking them questions."

Jessie smiled, chuckling under her breath. "I was a lot younger when I lived in a community similar to this one. I'll be honest, I played with the other kids a lot, but I also had a tendency of hanging on Victoria's elbow, too, asking her what she was doing." She chuckled again, shaking her head at herself. "Victoria did *not* like that."

"What did she do?"

"Mostly? Tried valiantly to ignore me. Not sure she was successful."

Delyn shook his head, a smile on his face. "I was always interested in things everyone would have rather I not focus on."

"Like what?"

"How things work? As I got older, I was really fascinated with genetics, especially after I left home. Seeing other species really made me wonder about the differences between us, you know?"

"I could see that. As a shifter, I often wonder about that type of stuff. I don't shift into other shapes very often, but I always wonder exactly how I'm changing." She waved her hands in front of her, indicating her body. "So much is done without conscious thought. You just picture it in your head, and it happens. I don't think anyone knows how it really works. I'm just glad it does."

"What's a shifter?"

"Oh, have I never told you that?"

He shook his head, leaning forward with interest.

She leaned in herself, like she was sharing a secret, which she supposed she was. It seemed to her that this was the perfect opportunity to tell him she was trans, too. She didn't always mention it. Sometimes, it just never came up naturally in a conversation. But this was the perfect opportunity, and she hoped her trust in him was well founded, that he would take it well.

"So, on Earth, there are two sentient species." She counted on her fingers. "Humans look like me, but only have one possible form. They can self-heal, within reason, using innate healing systems. They usually have lifespans around eighty-something years. They age gradually over time.

"Shifters, on the other hand, can look like humans, especially if their father is one. But they can also look like pretty much any other species, so long as mass is consistent. We can change forms, but we have no innate ability to heal. Our ability to heal is dependent on our ability to shift. We literally change our biology to fix whatever defect is there. It's a little weird. I don't think most species do anything similar, but it works really well... when it's working.

"The downside is that it is really easy to end up in a circumstance where you just don't heal. You can die that way. Starvation is really dangerous for a shifter. It's probably why you are more likely to see an 'overweight' shifter." She looked down at her body. "I'm scrawny as hell," she smirked at herself, "but not for lack of trying."

"I've noticed."

"What can I say? I'm a bottomless pit."

He laughed, drawing the gaze of some of the other residents of the table. "That you are."

"Another interesting thing with shifters," she said, teeing up for her reveal, "has to do with body image. Because we can practically shape-shift however we want to, it can be really beneficial with improving self image. It can also hurt, though. A shifter with an eating disorder can put themselves in a dire situation really quickly, but it can also be really beautiful for people with dysphoria."

"Like gender dysphoria?"

"Yeah, exactly that." She rested her chin on her hand. "I changed my physical sex when I was five and never looked back."

"So you're trans."

Jessie nodded. "My sister was really good about it." She smiled, her face almost hurting from its breadth. "I just told her I was a girl, she said, 'Okay,' and she never called me a boy again."

"So you," he paused, "you could just change your shape and be done with it? Man, I bet my sister would have liked that."

"Is she trans, too?"

"Yeah, you met her. Tesa. I don't remember how old she was when she announced that she was trans. It was before puberty because I know she went on blockers, and she started the rest after she hit the age of majority."

"That's nice that she could do that."

"What do you mean?"

"Well, not everyone has that option."

"Really? Everyone does here. I mean, sometimes you might need to go to one of the cities for treatment. We don't have anything here in Valana for corrective surgeries and such, but it's available to all."

"That's nice. On Earth, there's still a lot of places that aren't that accepting. Some don't accept it at all, others put a lot of strings on it that are a bit absurd."

"Well, that's just not right," he said, frowning.

"I agree. I was lucky. Being a shifter, I could choose how I wanted to express my body, choose what I wanted to look like. I could experiment until I felt comfortable in my own skin. Most people don't have that option. I have a lot of respect for people who have to go through it the hard way. That can be a very long process with a lot of difficulty along the way, both physically and emotionally. I'm glad I didn't have to go through that."

"Yeah, I've never really thought about it. I mean, for me it was just accepting her, taking her at her word, and calling her what she wanted to be called. Not a lot involved there."

Jessie nodded. "Cool. Okay, I have a question and maybe the answer is self-evident. On Earth, historically one of the things that affected trans people when it came to affirming health-care was fertility. People, especially cis people, tended to balk at the idea of someone basically destroying their ability to reproduce. I always thought it was silly, but how is that in your society?"

His eyebrows rose at the question as he chuckling slightly. "It's not an issue. You do remember that most people don't reproduce in my society, right? You have Seeders and technically anyone with a womb can be a Birther, but it's perfectly possible for most people to never be involved with the reproductive process in the community. Which brings me to a question? You were considering surrogacy. That means you have a functioning womb?"

"As far as I know. I should. Whether I can have my own biological kids, that's another thing entirely." She got quiet for a moment. She often didn't like thinking about it. Male shifters couldn't have children except with other shifters. They didn't have the appropriate processes to allow cross-species procreation. In the rare instances when she let herself think about it, she wondered if she would be fully like a female shifter now, or locked into the male biology of her natal form.

"Why's that?" he asked, reaching out to touch her hand on the table.

His hand was warm and solid, a comforting weight grounding her when her thoughts wanted to run away. "Well, I'm a trans woman. We do understand certain things about shifters from experience. We know they can breed with other species, but only women can. Men can't. What we don't know is if that is true of trans women or not. There's no research. The shifter community has refused every research attempt, afraid of what has been done to them and others in the past. As such, we just don't know. There's not enough information. And there're not enough trans shifters for anecdotal evidence." She shrugged, but no gesture could fully encompass what she was thinking or feeling.

He rubbed the top of her hand. "I see." He smiled. "Well then, I think we make a perfect pair."

"Oh?" she said, raising her eyebrows in question. "Why's that?"

"Well, we get along well, and fertility wouldn't be a problem with me."

Jessie shifted more upright, moving her other hand from her chin to rest on his hand. "Except, your culture and mine have very different ideas on raising kids."

She sighed and removed her hand. Leaning back and looking around, she realized the meal was winding down. People around the table were removing dishes and bringing them to what she assumed now was the kitchen area. She stood up and started to grab some plates, but someone next to her stopped her, saying, "I've got it. You just have a seat."

"But…"

"I told you," Delyn said.

She turned and gave him a dirty look, but he only grinned in reply.

Then Tesa walked up to their end of the table. Jessie hadn't realized that Tesa was a farmer, but she supposed Delyn *had* said that much of his family were farmers, so it was likely.

"Hi, Tesa," she said with a smile.

Tesa looked at her assessingly, then turned to Delyn. "I'm told you two will be staying here for a bit. Come on, I'll show you to your rooms."

Delyn stood, and Jessie took up the tail end of their group as they went up a flight of stairs and turned right, walking to the end of a hallway.

Tesa turned to face them. "Bathroom's at the end of the hall." She pointed at the door, then pointed a thumb behind her. "You'll be staying in these two rooms. Need anything else?"

Jessie shook her head and looked at Delyn, who said, "No."

Tesa nodded and walked off, leaving them to their own devices.

Delyn didn't know what to do now that he was back in Valana. Up to this point, he'd been sort of swept up in the momentum of being "welcomed" home, but now that they were alone, he couldn't help thinking, "Now what?"

He rubbed the achy bruise forming on his cheek, the skin hot to the touch as he opened both doors, staring in at the nearly identical rooms. They were clearly either guest rooms or rooms intended for new Farmers as they had no personal touches, just plain wood furniture and some sheets and pillows stacked on each mattress. A window let light into each room from behind the headboard and, once darkness settled in, a single lamp by the bed would provide illumination.

It was a little strange to him, being here after being in space for so long. When living in the community, it was easy to forget that their species was so advanced, with interstellar travel and state-of-the-art technology and science. This room felt like it could belong to someone completely out of touch with the modern world, somewhere remote and quiet, at one with the natural world beyond those panes of glass.

"Help me make the bed?" Jessie asked, looking at him imploringly with a smile.

"Right, yes." He shook himself, surprised he hadn't thought of it. "Sorry about that. I guess I'm just feeling a little out of sorts, being back and all."

Jessie crossed the room and dropped the pillows on the floor. "I can understand that. That ship is tiny. And you usually live on it by yourself. I can certainly understand feeling discombobulated by the change. Hell, *I've* felt like that just from touching down in the *Trojan*, and that ship is *way* bigger than yours."

"The *Trojan*?" he asked as he took one of the sheets and sent it soaring over the bed to unfold. With his two hands as anchors, it floated above, coasting to the mattress.

Jessie grabbed the other side, straightening it out and starting on the corners, where they would need to fold it into position. "That's my sister's ship. She's a pirate." She looked at him and winked.

It was a deliberate gesture, but he wasn't sure what it was supposed to mean. He chose to ignore it, instead focusing on her words as he smoothed his first corner out. "A pirate, huh? You don't seem like someone who grew up among pirates."

"Well, we *do* have a code. And she's more of a privateer now."

He looked up, confused. "I don't know what that means."

She stood straight, patting her second corner. "A pirate works for themselves. A privateer works for another party. In my sister's case, a business."

Delyn frowned. "That doesn't sound like a worthy place to work for."

"You'd be surprised. I've met the owner, and he's pretty rock solid. Real good guy. He helped save our friend, Victoria. And the only reason he *hired* a privateer is so he could address his competition's less than aboveboard tactics."

"What were they doing?"

She sat down on the edge of the bed. "I think the *better* question would be what *weren't* they doing. Stealing shipments, hiring mercenaries, kidnapping, blowing up ships. These are just some of the things that me or my friends have personally experienced or seen."

"Wow." He shook his head. He had no idea what company she might be talking about, but it certainly seemed justified to fight back against them. "And what does your sister do in response?"

"Mostly? Steal back what was stolen. Although, how we got started is a pretty good story." Jessie started moving her hands animatedly as she talked. "So, here we are, pirates. Cass, my sister's name by the way, has picked her target and we've shut down the ship and put the crew to sleep. We board and look for something worth taking, right?"

He nodded, sitting on the bed himself.

"We find this really beautiful glowing blue rock. We know we can get some green for this thing."

Delyn suspected she was referring to money, but he had no idea why she made that word choice. He wanted to ask, but didn't want to interrupt her story.

"We snatch it and are in the process of leaving when, honest to God, the biggest, scariest security guard you have ever seen starts chasing us. We race through the ship, go through the airlocks, and Cass has her weapons aimed at him while he's barreling forward like a freight train. He is not stopping, and *my* sister has never shot someone in her life. I can see she doesn't want to do it. So me, I rush over to the airlock controls and slam the button to close the inner door.

"Unfortunately, he's still in the airlock. What the fuck do we do, right? Cass is trying to talk him into leaving and going back to his ship, but he's not having it. Oh no. Finally, probably out of frustration, knowing my sister, she closes the outer door and takes off with him still in the airlock.

"We're ready to separate from the other ship, right? We do so, we're in the process of going into sub-space and would you believe it, we get attacked! Out of nowhere! Boom!"

Delyn had so many questions, like what was sub-space, for starters.

"We were hit right before entering sub-space and almost immediately dropped back out of it. We have no idea where we are and the ship is *badly* damaged. We end up *crashing* on some nothing planet. So now, we have to repair the ship. The comms don't work, the engines don't work, the water filtration systems don't work, practically everything is either on emergency power or turned off.

"And we still have this guy in our airlock." Jessie pointed her finger multiple times while saying that sentence. "He got badly injured during the crash, and we end up having to take care of him. But that's not the end." She clapped a couple of times for emphasis.

"The guys that shot us down are still after us." She was really getting excited now. "They follow us to this no name planet and try to force us to give up the rock we stole. My sister, like a total badass, tricks them, throws a grenade at them, and then has a shootout.

"Anyway, we manage to fix the ship, but now what?

"Clearly, these guys are not gonna stop. So now working with the security guard, Kou, they blow up the enemy ship, and we end up bringing the rock to Inia Intergalactic, which is the company Kou *was* working for, and the one my sister *now* works for. The bad guys, though, sent mercenaries to retrieve it. They shot me, infiltrated the station, and caused two shootouts on board." She sighed, finally taking a deep breath.

"That's quite a story. I'm afraid I don't have anything of the sort in my own history. I've been pretty boring."

She shrugged. "There's nothing wrong with boring, although now I can't remember what we were talking about."

He laughed. "I can understand that. It was a long story. Actually, I'm not sure what we were talking about either."

"Well, I guess it doesn't matter." She stood up. "I suppose we should work on your bed next."

"I suppose you're right." He stood as well, and they moved next door, repeating the process.

"I miss her," she said. Her hand gripped the sheet as she sagged against the bed, her hip pressing into the edge of the mattress.

"What?"

"My sister. She drove me nuts living with her, but she also made things interesting. Like, I wanted to get away so I could become my own person, but I'm not sure I know how to do that. I was definitely making progress on some fronts. People appreciated my art. I even had some commissions, but I feel like I could have done that anywhere, even on my sister's ship.

"I guess what I really wanted was to find a partner, ya' know? Someone to grow old with. But I was having *no* luck with that. Although, maybe I'm being too hard on myself. After all, it had only been a few months. These things take time."

Delyn stopped what he was doing. "I can't say I know exactly what you're dealing with. Partnering is not really something the Pardus do, but I know what it's like to have expectations of yourself that you aren't meeting." He looked over at her and felt like his entire world was off-kilter. He *said* the Pardus didn't partner up like other species did, but he felt it. Some part of him *wanted* to partner up… and with Jessie specifically. He'd *said* he didn't know what she was dealing with, and intellectually he didn't, but something buried deep inside did. It was as if some long forgotten instinct was rousing for the first time, yawning its first breath of wakefulness and still groggy from its long sleep.

He felt compelled to comfort her, to reassure her. He even found himself crossing the room, scooting around the end of the bed and approaching her. She didn't even question it when he reached out and hugged her, pulling her into his warmth. It felt right, like two halves coming together. All his muscles seemed to relax, and his mind cleared, at peace with itself.

They stood like that for the longest time, just *being* with each other. Neither of them spoke. Neither of them moved. Occasionally, he would hear breath whistle out of her nostrils or fabric brush against fabric. In the distance, he could hear members of the household moving around and talking, but it felt muffled and distant, too distant to be relevant to them in this drawn out moment.

Eventually, they separated, though he couldn't say who initiated the movement. They stared at each other, and he wanted more, though he couldn't say what *more* entailed.

Maybe it was better to say he wanted everything.

But did she want it, too?

<hr>

Jessie was reluctant to leave afterward. She walked back to her room in a daze, closing the door behind her with a gentle click. The sun had set, and the room was fairly dark, just gentle moonlight lighting the interior.

She leaned against the door, the solid strength pressing against her back.

She'd wanted to kiss him. Jessie pressed her fingers to her lips, wondering if he would have let her, if he would have even understood. He'd said himself, the Pardus did not partner up like other species did. It was a futile fantasy, but it was a fantasy all the same, and at least for the moment, she wanted to wallow in it.

Today was the first time she'd been with a person, someone who wasn't family, and felt so strongly connected, almost like coming home. And when he'd moved around the bed to hug her, it had felt perfect. She'd never wanted it to end.

In fact, she'd wanted more. Separating had seemed the hardest moment of her life. She'd wanted to lean in, to kiss him, maybe even more, and as she stared at the plain white wall, she couldn't figure out when that'd happened. When had she started seeing him as more than a friend or someone she wanted to help? When had she started having romantic feelings for him? Could he even have them for her? He'd said many times that the Pardus didn't form pairs. She knew how their society worked.

But she also knew that that structure was a lie. She knew that reproduction on Wesa used to be very different. She was struck with the urge to go back to the Archive Vault, to look up more about what it was like back then. Stupidly, she hadn't looked much further than the mention of the Drone Policy. She'd been shocked by the lie, by the deceit on the part of Delyn's government. She'd been angry, and she'd mostly stopped looking after that.

Unfortunately, there wasn't anything she could do about it now. Her computer was back on the ship. She didn't even have a change of clothes, which might get awkward in the morning. She sighed. Those were problems for tomorrow.

But that still left the here and now. She touched her lips again, wondering what it would be like to kiss Delyn. Would he allow it? Would he like it? Maybe it was her imagination, but she felt there'd been something different about him in the other room. She couldn't say what, though. They'd grown close since first meeting on that Ateles colony, and like most relationships, there were no clear-cut lines. You knew who was a stranger, who was a friend, but not when they became those things. There was often a fuzzy area where people didn't quite fit neatly into one category or another. It could be maddening, and she felt herself dealing with that now.

She supposed the best thing she could do was ask, but her mind went back to that fateful moment a few years ago when she'd tried to entice Kou. Admittedly, it had been a rash teenaged attempt at flirtation, one doomed to failure by their age difference, but it had still left a mark.

What would Delyn say?

What would he do?

And if she got what she wanted, would it make her happy?

———

The next morning, Jessie ate breakfast with Delyn and the farmers. She'd resigned herself to not helping, though it rubbed her wrong to do nothing.

Frustrated, she glanced over at Delyn and couldn't help seeing him in a new light now. He sat next to her, looking handsome and stoic, though maybe that wasn't the right word. She was better with drawing and painting than words. There was something *strong* about him, even though he was shorter and leaner than almost everyone at the table except her. There was something solid about him, even though he lived on a ship and had no real home.

Each time he looked her way, there was a smile on his face, and he often leaned toward her, as if he couldn't get close enough. She wanted to believe that was true, that he had romantic feelings for her as well, that he might be open to a relationship.

Things were different now, weren't they? She *felt* different, though again, she couldn't say *how* any more than she could say how Delyn *seemed* different.

"If it's all right, I'm going to go to the ship this morning to get some of my stuff."

"Oh, of course," he said with a nod. "I'll take you."

She smiled shyly. "Thanks."

The rest of the meal was spent mostly playing with her food. She didn't want to waste it, and she forced it down, but she was distracted and didn't really have an appetite.

When the meal finally finished, she bounced up, waving to the farmers at the table as she followed Delyn out the front door. It was busier outside today. People were spilling out of their homes after breakfast. She watched as they greeted each other and talked loudly about matters of the community.

They left, the voices turning into a background mumble as they took the path between buildings toward the ship. In the distance, the sun blinded her, almost seeming to be amplified by the narrow pass. She covered her eyes, blotting out the worst of the rays, and at first, it made her think they were heading east, but then she remembered she was not on Earth. She had no idea how they defined their directions here.

Before long, she found her feet pounding on the metal ramp and walking up into the ship. She lowered her hand and followed Delyn as they both made their ways to their respective rooms. Jessie paused when she reached her closet, not sure what she wanted to bring. She definitely wanted her computer. She had research to do, after all. But what about her art supplies? Her easel? How long would they be here? She had absolutely no idea about their plans. Neither of them had talked about them once they'd both agreed to forget the contract they'd signed.

Jessie looked back through the door, where she could just barely see Delyn packing a bag from his closet. "Delyn?" she asked, leaning back to get a better view through the door.

He turned. "Yes?"

"How long are we gonna be here?"

He frowned, and Jessie already knew the answer. He hadn't thought that far ahead either. "How long would you like to be here?" He looked almost hopeful.

"Well, it's a new place. I'd like to see more of it." *And more of you*, she thought. "I was trying to decide if I should bring my art supplies."

"Oh, absolutely. I'll help you carry them."

She smiled, loading up her bags and grabbing her easel. It wouldn't hurt if she lugged them back and forth for no reason. And besides, it would be nice to get out and capture the planet some, even if it was only the local area.

Delyn took her heaviest bag off her shoulder, allowing her to carry the more awkward bundles.

"Is there somewhere specific you'd like to see?" he asked as they stepped off the ship. The area was still bleached by the sun's rays, but at least it wasn't in their face. It did radiate warmth onto her back, though, which was kind of nice.

"No, not really. I'll probably start by just drawing some scenes nearby. I was planning to spend some time this morning on the computer." Hacking the hell out of his government's secret archives. "Then maybe check out the surrounding areas this afternoon?"

"Sounds like a plan."

"What about you?"

Delyn paused. He probably hadn't thought that far ahead. "I guess I'll probably catch up with some people."

"That sounds nice."

They reached the Farmers' house, and he opened the door for her. "Follow me. I think I know a place you'll like to set up."

She opened her mouth to protest. She'd been planning to work from the bedroom they'd given her as it would afford some privacy, but she couldn't come up with a way to voice that without arousing suspicion. "Okay…"

They crossed through the ground floor, walking past the dining room and the stairs until they reached a room on the back of the house. Delyn opened the door, revealing a small room with big windows, a comfy couch, lots of plants, and a view of the fields in the distance. It was beautiful, and she couldn't help wondering what they were growing in those fields. She didn't recognize them, but then again, why would she?

She shook her head. "It's perfect."

He leaned in, smiling, and again, she was tempted to kiss him, to just smack one on his lips in gratitude for his thoughtful gift.

"Thanks," she said instead.

He nodded. "Which bag has your computer?"

"This one," she said, tapping the one on his shoulder.

He offered her the bag and hefted the rest of her things onto his shoulders. With a final gesture in farewell, he disappeared out the door.

Jessie pulled her computer from its bag and powered it up, quickly making her way to the Archive Vault for answers.

———

"Hello," Tesa said, making Jessie jump and slam her laptop shut.

She turned to face the newcomer. "Hello, Tesa."

Tesa sat down next to her, her expression unreadable. "So, Delyn informed me that he told you I was trans."

"Yup. If it makes you feel any better, I am, too." Her mind drifted back to the page she'd been on when the other woman walked in. She'd been reading about relationships before the civil war. She was having trouble processing what she'd read. Looking away, she stared out at the fields in the distance. The sun was higher in the sky now, changing the shape of the shadows.

"He also told me you're a shifter?"

Jessie turned back to face Tesa again, gripping the hard metal of her computer protectively even though Tesa couldn't see inside. "Yup."

"So… you…"

"I realized I was a girl when I was five and never looked back."

"So, you've looked like this since you were five? No hormone treatments, no surgeries." For some strange reason, Tesa's face seemed to be growing darker, like she was angry or upset or something.

"Yes…" Jessie said, drawing out the word hesitantly.

"Isn't that nice for you."

And now, Jessie was certain Tesa had her panties in a bunch over *something*. The sickeningly sweet way she'd spoken those words *screamed*, "I'm gonna cut a bitch."

Jessie wanted to escape, but Tesa was between her and the door. She didn't even care what Tesa thought of her at the moment, though she would probably be agonizing over the conversation later tonight. She stood up, clutching the computer to her chest.

"Where are you going?" Tesa asked, a look in her eyes that seemed almost evil.

"Gonna go get some art supplies and maybe do some painting outdoors. Thanks for the chat." She scooted sideways for a few steps, instinctually nervous about showing her back to

Tesa right now, then nearly ran out of the room and up the stairs.

When she reached her room, she closed her door a little too aggressively, the slam echoing down the hall. "What the fuck?" she said, letting out a slow breath to calm herself. She crossed to the bed, dropping the computer on the mattress's soft surface. It bounced before settling into place peacefully.

Jessie sat down next to it and fell onto her back, staring up at the ceiling.

"What the fuck was that about?"

The Keeper jumped when his computer alerted him to another breach, sending his anxiety spiking. He had a momentary fear that yet another opportunity to catch the culprit would be wasted. He didn't look forward to the censure that would follow if it did.

Already, the Magistrate hadn't been happy with his latest update, though he thought the other man was being unfair. After all, he *had* discovered that the ship belonged to the Pardus government, was on a trajectory to Wesa, and he'd already put in a request to the Hardware Registration Office. Since then, he'd learned that the hardware was registered to the Reproductive office, though he still hadn't received an answer from their office as to who they'd assigned the ship to.

He'd been practically chewing his nails off waiting for answers from the various departments he'd been reaching out to lately, and his office was feeling increasingly claustrophobic. There wasn't a single surface now that wasn't covered in printouts. He kept hoping that if he only arranged it in just the right way, he would have the answers he was searching for without having to wait.

So when the computer chimed with the notification that the hacker had accessed the Vault again, his mind had been otherwise occupied. He'd scrambled to get in front of the computer, and the first thing he'd noticed was that the coordinates weren't changing. Each update provided identical ones, right down to the smallest digit.

They're parked. We know where they are.

He quickly started pulling up the coordinates on his digital maps and excitement ran through him when the program gave a location here on Wesa. He didn't breathe for a moment, just staring at his vindication. It was on the other side of the planet, far away from the capital, but it was here. At least, for the moment, it was. He touched the screen where the indicator dot was, feeling the smooth surface and slight electrical field it generated.

"Right there. I've got you," he whispered.

CHAPTER THIRTEEN

*J*essie tried to go about her day as normal. Delyn guided her to a spot he thought she might like and left her to her own devices. He was right, of course. The spot was beautiful. The sun was behind her, so the lighting was great. A sea of wildflowers abutted a forest in the distance and even farther out, she could make out a mountain kissing the clouds. To the right, a river or creek bubbled along, its rushing water a constant gentle song as she set out her supplies.

She pulled out a canvas, touching the tightly woven fabric as her mind remained with the things she'd learned today. She couldn't believe how much Delyn's society had changed. Sure, cultures changed, people changed. Worlds evolved and technology advanced, but this was different. Before the war, the Pardus lived in individual tribes, what the communities were now. They'd been run by magistrates then, too, but those magistrates had only worked together as much as they wished, like separate governments making peace treaties and trade agreements.

Then the war had broken out. It was described as a civil war in the Vault, but it hadn't really been a civil war back then. They hadn't been one people back then. Same species, but separated. Like humans were. The war had been nasty, devastating. Before long, the magistrates, with the support of their people, had decided to start using drones.

It wasn't until she'd dug this deep that she'd really understood what drones were. Before the war, producing drones was rare. So long as men had sex or masturbated, they couldn't even produce them. It was theorized that the function evolved to rebuild populations after significant hardship that reduced their numbers. Gestation was reduced, time to maturity was reduced, and significantly more offspring could be produced with each breeding session. It could even be accomplished if no females of the same species remained in the population.

But it also meant that 50% of female young failed to develop, causing a gender disparity. It was why she'd only met a handful of women so far on Wesa. And one of them had been assigned male at birth.

But that wasn't the worst of it. No, when she'd really started digging, she'd found something her heart had been secretly hoping for, but she'd never expected. Their society had been structured entirely differently before the war, even removing the drone business and new government. Before the war, the Pardus had formed some of the strongest pair bonds she'd ever heard of.

And it was also unusual because those pairs weren't all romantic or sexual in nature. Some of the stories, myths, and legends she'd found had been these profound love stories or stories of unending passion. But others had been of warrior brothers who would die for each other, or queerplatonic partners who happily lived their lives together. Some pairs were procreative, some weren't. Some adopted children, while others served various supportive roles in the community. Everyone was accepted, regardless of their bonds.

And the bonds were lifelong. Once a bond formed, it couldn't be broken, even by death.

Which was how the war fucked things up so royally. Warriors were dying left, right, and center, and people were afraid to form pair bonds. Even staying behind didn't keep them safe, as sometimes the fight would get beyond those fighting it and reach the people huddled in their homes. Losing loved ones was a fact of life back then, and losing a bonded partner, should it happen, was life shattering. No one wanted that, and the tribes couldn't afford the devastation that inevitably followed. So, like an unspoken agreement, people stopped forming the bonds. It didn't say what people did to stop them, but from what she'd learned about pair bonding, she had an inkling. Documents described what the initial stages of a bond felt like, those first stirrings that would have once been seen as a blessing but soon became a curse. She imagined people during the war would get scared if they felt it, changing duties in the tribe to keep away from their partner and let the bond whither into dust.

Jessie paused in her ruminations. She had a paintbrush in her hand, but hadn't touched it to the canvas. It just hovered there, useless and waiting. She thought of her and Delyn spending weeks together with no one else for company. Could they have started bonding? She tried to go through her memories, looking for signs, but the historical texts hadn't been specific about what to look for. The documents were written from the perspective that everyone would know what bonding meant.

But could that be it? She'd thought they were growing closer, but she'd continually ignored it because he'd said himself that the Pardus didn't form pair bonds. But now she knew they did.

Could she have been missing something obvious? Could Delyn have missed it, too? After all, he didn't know about this stuff. He didn't know what his own government had been hiding from him. He wouldn't have known what he was experiencing and might have been shoving it aside as unimportant.

But she remembered some moments along the way where she'd believed more was possible. She stared at the blank canvas, seeing her and Delyn's relationship in it, a blank canvas waiting to be filled with color and life.

What could they have together?

What could this be between them?

Could it be everything she'd hoped for?

Delyn felt like he was having a productive day. He'd taken Jessie to the ship first thing that morning to get her things, shown her the nicest place in the house to hang out, told his sister he'd mentioned her being trans to Jessie, and shown Jessie a place to paint later that morning. In between, he'd helped the Farmers in the fields. It had been a long time since he'd last been out here, and he didn't remember it being such hard work. He could see now why he hadn't been chosen as a Farmer. He just wasn't built for it.

When the sun dipped low over the horizon, they all went inside en masse to clean up for dinner. Delyn felt grimy in a way he didn't ever remember feeling before. He had dirt in places he didn't even know existed and sweat stuck to him and ran in rivers down his body.

When the shower was over, he felt like a new person, though with sunburn. He rubbed his forehead, feeling the dry skin there. One downside of living in space was that sun exposure wasn't usually an issue. You got used to not needing to worry about it.

"Oh, you're really red," Jessie said as he entered the dining room.

He rubbed his forehead again. "Yeah, I didn't consider the sun. You look perfect, though." She looked like she might have gotten a little color today too, but only enough to give her skin a golden hue. It made her look like a goddess.

She smiled, ducking her head a little. "Thanks."

When he sat down in his seat next to her, she leaned over and whispered in his ear. "There's something I want to tell you after dinner."

He looked over at her, wondering what she needed to say that she couldn't say here, but she just sat up straight again and started serving herself when the food came.

The rest of the meal was a test of his restraint, looking at Jessie constantly and wanting to ask her what she wanted to say, but he suspected pestering her wouldn't do him any good. After all, she'd felt the need to whisper to him when she wasn't even giving anything away. Clearly, she didn't want anyone else to know.

The sound around them picked up as everyone dug into their food and started talking animatedly in the background. It was a raucous affair, filled with life and energy, but Delyn was distracted. He could smell some of his favorite foods on the table, but couldn't remember what he'd eaten, let alone what it tasted like.

When the meal ended, and Jessie stood up from the table, he was eager to follow her, nearly trampling her heels. "Sorry," he said absently.

She looked back, but didn't say anything, just shrugging before continuing onward.

They reached his room, and she pushed it open, encouraging him to follow. She closed the door behind him, standing with her hand still on the door handle. She licked her lips and didn't look at him.

"Anything I can do to help?" He sat down on the bed.

She shook her head. "No, just gathering my thoughts, I guess." She crossed the room and sat down on the bed facing him. Her hands moved like serpents in her lap. "So, I should admit that I've been doing some research on your people."

"Oh?"

She looked down, staring at her hands. "I found something interesting."

Delyn waited, wondering what this was about, but she didn't speak at first. She bit her lip, wrestled her hands together, and generally looked uncomfortable, so he reached out and held her hands, hoping to comfort her. He watched her, looking for signs of distress, but instead, she looked up at him and seemed calmer than before. "Go on," he said.

She nodded, taking a deep breath. "I assume you know about the war?"

"Of course, everyone does. The tribes fought each other, bent on each other's destruction. Eventually, they came to a peace agreement, forming a unified government."

"Yeah, that's right. But it's not the *whole* story."

"Oh?" He rubbed her hands soothingly. "What else is there?"

"So, I found a source that tells a bit about what things were like before."

When she said that, Delyn realized she probably knew more about the before times than he did. Growing up, they were taught that learning about those barbaric times could only taint modern society. They saw the unifying of the government as a rebirth of sorts, and nothing before it mattered.

But did it? As he stared at Jessie, who was watching him carefully for a reaction, he realized it just might. What if there was some valuable lesson to be learned from the mistakes of old? How would he know? How would anyone know? "Go on," he said, compelled to know more.

Her lips curled up in the barest of smiles. "So, before the war, the Pardus formed pair bonds. It was a basic part of society. It was lost during the war because losing a bonded partner was devastating. It was an eternal bond, not even breakable in death, so people avoided it at all costs because so many people were dying.

"And the war went on for so long, I think it slipped out of living memory."

Delyn sat there, his mouth slightly agape. Was this what he'd been feeling of late? He'd dismissed it over and over again, but what if that was what he'd been feeling for Jessie? "What does it mean?"

"It can mean just about anything, I think. From what I read, it can literally be any form of relationship. You just have to see where it takes you."

Recovering a little, he leaned forward, now curious and just a little excited. "How does it work? How do you... make it stronger?" He could feel it, like a magnetic pull between two objects. But it also felt fragile, like it would dissipate into nothing if they weren't careful. It felt like a gentle sprout, just seeing its first sun. Without water, it would wither and die, never providing the promise of a fruitful crop.

Jessie shrugged, shaking her head. "I don't know. It didn't say. I got the feeling that separation would stop it, but didn't really read anything about how to make it stronger."

He frowned, leaning back to think. "Then what do we do?"

"So do you think we're…"

He nodded, remembering all the times he'd felt drawn to her or different about her. The times he'd felt the need to protect her, the times he'd felt this strange energy while in her presence. In fact, just yesterday, he'd felt compelled to comfort her, to draw her into his arms. And compulsion was absolutely the right word. Theirs was a subtle drawing together of two people, something slow and nebulous and undefined. He couldn't say when all this had started. There was no eureka moment when he knew, but he felt it all the same. There was something between them, and he wanted to explore it. "I'm not sure I understand it, but yeah, I do. I think there's something there, a bond between us." He looked at her, trying to imagine being bound to her as she'd described.

An eternal bond. What did that even mean?

"So, what do you want to do?"

"Experiment?" She looked hopeful, like she wanted him to do something specific.

"Like what?"

She looked away, and there was something about the way she looked in that moment that was truly captivating. "Jessie?"

"Hm?"

He smiled, shaking his head at her. "What do you want to do?"

Her hands started moving again. "Have you ever kissed someone?"

Kissed? Yes, when he was a kid, but he was certain she meant something else, something more. He leaned in, feeling unbelievably awkward, but also like he was being urged forward. Again, the magnet analogy came to mind.

She smiled, leaning in as well. She rested a hand on his shoulder, the gentle weight feeling grounding. He lost some of his uncertainty and pressed his lips to hers.

It was… just right. Her lips were soft, moving gently against his. The world slipped away, and he lost track of everything but her lips. He didn't even notice when the kiss deepened. He just felt the need to continue. Breath didn't matter. Nothing mattered. Nothing but this.

When Jessie pulled away, he protested, leaning forward to get another taste.

When he looked into her eyes, they were glazed. Her breath was uneven, ragged. But there was also a certain determination there, like she wanted to dive in for more.

"Yes," he whispered, as if in agreement.

He'd never actually been here before. The Keeper straightened his clothes, dusting off imagined dirt, and tried to stand taller. It was one thing meeting the Magistrate at his home or the Magistrate coming to his office, but this was a place of respect, of dignity. This was where things in their society were decided. This was where the Magistrates ruled on matters of importance.

He wasn't sure he was worthy and wanted nothing more than to return to his own little office on the other side of the complex.

When the door opened, he gulped. A voice he recognized said, "Enter," and he did. The room was ornate, with large windows overlooking a central garden, one not visible from his own office. The desk, which took up a large portion of the surprisingly cramped room, was ornately carved of a dark wood. The chair the Magistrate sat in was similarly carved, with thick cushioning that spoke of comfort.

There was not a single personal effect in the entire room, in spite of the room being far from empty. Instead, everything spoke of elegance rather than personality. There were expensive paintings, fancy nicknacks, and various accoutrements of his trade, but nothing told anything about this man's life or personality.

"Please, sit," the Magistrate said, indicating one of the guest chairs.

He looked down and uncomfortably sat on the, likely expensive, seat. He waited awkwardly, his back stick straight, trying to touch as little fabric as possible.

"So, what's the news?"

"I've located the hacker, and they seem to have stopped."

"Where are they?" The Magistrate leaned forward, folding his hands together in front of him on the desk. He was the picture of authority, and it unnerved the Keeper greatly.

"Here, on Wesa." He pulled out a tablet, bringing up a map. "This is where the signal comes from." He pointed his finger at a dot on the screen. It showed a small, mostly agrarian community on the other side of the planet. He'd never heard of it before today.

"Hm," the Magistrate said, leaning over the tablet thoughtfully. "We can have forces there within a few hours."

He frowned. "Do you really want to do that, sir? The Archive Vault is supposed to be secret. Wouldn't it raise suspicions if the Fighters swooped in and took out this hacker?"

He sat up. "Yes, yes, of course. I'm getting ahead of myself." He laughed, shaking his head with a smile. Rubbing his chin, he reexamined the map. "There's good cover here, though I'm not a tactical expert. Perhaps we can take the person at night, when we wouldn't be spotted."

"I suppose it depends on the person's movements, but I don't have access to satellite footage, so I couldn't say. I'm just responsible for the databases."

The Magistrate nodded. "I'll send a squad. Discretely. Have them observe for now. You made a very valid point." He rewarded the Keeper with a thin smile. "This needs to be covert."

CHAPTER FOURTEEN

*D*elyn woke up before the sun the next day. Sitting up, he looked out the window, but there was only the barest of red tinges in the sky with no sign of that magnificent orb in sight. The house around him was quiet, still resting under the night's comforting embrace. There was a slight chill in the air that had him pulling a blanket around his shoulders as he continued to look outside.

It was truly too early to get up, too early to be moving about. Everyone else was asleep, but he found he was raring to go. He wanted to jump up and rush to Jessie's room just to see her face. He wanted to do everything and nothing all at once.

In fact, Delyn had so much energy, he felt like he could do laps around Valana, but he didn't. That wasn't really what he wanted to do. He wanted to see Jessie. He wanted to maybe kiss her again. Or maybe something else. What else could they do together? He wasn't sure. Maybe he could research what other species did as couples?

Was that what he wanted? To be a couple? A pair? What did that even mean? He felt simultaneously like everything was possible and like a great big terrifying void yawned before him, ready to swallow him into all the unknown that existed in the universe.

Delyn had always known what was expected of him. He'd always been told. First, he'd had the guidance of his Carers, teaching him and moving him through childhood with love, sternness, and kindness. Then, he'd been assigned the responsibility of Seeder, where he also received training, though probably nowhere near as much as that of a Farmer, for example.

He sighed and looked away from the window. There was nothing to see except the swaying plants greeting the dawn. It made him realize just how little he knew about farming, and how much they had to learn to be proficient. They had to know about watering needs, planting, harvesting, weather effects on plants, and probably countless things he couldn't even fathom. What did he, a Seeder, have to learn by comparison?

Even as that thought should have brought him down a bit, pulling him into the very depths of his inferiority complex, he couldn't seem to dwell on it today. No, instead, he couldn't help thinking about the promise of the day and that Jessie would soon be awake.

Was it too early to check? Maybe she was an early riser? He really didn't know. It was hard to say on a ship. You couldn't get a real sense of night and day, and you lost most of the environmental cues that told you when to get up, sending your circadian rhythm completely out of sorts. He looked at the intervening wall. Should he? Or should he wait a little longer?

He thought of the kiss again, touching his lower lip gently in awe. Would it be just as good next time? Would it be better? He lay back down on the bed, thinking about that moment yesterday. It had felt like everything had changed.

He couldn't wait to see what happened next.

Jessie woke up with the first rays of the sun. She groaned, not wanting to be awake. She'd stayed up late contemplating the new dimensions to her relationship with Delyn. For the longest time, she'd stared at the ceiling, remembering the kiss and wondering what would come next. Intermittently, excitement would race through her, making her giddy, but also completely thwarting her attempts at drifting into restful sleep.

Now she lay in bed, staring up at the white ceiling, currently gilded with sunlight. People were banging around downstairs, and the aroma of breakfast was drifting up to her room, telling her the meal was imminent.

She'd slept late.

How the hell was this sleeping late?

Another groan escaped her, and she rolled over, pushing the sheets aside as she slowly made her way out of bed. Looking out the window, she spotted a few people already outside and getting ready for the day. There was a big figure, possibly a man, walking toward a barn while another was laying out tools for everyone.

She looked away, not liking being reminded of her lack of a role here. It felt wrong to just live off their generosity without finding some way to repay them. Even her situation with Delyn had started out as a contractual agreement, though now maybe it was more? She certainly had hope in that direction, and Delyn seemed to as well.

Jessie stopped and stared at the wall separating their rooms. Was he there right now waiting for her? Was he just now getting up just like her? Or had he already gone downstairs?

She was suddenly desperate to find out. She rushed through grabbing clothes from her bag and pulling them on, not caring what she looked like. Only a small portion of her brain warned her she might regret this, but she pushed it down ruthlessly in favor of expedience.

In moments, she was dressed and rushing out the door. She stopped in the empty hall, wondering if she should knock on Delyn's door. She stood there in front of the portal, staring at its wood surface, indecisive about her next move.

Just do it, stupid.

She knocked, and a loud racket, like a great many things falling to the floor, came from the other side. Then, a moment later, Delyn appeared, a smile on his face.

"You're awake," he said, looking pleased.

She smiled and nodded. "Yup. Want to walk to breakfast with me?" she asked, offering her arm.

"I would be delighted." He looped his arm with hers, and they made their way carefully down the stairs.

There was a happy silence between them, neither of them feeling compelled to talk. There was also a weird energy, like she could break out in giggles at any moment. It wasn't like her. She wasn't the giggling type. Ebullient? Sure, but giggly? Not a chance. Still, this felt like more than her normal effervescent nature. She felt positively bubbling with sparkly energy, like she wanted to just bounce her way down the stairs.

And yet there was nothing she wanted more than to just curl up against Delyn and enjoy the moment. It was contradictory, and *she* certainly couldn't make any sense of it, but she couldn't control how she felt. Now that she'd let loose her hope, she suspected it was running wild, like an unsupervised toddler.

They separated briefly as they reached the table, then sat down shoulder to shoulder.

"So, what would you like to do today?" he asked as he scooped some food onto her plate.

She smiled, seeing how he chose the things she had gravitated toward most, even a few she'd only tried since arriving on Wesa. She looked over at him, her heart swelling with emotion. "I don't know. I hadn't really thought about it."

He turned to her after loading his own plate. "Well, did you have a productive art session yesterday?"

She shook her head. "Not in the slightest. My head was so full of the stuff I'd learned earlier that day that I ended up just standing there looking stupid with a brush in my hand and a blank canvas in front of me."

"Well, maybe we can go out, and you can try again today."

"We?"

He shrugged and put the first bite of food in his mouth.

She watched him, but he didn't say another word, so she shrugged as well.

I guess we're going painting together.

Tesa stared at her brother and Jessie. Delyn looked happy, possibly for the first time since reaching maturity. He'd never taken to the Seeder role he'd been given, and she'd always felt sorry for him because of it.

But she couldn't believe that *Jessie* was the cause of that happiness. Tesa would be the first to admit she wasn't always the most open with people, especially when meeting someone new, but something about Jessie had rubbed her wrong from the first. When she'd found out that Jessie was not only "trans" but something called a shifter, she'd been simultaneously envious and skeptical.

On Wesa, trans people were widely accepted, but transitioning was an essential part of that acceptance. You were accepted from the moment you declared yourself, but that acceptance was different before you finished your transition. There was this feeling of anticipation, like they were always waiting for you to change your mind, that it wasn't set in stone yet.

That had been a tense time in her life. It had made her feel separated from people who should have welcomed her with open arms. They didn't seem to know what to do with her until her transition was complete. And it made finishing her transition feel like a triumph, like she had officially achieved womanhood.

Looking over at Jessie as she laughed and piled food into her mouth, she couldn't help associating her with the trans person who had declared themself, but still hadn't finished their transition. After all, without surgery, Jessie could turn back and decide to be a man at any time. And really, wasn't five years old kind of late to realize that? That was the age of maturity here on Wesa. Tesa had known *years* before that.

So, yes, she was skeptical of Jessie. She didn't trust her dedication to her gender, and she hated that *Jessie* could just *choose* her sex while *Tesa* had to spend years transitioning and would spend the rest of her life on hormone replacement therapy. True, she had it pretty easy there. It was a time released implant in her arm, and she just had to go into the city every once in a while to recharge it. It was effortless and rewarding, but it also left a constant reminder of her otherness, a small lump on her upper arm that felt like some sort of beacon saying, "You're trans."

Sure, Tesa was accepted and had never known otherwise, but it still made her feel different, like that part of her was always whispering at the back of people's minds, influencing how they saw her. She was constantly struck with the feeling that she might not be good enough, might not be feminine enough. And being a Farmer didn't exactly help. You were expected to get your hands dirty, and many of the women here looked disturbingly like the men. It was sometimes hard to tell them apart. They were often tall, muscular, and sometimes with identical haircuts meant for practicality rather than style or gender presentation.

What's more, their work meant that there were limited opportunities for gender expression. Clothing tended to be pants (skirts would get snagged by plants or tools), breathable long-sleeved shirts (to protect from sun and overheating), boots that protected the feet and ankles, and hats with wide brims (again for sun protection). Even differentiation with colors often didn't work because colors faded fast in the sun, and you often found yourself covered in mud, dirt, and dust.

She envied the Carers who could just wear whatever they wanted every day with little consideration for their work. Tesa *wanted* to be able to wear dresses every day, to doll up with jewelry from time to time, to feel pretty, even if it was only for herself. But she'd been assigned Farmer, and that always came first in everyone's eyes.

Chairs scraped, and she watched as Delyn and Jessie stood and left the table. They connected arm to arm, and she couldn't help noticing how feminine Jessie looked, even with her mismatched pink shirt and brown pants. There was an adorable creature printed on the front of the shirt, enhancing her femininity. Her hair was long and seemed to effortlessly declare her gender. Her face was cute, her body thin and fragile. She was delicate in a way Tesa could never be, no matter how much smaller she was compared to other Farmers.

She gripped her utensil, the hard metal digging into her palm and fingers, resisting the urge to do something drastic.

"Sir?" one of his subordinates said, walking up to him with a tablet in hand. Heat radiated off the cooling engines, and birds chirped nearby, reminding him of their location. Dappled light and shadow painted their surroundings, including the tablet screen offered to him.

"Yes?" He looked down at the tablet, noting their positioning in relation to the location of interest. The map showed a series of buildings in a circle, with woods on one side and open fields on the other.

The subordinate spoke up. "This was the data we were given by the Magistracy. The signal originated from this building here." He pointed at the dot, then moved on to a more up-to-date thermal mapping of the area. "This is a readout from last night. You can see there's easily a dozen or more people in that building. It's hard to determine an exact count. From drone imaging, there are two, possibly three, floors based on the shape of the roof."

"So, all we know is that at one point, our hacker was in that building. Can we get a trace on the hardware without them having a live connection to the classified information?"

"I'll see what I can do, but won't we need more information to identify the hacker?"

He paused. He knew that tone. "What do you have in mind?"

The subordinate frowned, looking off into the distance as he thought. "If we can infiltrate the software, install a tracker, we should be able to pinpoint its location so long as the hardware's powered up."

He shook his head. To think that hadn't been done already. He was disgusted to think that this hacker had apparently been accessing confidential files for so long and yet no one had thought to act proactively. Or even tactically. The additional hardware and software they'd installed had been a good first step, but they'd never gone beyond that, leaving a great deal more work left to do.

"Get to it," he said with a nod. He looked back out into the distance. The series of buildings from the map jutted out over the thick fields in the foreground. Just beyond the angular roofs, the outline of a parked spaceship greeted the sky.

There was something weird about standing there in front of an easel while Delyn lounged off to the side as if he were posing for a portrait. And yet it also felt like he was encouraging her. He would often ask her questions about what she saw, what she wanted to paint, or how she would portray it.

She wasn't sure if she loved his presence or hated it. It make her a little self-conscious.

Jessie stared out into the field the same as she did yesterday. It really was a beautiful sight. The wind moved the tall flowers in a swaying motion that reminded her of dancing. She wanted to somehow catch that motion, but was stuck on the how.

Also, just like yesterday, the water serenaded them when they weren't speaking, and she found herself more inclined toward talking than painting. Delyn was propped up on a large rock, sunning himself in the morning heat, which would only get hotter.

"You should be painting," Delyn said before taking a swig of water.

Jessie looked over at him with a fake scowl.

He smiled, motioning his eyebrows and head to indicate the still blank canvas.

She huffed good-naturedly, but turned around anyway, lifting a brush to the canvas. She started working on the easy stuff, like the mountain and trees in the background.

"What do you think makes a good relationship?" he said out of the blue.

She turned with brush poised over the canvas. "Why do you ask?"

"Well, my only experiences are really with other types of relationships. Carers, teachers, siblings, friends."

She nodded, putting the brush down, and faced Delyn. "I think it depends on the person. There are some basic things."

"Like?"

"Communication. Doesn't really matter what type of relationship, communication is key. If you can't voice your wants and needs, it won't end well."

He nodded. "That makes sense. Some of the worst relationships I've ever had have been with people unwilling to listen."

"Your father?"

He laughed. "How did you know?"

She raised her hand, pinching index and thumb together. "The little fight when we first got here kinda gave it away."

He bent over, holding his belly, as he laughed again. "Oh, I'm so sorry about that."

She shook her head. "Don't be. After all, how is this any different than my situation with Rae? You were just *there*, and that was enough to set him off. That's not your fault."

"No, I suppose it's not."

Jessie stepped up to him, kneeling and touching his knee. "Hey, sometimes you can't please people, and it's not your fault. *Sometimes*, the best thing you can do is accept that a relationship cannot be fixed if both sides aren't working at it." She stood. "Which I guess brings us to the second thing that makes a good relationship. Both people need to be willing to work at it. If not, it'll fall apart."

"Fair," he said, nodding. "I suppose common interests would be required, too?"

"Not especially. People can have wildly different interests and still make a good couple. But it also means they have to give each other space to indulge those interests. *Wanting* to be together is more important than having interests in common.

"Though," she raised her index finger into the air, accenting her point, "common life goals *are* important. You can't expect someone to change their mind about what they want out of life in a healthy relationship. If they say they want kids and you don't, not having kids will make them miserable, and having kids will make you miserable. There's no middle ground."

"Do you want kids?"

"Hm." She sat down on the rock next to him. "I don't know. I know I don't want kids right now. I'm too young. Don't really know myself well enough yet. I don't think anyone does at this age.

"I guess that's why the surrogacy agreement appealed to me. Sort of like a trial run. No strings. No responsibility. But that doesn't mean I won't want them in the future.

"I'm certainly not *opposed* to having kids eventually, and I'm definitely curious. But then again, it's kinda hard to imagine a life with kids considering how I grew up. I spent my teenage years on a pirate spaceship. That's not exactly an ideal place for a kid." She looked over at him. "Of course, having kids means something different for you, doesn't it?"

"I guess… yeah. It's always been a duty for me and, like you said, doesn't have the responsibility afterwards. That isn't to say that I don't know how other species handle children. I've researched it, seen it." He sat there, seemingly lost in thought.

"And what did you think?"

He shook his head. "I don't know. On the one hand, I'll admit that the way we do it is really efficient. The children get good care, are loved, and they're never without a purpose."

Jessie thought of her own research, about the changes the Magistracy had made, manipulating their people for their own selfish gains. "But it doesn't give people a choice."

He turned to her. "Is that a bad thing?"

"Well, are you happy?"

He smiled. "I am now."

She leaned in. "But your society has forgotten about this bonding experience. It's not part of the system. The system did nothing to make you happy." She leaned back, shaking her head. "It's too rigid, and a system that's too rigid will always cause problems."

"Is it really too rigid?"

"Yeah. I don't know what the perfect system is, but any system that doesn't play to your strengths, that doesn't allow you to change when you're not happy or as you grow and evolve as a person, is not an effective system."

"I guess I can see that, but do you think it can be fixed?"

"Anything can be fixed, if enough people want it to be."

They grew quiet and looked away from each other. Jessie couldn't help wondering if Delyn *wanted* things to change, if *any* of the Pardus did. She figured he would probably be more motivated than most to see change, but social mores were hard to escape.

Her gaze moved off to the distance, her mind struggling with the desperate need for change she saw here on Wesa as something shined briefly in the shadowed woods.

After Jessie finally gave up on painting, they went inside, settling on his bed for the rest of the afternoon. Before long, they each had their computers propped up on their laps while they talked or traded little bits of information they found.

Daylight shined in through the window while muffled voices from outside served as a backdrop.

"Do you think we'd make a good couple?" she asked, continuing their conversation from earlier.

He wanted to say yes enthusiastically. After all, he *wanted* something more with her, but it would do her a disservice if he didn't think it through.

But what if you don't like the answer?

The talk about kids earlier had thrown him a little. It had never occurred to him before that what she wanted in life could have been so different from anything he'd imagined. Admittedly, he'd already been confronted more than once with their different worldviews, but this was different, real, not some abstract thought with no connection to their lived experiences. She didn't know if she wanted kids, but what if she did? Would he be the right partner then? Could he turn his back on his society's traditions and structure to make her happy? His chest tightened even at the thought.

Yes, yes, I could.

If he had to leave Wesa far behind, never see another Pardus, he could do it. He'd already left Wesa once before. He'd even taken jobs off-world, so he could handle it. Delyn would miss his family and friends, but Valana hadn't truly been home for him for quite some time.

And if she wanted children, he could raise them with her even though the only experience he had with children was being a child himself. They could figure it out together. He'd always been fond of seeing the children frolic and play in the parush. He could find a great deal of fulfillment in raising children together.

And if she didn't want to have children, that would be okay, too. He knew she was an artist. She seemed passionate about it, and he could easily see her being successful at it.

And suddenly, he wanted to make that happen. Delyn wanted to see her sharing her art with the universe. He wanted to see her mouth stretched in a broad smile as she accomplished the goals she set for herself. He realized he didn't much care what she wanted out of life, only that he was there beside her and helping her achieve them, whatever they might be.

And he knew without a doubt that she would support him in kind. He didn't really know what he wanted. On Wesa, he'd never been given the opportunity to explore such concepts as "life goals," but he knew she would encourage him and believe in him while he figured it out. More than that, she would encourage him like she encouraged him to try painting. She would push him to discover himself, to find his happy place.

"Yeah, I think we would make a great couple." His voice was soft with emotion, like he was speaking something sacred that would be tainted if anyone else heard.

She smiled and set her computer aside.

"Jessie?" he asked, suddenly wondering what she was up to.

"Move the computer, Delyn," she said, leaning toward him.

He moved to do just that as Jessie loomed over him, a certain spark in her eye. "What is it?"

"Nothing." She smiled, shaking her head. "You know, another person might have been worried about how long it took you to answer my question." She straddled his legs.

"Oh? Not you?"

She shook her head again and touched his cheek, her fingers gentle as feathers. "Nope. You thought about it, long and hard." She snorted and looked away, and he wondered what was so funny. "Sorry." She settled and looked at him, a soft contented smile on her face. "You weren't just trying to placate me. You really thought about it, gave me a real answer." She kissed his nose.

It was odd, and he touched the spot she'd kissed, wondering what she meant by it. It wasn't like when she'd kissed his mouth. By the look on her face, he would say it was an almost playful gesture.

"I agree, by the way. I think we'd make a great couple." She leaned in and kissed him for real.

It was almost exactly like last time, only more. This time, their bodies were pressed together, and heat blossomed between them. He didn't know what he was doing, but he deepened the kiss, twining his fingers into her hair as she moaned in encouragement.

Delyn wanted everything, his impulses telling him to move, to touch, to act, but he didn't trust his instincts. He wanted to rely on Jessie, to let her guide him. She, after all, seemed to know what she was doing, and he wanted to please her. He wanted to give her everything she wanted, and he wasn't sure what all that entailed.

Then their mouths opened and her tongue met his. He groaned, simultaneously confused and becoming increasingly absorbed by the acts. His hands started moving of their own accord, and Jessie encouraged them, moving them under her shirt until his fingers met bare skin. She rubbed against his hands, like a pet begging for attention. He couldn't deny her and started moving his hands experimentally, trying to find what affected her most.

Delyn broke the kiss so he could watch what he was doing, but that didn't deter Jessie. She kissed her way across his cheek, nibbling at his ear before moving down his throat.

Meanwhile, he ran his hands up her sides, feeling the soft skin underneath her shirt. He moved farther north and as he approached her breasts, she took in a long, shaky breath, forgetting entirely about her progress. He took that as a good sign.

"What do you like?" he whispered against her ear.

She didn't speak, though, her jaw hanging open in anticipation. He ran a thumb gently over the fabric there. The material was silky soft, almost as soft as her skin. She leaned into his touch, silently begging him for more. He moved his hands farther, cupping her flesh so he could run a teasing thumb over the sensitive flesh at its center. A small smile crossed her face, and she pressed against him, cheek to cheek.

She stayed like that for a moment before moving her hands behind her. He couldn't see what she was doing, but soon after, the fabric in his hands loosened, and he gained access to the skin beneath. If her skin before was soft, the skin that tipped her breasts was the silkiest thing he'd ever touched. He was fascinated as he moved his fingers over it, loving the luxury of it.

Then the texture started to change, and he pulled back, surprised. But she quickly grabbed his hand, pressing it back in place. He felt suddenly awkward and self-conscious, but she urged him onward. The skin there puckered up, and he ran his fingers over it again, studying the new sensations there.

Then she leaned back, sitting up straight. She looked empowered, like she was completely in control, and he suspected she was. She smirked. "You wanna try something else?"

"Else?" he said, his voice squeaking.

She laughed, and he relaxed, feeling more comfortable with this playful side of her.

"What did you have in mind?"

She shrugged, looking away. "It would require removing more clothing."

He tried to understand what she was getting at, but all his training had been focused the end goal of implantation. He was enjoying this so far, but he had no idea where this was going. "Whatever you think is best."

She looked back at him and frowned. Her brown hair had started to come out of its ponytail, with little loops of hair curving around her ears and others caressing her neck. "What was that supposed to mean?" she said, looking confused and snapping him out of his reverie.

He opened his mouth to answer, but his jaw just bobbed up and down, ineffectually forming shapes that had no words to back them.

"Delyn?" She leaned in, looking concerned.

He shook his head. "I really don't know what I'm doing."

She relaxed. "Neither do I, silly. Been on a lot of dates the last few months. Mostly first dates. None of them went anywhere. I have a lot higher hopes for this, though."

"Me, too." He leaned in and gave her the briefest of kisses. "You had something in mind, yeah?"

"Yeah. Clothing not allowed."

"Okay then." He reached for his shirt to start removing it, but Jessie stopped him. He looked at her, confused.

"That's my job," she said with a smile.

She reached for his shirt, skimming her fingers over his flanks as he'd done to her only moments before. His muscles jumped, twitching under her touch as she pushed the shirt out of the way, exposing the vulnerable skin beneath. He lifted his arms, never taking his eyes off her as she continued. They were briefly separated by fabric before it popped off his head, and she threw the offending garment across the room carelessly.

"My turn?" he asked, dropping his hands to tease her hem.

She nodded with a smile, lifting her hands into the air.

He made quick work of her shirt. After all, he'd already made slow work of caressing her, and now he was curious about where this would go. He was eager for the next stage.

She laughed as he dropped her top on the bed beside him.

Jessie pulled the loose breast covering off her arms and said, "Next come pants," pretending at disappointment. She lifted a leg over his lap and shifted off the bed, standing beside it to disrobe.

He watched, mouth dry, as the material caressed her curves. A few moments later, she was wearing nothing but a single tiny piece of fabric.

She tilted her head, moving her fists to her hips. "Delyn, focus. You're behind."

He looked down and yes, he was, in fact, behind. He jerked into action, fighting with the fastening at his waist, then shoving his pants down his legs with frustrating difficulty.

Jessie laughed, but stepped forward, grabbing the ankles of his pants and pulling to ease the process. "There, that's better," she said as she dropped the pants on the floor.

"What about those?" he said, pointing at her last remaining garment.

She reached down, pulling the elastic waist away from her body and letting go. It snapped loudly against her skin in the otherwise silent room. "Are you sure?" This time, there were no smiles, no laughter, just a serious question requiring an honest answer.

Delyn didn't really know what he was getting into exactly, but he knew he wanted to proceed. He nodded. "I'll tell you if I change my mind."

"And so will I." Jessie pulled down the stretchy material, and once it passed her hips, it fell to the floor at her feet. She stepped out of it and resumed her position straddling him on the bed. She laid her hands on his shoulders, massaging gently. "What feels good to you?"

"I'm not sure what you mean."

"Okay, let's back up a little further. What have you been taught about sex and pleasure?"

Delyn struggled to focus on the question. There was something about so much skin to skin contact that seemed to short out his brain. It took long moments for him to form words. "Um, women have arousal tissue at the rim of or just inside the vagina, which gets stimulated during penetration. If a woman is not aroused beforehand, you should manually stimulate that tissue. Also, you should pay attention to what speed or rhythm gets the best response, as women have different sensitivities."

"I *meant* about your *own* pleasure, Delyn."

He shook his head. "I don't understand." Seeders pleasured a female to encourage Birthers to come back for repeat performances. A well-skilled Seeder could have women lining up for the process without effort. Delyn, on the other hand, had never had the opportunity to prove himself, and he realized now, his father had been sabotaging him with the women of Valana since the moment he received his role as Seeder.

One hand reached up, dipping into his hair and scratching gently against his scalp. It sent pleasurable chills through him. "Delyn, sex is about both people, not just one. If all I cared about was my own pleasure, I could just masturbate."

"What's masturbate?" he asked, distracted by the hand massaging his scalp.

Jessie's eyes rounded, and she pulled back from him slightly. "What's masturbate? Have you never masturbated before?"

"I don't... think so." He would know better if he understood the word.

She sighed, rolling her eyes. "It means self-stimulation. Pleasuring yourself."

"Why would I do that?"

"What?!"

He looked around the room, suddenly feeling uncomfortable with the conversation, like he was somehow defective.

"Oh, oh, Delyn. No. No. Look at me."

He did. She looked sad, like she'd done something wrong.

"I'm sorry." She shook her head. "I reacted badly. I mean, people can do or not do whatever they want to, especially when they're the only person involved. There's nothing wrong with not masturbating. I shouldn't have reacted that way. That was stupid."

Now *he* felt bad. He'd made her feel guilty with his reaction. He couldn't leave things that way. "No, you have a right to your own reactions, just like I have to mine. Okay, so I didn't understand this 'masturbate' word or why you would do it. And you reacting so strongly does make me wonder if maybe something is wrong with me, but that's not your fault. Maybe we could start over? Why don't you tell me why *you* masturbate?"

She nodded, looking away as her cheeks grew bright red. "Um, well, like I said, for pleasure. If you're wanting to feel good, then you can stimulate yourself by touching your eroge- nous zones. Sometimes, it's a pick-me-up. Sometimes, it's to satisfy a biological urge."

"What urge?"

"Sex drive? Is that a concept in your species?"

He shook his head.

She frowned. "Hm… Well, um, a sex drive is basically a biological drive on my planet, probably others, too. It's associ- ated with reproduction, and the drive can be stronger or

weaker, depending on the person. Some people don't experience it at all."

"Huh. I mean, I've never heard of anyone seeking reproductive contact other than Birthers and Seeders, at least here on
Wesa."

She leaned forward. "Well, I suspect that drive has been
circumvented or even bred out of the Pardus. After all, you've
created a society that revolves around socially constructed
breeding patterns. There's really nothing biological about
those choices anymore, is there?"

"No, I supposed there isn't. Most males aren't Seeders, so they
never do any of that. The only biological trigger I can think
of is the feeling when new seed is ready, which can take
months between implantations. Or so I'm told. And even
then, there's no real *drive* to act on it."

She nodded. "Interesting. For us, we have physiological and
neurological triggers that can encourage sexual contact. But
I'm not exactly an expert on the subject."

"That's okay."

She laughed. "I can't believe we're having this conversation
naked."

He looked down, seeing the way skin met skin. He was
surprised himself. It had come to feel so natural for the two of
them to sit here without a stitch on. "Is there anything that
can't be talked about while naked?"

She chewed her lip before answering. "I suppose not. Still,
getting back to the topic at hand, I guess I should ask you
again if you want to continue."

"What are we doing?"

"Pleasuring each other, hopefully… eventually."

"Okay."

She pointed at him. "But you always have the right to tell me to stop."

He nodded. "Of course."

She took a deep breath. "Now, I'm going to touch you."

"You are touching me."

She laughed. "I meant down there." She pointed a finger twice at his crotch.

"Oh." Now, didn't *he* feel like an idiot. He nodded.

One of her hands slid down the midline of his body, moving slowly closer. It felt a bit like a string being pulled tauter and tauter. It felt like it would break, like he was being pulled upward by the force of her gentle caress. He held his breath as the back of her hand glanced against the sensitive skin down there. It felt… good, like he wanted more.

Then her hand turned and surrounded that hard flesh. It was warm and dry, firm, providing pressure that he imagined must be similar to the experience of implantation. She watched him for a moment, maybe waiting for a reaction, then dragged her hand upward, toward the tip. He gasped, his breath quavering as it sucked into his lungs.

He couldn't describe the sensation. It was like his brain and skin were on fire, but nothing burned. It felt tight, but nothing was constricting. He wanted to move, but there was nothing in the universe that could drag him away from Jessie's hand right now. "More," he said, his voice feather soft in the aftermath of her exploration.

"Aye, aye, sir."

He barely registered the words. They just filtered in and dissipated, becoming nothing in the waters of his mind. She experimented with firmness and speed, even licking her palm at one point, but Delyn barely noticed. He was too absorbed in the sensation to process her actions as anything more than good or bad.

Then it got to be too much. He couldn't think. His mind and body were screaming for something to happen, but he couldn't say what. Then it snapped. He wanted to roar his approval, but his throat locked up, trapping the sound inside.

There were moments there where he didn't process anything at all, just this lassitude, a sort of boneless bliss where all was right with the world and nothing else mattered.

Eventually, the world started to come back to him. Jessie was leaning over him with a smile. "I wasn't expecting that," she said, lifting her hand, which was wet with a creamy, lumpy liquid. Her fingers rolled the little beads back and forth, seeming fascinated.

My seed.

A part of him froze, having never seen them before. He'd learned about them, knew they existed, could even feel them waiting inside him, a full feeling he'd had since shortly after reaching puberty. A feeling that was suddenly gone. "I shouldn't have done that," he muttered under his breath, unable to take his eyes off them. They were seeds of new life, life that would never be, life his people had counted on him to bring into the world.

"Why not?" She turned to him, seeming to finally notice the direction of his attention. She looked back at her hand, then up at him again. "What was wrong with what you did?"

He shook his head, finally looking away. "It's nothing."

"No," she said forcefully, dragging his attention back to her. "It wasn't nothing. Now answer my question and don't lie."

Her intense gaze bored into him, revealing a side of her he'd never seen before.

"It was a waste." He could barely speak the words, his mind echoing *failure, failure, failure* on repeat, like those were the real words he needed to say.

She looked down again, running an index finger over one of the seeds. She turned her gaze back up to him, her finger still hovering over the seed. "This is a waste? Was it? Were you planning on doing this with someone else?" Her expression grew dark at the question, and she wiped her wet hand on his leg, as if dismissing him.

He reached out to her. "Jessie, no. That's not what I meant. It's just… that's how I was raised, how I was trained. You're the only one I want to be with." He looked down at the mess they'd made. He *did* see it as a waste, as people who now would not be born, but he also recognized that he wasn't exactly on any path to see them born. And in the grand scheme of things, what did it matter? Should they want, there could always be future batches. This wasn't something final. "I'll admit I feel conflicted. I don't think you get over your childhood and training in a moment." And he wasn't really ready to talk about it.

He looked over at Jessie and smirked, seeing a way out of this awkward conversation. "But I think, more importantly, *someone* is still owed some pleasure."

Her smile became huge, and he took that as permission. Carefully, he followed the same path she had, running a gentle hand down her midline until he reached a grouping of curls. He dived in, finding wet flesh.

She took his hand, guiding his fingers. "I'm not quite like Pardus women. This," she said as his finger connected with a tiny bit of flesh that made her jump, "is the money spot." She released him, then moved both hands to his shoulders, steadying herself for the experience ahead.

He hoped he could give her an equal experience to what he'd felt. Leaning on his training, he experimented. Hard or soft. Fast or slow. Different motions and patterns. Her whole body jerked when he did something she liked, and if she really liked it, she would squeak. He decided then that it was his new life goal to make her squeak like that. It was so cute and adorable and completely unselfconscious.

Delyn continued fine-tuning his technique on Jessie's body, watching as her head fell back, exposing her neck. He leaned in, kissing her there as she'd done earlier to him. She moaned, her movements getting more frantic.

His unoccupied hand didn't know what to do. At first, he just held on, his hand supporting her back. There was something graceful about the way it curved around his fingers and palm. But as the session continued, he wanted to do more, and he moved that hand toward her front, returning to her breast. He played with it in time to his work at her apex, using the two in combination to drive her wild.

When she came, it wasn't with a strangled, soundless scream. It was high-pitched, an exclamation of joy that threatened to call every person in the house down on them. He quickly covered her mouth, hoping to extend the moment, hoping to preserve their privacy a little longer.

She collapsed against his chest. "That was… perfect."

CHAPTER FIFTEEN

Jessie spent quite some time, it would seem, just laying there against Delyn, feeling his firm muscles as her damp skin slowly cooled.

"Is everything okay in there?" a voice said, startling her out of her post-coital brain fog.

She jumped, throwing the covers over her to hide. Her cheeks flamed with embarrassment, suddenly feeling like a teenager caught making out with her boyfriend while her parents weren't home.

I'm not here. I'm not here. This isn't happening.

"Everything's good," Delyn said loudly, speaking to the person on the other side of the door.

There was a pause before footsteps slowly walked away.

"Phew."

Delyn wrapped an arm around her shoulder under the blankets, pulling her close. "It's fine. Someone just wanted to make sure no one was hurt."

Jessie pulled back the blanket and glared at him, annoyed at both his practicalness and the invasion of privacy. She supposed part of her annoyance was with the rather abrupt ending to the afterglow. She'd been reveling in it, wanting it to last as long as possible. Nothing had ever felt like that before. It made every time she'd masturbated in the past feel like an utter waste of time. Not when she could have had *this*. Masturbation was a relief, scratching an itch. Sometimes, it was just a great sleep aid.

But this? This was a revelation. It was a celebration of two people connecting on a profound level. If she'd had the energy, she would have sung at the top of her lungs like a hallelujah chorus or something. That's how she'd felt in that moment. Both perfectly at peace and like she'd found the ultimate thing to fight for.

Although, she supposed she'd known he was important beforehand. She wouldn't have done this otherwise. But it was like the exclamation point on the end of a strong sentence. It probably didn't *need* the exclamation point if it was well worded, but it definitely slapped you across the face with the point it was making.

She looked over at Delyn. They were nearly nose to nose in the bed. "So, what'd you think?"

"I think we might need to do that more often."

She laughed, a big smile stretching her cheeks taut. "I think I agree." She turned over on her side, running fingers over his arm. "I'm glad we did this. It feels right."

He nodded. "Yeah, it does. I still feel like I have some work to do… here." He pointed at his head. "It's hard to reconcile what I've been told all my life with what I feel now."

She moved her hand to his hair, feeling the silky strands and pushing them out of his face. "That's okay. Take all the time you want. That's what a relationship's all about, right?"

"We've got something," a voice said from across the shuttle.

The team leader looked up from his console, seeing a confident female urging him over with her eyes. Behind her, a view of the woods they'd cloaked themselves in stretched from one side of the room to the other. In contrast, the interior was all cool metal and hard edges. He stood up and crossed the space, leaning over her shoulder to see her display. "What have you got?"

"We got a signal from this location in the building. I also took the liberty of sending out an unmanned vehicle so we can get a visual."

"Good initiative," he said with a nod, watching as she beamed with pride. "How far out is it?"

She changed screens, pulling up the vehicle's camera. It was approaching one of the buildings, having managed most of the distance on autopilot. Because of its size, it was an ideal tool for covert ops. Smaller than a person's palm, it became almost impossible to see with the naked eye if it was sufficiently high and easy to mistake for a bird. It also could not be tracked using conventional methods for controlling airspace.

"Okay, I think we got something. A window." She zoomed in with a control device at her side.

The screen showed a bedroom outlined by slim pieces of wood. Inside, he could see a bed with two people on it, one straddling the other. "Is there any way to see both their faces?"

She pressed a button, taking a screenshot and capturing the woman's visage. "I'll try. It'll be hard with the second person. The angle's not very good."

She moved the drone, shifting it farther to the side. The scene rotated, giving a narrower and narrower view through the window. He frowned, getting frustrated with the poorer image, but then the woman in front of him exclaimed excitedly, hitting the button to take another screenshot.

"What'd you find? What'd you see?" He leaned farther forward, his hands pressing into the thin padding of the chair.

"One sec. I'm going to put the vehicle in standby. It'll get it out of sight until we're ready to move it." The camera screen disappeared, and she opened the screenshots folder, pulling up the two pictures she took.

One showed a woman's clear face. The clarity was good, undistorted, and while her hair was in a bit of disarray, it didn't obscure her face or alter her bone structure for facial recognition.

The second showed a closeup of a man in profile. He was more in shadow, and while the camera was quite powerful, there was some loss of clarity in this picture. Still, it should be enough.

"Okay, good. Let's try to identify these people."

She turned in her seat. "But isn't only one of them the hacker?"

"Doesn't matter. We've narrowed it down to two people. Let the Magistracy figure out the rest."

<hr>

The next morning, Delyn woke up in Jessie's arms. It was a weird feeling, both awkward and unfamiliar, but also warm and comforting. He couldn't decide if he liked it and wondered if he should move or remain still. On the one hand, he didn't want to disturb her sleep. On the other, sunlight was already streaming through the window, and he could smell breakfast fumes rising up from downstairs.

He looked down at her. She seemed so peaceful laying there with her head on his chest and her hand curled up under her chin. Then she snorted, killing the moment, and he wanted to laugh, but that would surely wake her. The emotion felt like a pressure in his chest, but he held it in.

"Stop it," she mumbled in her sleep.

"Stop what?" he said, a smile on his face.

"It," she said, as if that explained anything.

He kissed the top of her head, deciding she was probably waking up anyway. "Are you hungry?"

"Mmmm…" she said, her fist clenching against his skin.

"Well, if we get up, we can go downstairs to breakfast. What do you say?"

That got her curling up tighter, as if in protest of his suggestion.

This time, he did laugh.

She groaned and rolled over, sprawled out on the bed. "Couldn't I have had a *few* more minutes?"

He leaned over her. "You could have, but do you really want to?"

"Yes, yes, I do," she said, eyes still closed stubbornly.

He kissed her on the nose. "Well, get dressed when you're ready." He got out of bed and started donning the day's clothes.

"Delyn…" she whined.

He turned, shirt secured on his arms in front of his torso. "Yes?"

She was sitting in bed, looking pouty. "Oh, never mind." She got up and grabbed a shirt from the floor, pulling it on over her head. "I'll see you in a bit."

She walked from the room, the bottom of her butt cheeks playing peekaboo with each step.

Delyn couldn't look away until the door closed, blocking his view. He snapped out of it, pulling his shirt the rest of the way on and rushing through the rest of his dressing.

Within moments, he was dashing out of the room so he wouldn't miss Jessie when she exited.

"Well, damn, you beat me," she said as she stepped out of her room. She smiled, reaching out her arm to him.

He took it, and they went downstairs and to their seats at the table arm in arm like yesterday.

When they sat down, he was surprised to see quite a few peculiar looks sent their way. He wasn't sure what they meant, though when he looked over at Jessie, her cheeks were bright red, and she looked very uncomfortable. He reached over, taking her hand, hoping to make her feel better. She smiled at him, but there was a hesitancy to it he hadn't seen before. There was something wrong, but he didn't know what it was. Unfortunately, this didn't seem the right time to ask, so he would have to wait until later to find out and help fix it.

Letting it go for now, he loaded their plates with food and dug in. For a while, things seemed pretty calm. They ate in silence while people talked around them, filling the room with idle chatter.

But as the meal started to wind to a close, he noticed his sister, Tesa, looking at them. Or more specifically at Jessie. He was frankly surprised to see Tesa still hadn't warmed up to her yet. Usually, though not fast to befriend new people, she wasn't this slow either. There was a cold, critical expression on her face that he couldn't quite read, and her gaze never left Jessie, like there was something about the other woman that offended her somehow.

He decided he would talk to Tesa before the day ended. Maybe that was all she needed, someone to work through her feelings with. He looked over at Jessie, a woman he couldn't imagine not having in his life. They were both important to him. His sister. His partner.

He hated seeing them at odds.

Jessie leaned back in her seat, pressing her hands to her over-full stomach. She would be the first to admit that she should have stopped a while ago. But the atmosphere was friendly, and the food was delicious.

Even so, she couldn't get over her embarrassment, her cheeks maintaining a constant state of heat while surrounded by all these people, people who were important to Delyn, people who just might have heard her scream last night. She'd received looks that made her wonder what they'd heard, what they suspected. Did they know? Did they suspect? Or was she just imagining it? Maybe these were the same types of looks she'd received all along, and her imagination was just running away with her.

And yet, someone *had* knocked on the door, asked if everything was all right. At least one person *had* heard. Who was it? Were they here, wondering? They had to be, but she couldn't pick them out from the cacophony of voices at the breakfast table.

Someone knows. I just know it.

Still, in spite of all that, she'd been determined to have a good time, to enjoy this, and she had. Now she needed to move. She needed to work off some of this food she'd eaten.

"Want to go for a walk?" she asked Delyn.

He nodded with a smile, offering her a hand to help her to her feet. They left the table behind, stepping out into the early morning sunlight. There was a brisk feeling to the air, and it was bracing, making the full tummy feel not as uncomfortable.

They started out the walk in silence, just holding each other's hand as they made their way out of the circle of buildings and to the field that almost seemed like their "spot" now. This time, they made their way along the creek, enjoying the sound as it rushed over the rocks. Water spray touched her exposed skin in random patterns, a welcome coolness in what was set to be another hot day.

"You know, it's beautiful out here," Delyn said, drawing her attention.

She looked away from the water where it frothed over rocks. "Oh?"

"I've spent years in that ship. I think I'd forgotten what this place looked like. This place was home, but now I'm a stranger in it, a guest in someone else's house. It's surreal."

She bumped his shoulder. "I know there are strict hierarchies here, but you don't have to live by their rules, you know?"

He looked at her, but didn't say anything.

She continued. "I could call my sister. We could get out of here. Be beholden to no one. Go wherever we want. Just start a life together."

He smiled. "That's very tempting."

"But you're not gonna do it, are you?"

"I don't know what I'm going to do." He ran a hand through his hair, looking out into the distance. "So much has changed. I think I just need to adapt first."

She nodded in agreement, looking out at the distance along with him. Out of the corner of her eye, she spotted something shining and looked right. There was something there, in the trees. She squinted, adjusting her vision to try to see it better, but she lost it. Continuing to stare, she realized that wasn't the first time she'd seen something shining out there. Curiosity and anxiety rose inside her, making her big breakfast churn ominously.

What was it?

———

The Fighters froze, hiding behind trees when the female suddenly looked in their direction, staring at their hiding place like she could see right through the trees. They all held their breath, not wanting to make a sound or move until she moved on, even though she was too far away to possibly see anything of significance.

The Fighter controlling their unmanned vehicle gave a nod. As tension left their bodies, they touched the weapons at their sides, ones they doubted they would need since neither suspect looked dangerous, and slipped out from between the trees to get a better view.

The small stream cut off their path to the couple, making an extraction at this point problematic. Ordinarily, they would have been on the other side of the water, hiding in the tree line or crouched in the tall grasses. Unfortunately, they hadn't been in position when the two left Valana.

A quick scan of the area showed the two following a path along the stream. They couldn't cross without risking being heard and spooking their prey, so after a hand gesture from their leader, they moved on. Continuing to stay out of sight, they searched for a better position to lie in wait, hoping their targets would get far enough from witnesses for a successful extraction.

———————

CHAPTER SIXTEEN

———————

*J*essie felt optimistic about the universe as they returned to the Farmers' house. She was curious about the shining something she'd seen, but mostly she was just enjoying her time with Delyn. At times during their walk, they'd been completely silent, just comfortable in each other's company. Other times, they'd talked. It could be lighthearted or serious, and they didn't always agree, but it never boiled over into a fight.

She'd been a little worried about his stance on where to go from here, but as they'd continued in silence for a while, she'd realized that it made sense. He needed time to figure out what he wanted, and more importantly, what he wanted to do with his life. Turning away from his society or societal expectations was a huge thing for most people. The fact that she'd never had said expectations meant she had to work harder to understand that, but she did.

So when they reached the house and Delyn ceremoniously opened the door for her, causing her to laugh, she was in an exceptionally good mood.

Until Tesa.

She stepped through the doorway first, looking back at Delyn. She opened her mouth to say something, though now she had no idea what it might have been.

Because at that very moment, Tesa grabbed her by the shoulder, turning her around and practically spitting in her face as she spoke. "What do you think you're doing?"

"Excuse me?"

Tesa looked like she was about to explode. She'd noticed the simmering emotion in the other woman for a while now, but this was different. It had been unleashed, and she knew from personal experience that this type of anger couldn't be doused until it burned itself out.

Tesa was shaking, her body charged with energy, but at first, she didn't say anything more. The moment drew out uncomfortably, with each of them hesitant to speak or move for fear of setting Tesa off. Then she screamed, breaking the tension, and threw a punch.

Jessie squeaked, dodging the punch aimed at her head. "What the fuck?!" She didn't realize at first she was talking in English, but it didn't really matter. Tone said it all.

She backed up a step, but that didn't deter Tesa. She took another swing, this time with the other fist. Jessie deflected it with her palm, slapping it out of the way. This had her moving to the side and away from the door. She bumped into a piece of furniture with her hip, a sharp pain radiating outward, the first casualty of the fight.

"Tesa, come on. Stop it."

"Stop it? Stop it?" Tesa was becoming hysterical. "You come in here, like a savior for our poor Delyn, but you aren't, are you? You're just stringing him along, a fake through and through." She spat at her, stomping forward, winding up for another wild swing of her fist.

"Tesa, where is this coming from?"

She swung, this time using her punches to accent her words. "You're. An imposter. A freak. You don't. Belong. Here. You're not. One. Of us. Just get out. Leave us alone."

"Enough," Delyn said, stepping between Tesa and Jessie. "What has gotten into you?"

Jessie could no longer see Tesa, only Delyn's back, but she could feel her face getting hot, her emotions getting the better of her. She turned tail and ran, feeling the first tears welling in her eyes as the sun snuggled against the trees in the distance, giving the world a warm golden glow.

But Jessie felt cold inside. Only another trans person could hurt her like that. She tried to hold herself together, a single thought on repeat in her head.

I'm not a freak.

It wasn't looking like they would get an opportunity today. The sun was now setting, casting the world in golden hues that felt warm even as the temperature dipped in anticipation of night. Nocturnal creatures were waking up, warming up their voices for the songs they would sing to serenade the darkness.

From their observations thus far, it seemed the people would settle in for dinner, then not leave the building until dawn. They had not found an opportunity in the suspects' habits to allow them to snatch them without risking a witness.

So when the female came running from between the buildings at top speed, that caught their attention. While the team had been lazing about, relying on their one pilot to warn them of anything interesting happening, now, they were all at attention.

And a moment later, the male showed up behind her, running to catch up. They couldn't know why the two had abandoned dinner and run into the field, but they did know two things. One, the light was failing, casting deep shadows that worked to their advantage. And two, the community should all be preparing for dinner, each one inside their respective buildings, either in kitchens or dining rooms. No one else should be outside. No one else should see.

Their time to strike had arrived.

Tesa regretted her actions almost from the moment Jessie and Delyn rushed out the door. What had gotten into her? Was she crazy? She couldn't deny that she was jealous of Jessie, of her ability to change her biology without surgery and hormone treatments, but that wasn't Jessie's fault.

No, she didn't even think this was *about* Jessie. She was just a convenient outlet for something darker that Tesa had never acknowledged before. The whole situation made her notice parts of herself she didn't really like, and parts of her society she didn't want to look at too closely. Her brain had always skittered around that reality, not willing to really pull it out and *see* it for what it truly was.

The Pardus don't really accept trans people.

She tried not to cry as the thought popped into her head, but she was so unbearably afraid it was true. They were willing to accept people like her, but you were expected to rectify that biological mistake as soon as possible. You had to look the part, *be* the part, or you weren't good enough. Seeing her own reaction to Jessie, those deep-seated prejudices rising to the surface, made her realize that. Did everyone see Jessie that way, or was it just her?

She stood in the doorway, deep in thought, as she stared off into the setting sun, where she could see Delyn's silhouette dwindling as he ran after Jessie. Behind her, the commotion made by preparations for dinner served as a backdrop, a surreal taste of normalcy in a moment that didn't deserve to have any. She could even smell the warm and tempting aroma of today's feast, taunting her and trying to tempt her away from the door.

Except she couldn't turn her back on them, on Jessie, on Delyn. She'd made a mistake, a huge one. She couldn't even fully grasp why she did it. There was no way she could just go inside and forget what she'd done.

"I need to fix this."

She dropped her hand, at first just taking a single step out of the door, then she slowly built speed into a jog, then a run. Within moments, her muscles were burning and her lungs were screaming out for surcease. She didn't stop. She couldn't see either of them anymore, but she couldn't let that dissuade her. They were out there, possibly suffering from her actions and words. She couldn't believe the things she'd said. She wasn't even sure where they'd come from.

Freak?

Imposter?

Fake?

Some part of her recognized her own ingrained bias in those words, biases she'd been taught from an early age. But that didn't let her off the hook. She needed to reach them. She needed to fix her mistake.

Unfortunately, time and nature were not on her side this evening. The sun was dropping ever lower, casting long shadows and reducing the light. She reached the field, but couldn't see far enough to tell where they were at first. She squinted, scanning the distance, looking for movement. But the tall vegetation moved as well, making the task even harder.

Then she spotted something she thought might have been them, but she wasn't entirely sure what she was seeing. One shadow stopped while another came up behind it until the two seemed to become one. She suspected maybe Delyn was trying to comfort Jessie, which twisted something in her chest, making her feel even worse. She slowed, wanting to give them time before she barged in, but those weren't the only shadows she saw.

More shadows erupted from the tree line. Tesa was closer to those dark specters than the ones she suspected were Jessie and Delyn, but these sent chills down her spine. She hurried up again, opening her mouth as if to give warning, but of what? Shadows?

They moved like predators in a prairie, stalking their prey, and she couldn't get that thought out of her mind. She rushed ahead, pushing herself faster and faster, hoping she wouldn't be too late, though her mind blanked every time she tried to suss out what she thought might happen.

Shadows became people in Fighter's gear. She recognized the camo, the weapons. But they weren't local Fighters. Their equipment was too nice, too high tech. They must have been from one of the cities, where Fighters were sent out to fight and protect abroad.

So then, why were they here? Why come to this community in the middle of nowhere?

She got her answer moments later when the Fighters all converged on Delyn and Jessie. Jessie spotted them first. She could tell by how short the figure was by comparison. It looked like she grabbed Delyn and ran off toward the trees.

Tesa stopped and stood there, paralyzed as she prayed in her head, hoping they would escape to the woods, that they would be safe. But the chase only lasted a few moments before they were tackled to the ground. Tesa gasped, covering her mouth with her hands in shock.

She stood there as they were roughly pulled to their feet and marched off into the deep darkness of the woods, where she feared she would never see them again.

<hr>

CHAPTER SEVENTEEN

<hr>

*D*elyn was sore where he'd been thrown to the ground. He didn't know how Jessie had seen it, how she'd known. One moment, he'd been holding her tight, his heart aching at the tracks of tears running down her cheeks. The next, there'd been a look of horror on her face. She'd grabbed his hand, yanking him toward the woods.

"Jessie, what is it?" he'd said, completely oblivious to what was about to happen.

The tackle had taken him completely by surprise. A knee had ground into his back while his face pressed against the earth, his mouth sucking in grass with every breath.

He'd bucked like mad when he'd heard Jessie's cry of surprise, knowing she'd probably suffered the exact same fate. "Let me go!" he'd yelled, trying to use all his strength to his advantage, but it had been a hopeless endeavor. Not only was he far weaker than his opponent, but he was flat on his stomach, which didn't exactly provide decent leverage.

Next, they'd secured his wrists with hard metal and dragged him to his feet. He was terrified, craning his neck to try to get a look at Jessie, to make sure she was all right, but they barked at him, shoving him between the shoulder blades until he almost fell over. He stumbled forward, seething inside as they moved toward the trees Jessie had thought were salvation.

Clearly, they weren't.

His arms pulled tight as their captors whispered around them. The sun continued to set, leaving the woods before them looking dark and ominous. He was already having trouble keeping up with their brutal pace without the hazards the forest presented. He knew full well that the forest was filled with tree roots and half buried rocks, often hidden by thick underbrush.

His stomach sank with each step, and he had the bad feeling that once they entered the trees, all hope would be lost. He thought of Tesa, about their argument. He might never see her again. Would she wonder what had happened to him? Would she angrily go off to dinner, not thinking anything of them not returning for supper? He wanted to think they would immediately know something was wrong and come after them, but he'd been gone quite a while, and they didn't know him as well anymore. They didn't know what his normal patterns were. They didn't know he *wouldn't* just wander off and skip dinner. How could they?

He and his captors passed between the trees, the transition like entering through a dark shroud. It was immediately colder, making him shiver.

His toe slammed into something hard, and he stumbled, catching himself with a shoulder against a tree trunk. He stopped, turning to his captors. "What is this about?" he asked, afraid to move forward. He was lucky he hadn't fallen.

"Just keep moving," an angry voice said as someone shoved him with a gun.

They were getting more confident now that they'd escaped potential prying eyes. The forest provided protection, camouflage. It gave them an additional advantage over two people who were already at their mercy.

"Move it!"

A sharp blow hit him in the arm, sending pain shooting up and down the limb. He hissed in a breath, but did as he was told. He wanted to look back again, search for Jessie. Was she scared? Were they treating her as badly as him?

What did they want? Why were they even here? Nothing ever happened out here. It was a quiet, tight-knit community. Excitement just didn't come here. If anything, it ran far, far away.

So why were they here?

Tesa's heart was pounding. It was almost all she could feel. Even the pounding of her feet on the hard ground reminded her of it, driving her farther, pushing her to her limits.

You just stood there.

How could you just stand there?

She'd watched as Delyn and Jessie were dragged off into the woods.

What did the Fighters want with them? She shook her head. *Scratch that. It doesn't matter.* All that mattered was fixing her mistake. Her mind kept running through scenarios.

What if she'd yelled? Would they have stopped? Would they have run off into the woods alone? Maybe someone from the community would have heard and come running? Maybe even now they would have been coming to the rescue?

What if she'd run to them, run after them? Would she have been able to catch up and maybe do something? Could she have saved them herself?

She held no illusions about her own abilities. She was no Fighter, but that didn't mean she couldn't have done *something*. Maybe she could have given the two an opportunity to escape. A distraction? That might have been all it would have taken.

Maybe.

Maybe.

Maybe.

Stop it. Stop doing this to yourself.

She continued running, the field feeling larger than it ever had in the past. No matter how fast she moved, no matter how hard she pumped her arms and legs, the buildings felt so far away, like they weren't getting any closer.

Come on. Faster.

Everything hurt as urgency struggled against natural limitations. She just *couldn't* push herself any harder. There was no way to go any faster, and she very much feared she would hit her limit and just collapse, still too far away from salvation.

I shouldn't have driven them away.

What's wrong with me?

Why can't I ever get anything right?

A tear started trailing down her cheek, but it was quickly dried by a cool, bracing wind that matched the coldness she felt inside.

Please.

She finally passed the first building in the circle, one across from the Farmers' house. She could have sobbed with relief, but she didn't for fear of collapsing and never getting back up again.

Just a little more. A little more.

Her breaths came in gasps now, sucking in and wheezing out with all the effort she could muster. She rushed across the parush, dashing up the steps, then crashing against the door with a loud thud. She panted against the door, her muscles shaking with fatigue, unable to step back far enough to work the door.

"Please," she whispered, no longer having the breath to speak properly. She wanted to yell, to draw everyone to her, but she couldn't. Instead, she smacked a palm against the door. After a couple more breaths, she did it again… and again… and again. It was all she could do at that point.

Please.

With her breath sounds and heartbeat filling her ears, she didn't hear anyone approaching. She just dropped to her knees, sobbing with relief when the door opened and she spilled over the threshold.

"Tesa? What's wrong?"

She didn't see them as they touched her shoulders, kneeling in front of her. Instead, she stared at the floor, trying to get her breathing under control. It took far too long. She was painfully aware that each moment that passed was a moment where Delyn and Jessie were slipping away from them, never to be seen again.

Stop it.

Her visions of doom weren't exactly helping her calm down, making it all the more impossible to get the help they so desperately needed. She took several very deep breaths, trying to calm down. *You can do this, Tesa. You need to do this. For them.* "Delyn… Jessie… taken."

"What?"

She took another calming breath and tried again. "Delyn and Jessie were taken. Through the woods. People in black. Tactical gear." She looked up for the first time. It looked like the entire household had gathered around her. Worried faces filled the foyer. Some covered their mouths with their hands, some shook their heads, and some looked stiff and angry, like they wanted to hurt someone.

"All right, everyone. Calm down. Tesa, give us all the information you have," said Faelee from the back of the group, using her authoritative voice to its best advantage.

It immediately settled Tesa's nerves, and she nodded, describing every detail, even the ones that weren't so flattering to herself. Tesa wasn't proud of what she'd done, but she wouldn't leave out anything in case something was useful.

She would do that for them. She *had* to.

Shit, shit, shit.

Jessie looked around frantically, but no ideas came to mind. They were surrounded by big, brawny men in matching uniforms. They all towered over Delyn and made Jessie feel like a defenseless puppy. Trees surrounded them on all sides, with darkness creeping in around the edges.

Her hands were secured behind her back with tight cuffs that dug into her wrists. Even the slightest movement of her arms caused the metal to scrape against her skin, taking off a few layers. As they continued to walk, she had a hard time keeping her balance. She didn't hold any hope that she could stay upright long enough to run, even if she *did* manage to momentarily escape the iron grip of the one maneuvering her.

We're screwed, that's what… and it's all my fault.

Jessie couldn't deny it. She'd screwed up big time. Of all the moronic things she could have done, why did she think hacking a government database was okay, no matter how bored she was? She just *knew* that was why they were here now. She'd accessed something she wasn't supposed to, found out secrets *no one* was supposed to know, and now she was being silenced.

Thank God she hadn't told Delyn everything. The best she could hope for now was that they would realize he knew nothing important and let him go. He was no threat to them.

I'm the threat.

Jessie shook her head. She should have just stuck with her art. Why had she ever gotten into hacking in the first place? That was her sister's forte. Her sister could have hacked that government database and left no one the wiser. Her sister also could have probably escaped these meatheads without a backward glance.

"Go," the meathead holding her said right before her foot slammed down on a metal ramp, the material reverberating with the force. She looked up, surprised to find herself at a shuttle. She wasn't exactly sure what type. Cass was the expert there, too.

A couple moments later, she was shoved into a thin, mesh seat against the wall and strapped in place, her hands still behind her back, forcing her to lean forward. Delyn was dropped unceremoniously into the seat across from her. As he looked around him, their kidnappers filed in, taking their places in similar seats that made up two rows, one on each of the long walls of the craft.

"It's gonna be okay," Jessie whispered, nodding her head, trying as best she could to reassure Delyn.

He doesn't know anything.

They'll let him go.

It's gonna be okay… for him.

CHAPTER EIGHTEEN

*D*elyn couldn't believe Jessie was trying to soothe him. In the background, the engines alternated between humming and roaring depending on the pilot's maneuvering. The men who'd taken them exchanged ribald jokes and insults, even punching each other playfully, clearly secure in their success.

Meanwhile, Delyn was strapped in like an animal on a spit, his arms locked behind him in a punishing hold. Even the seat was uncomfortable, with no padding and a hard frame that dug into his legs after a while. Looking over at Jessie, he could see her fear, and her determination to stay strong. He wanted to save her from this, help her escape, even if it meant he could not. She was such a good person, an angel even. She didn't deserve this.

Then again, who did? Why were they doing this? What had been the trigger? Certainly, he'd done nothing warranting this type of action. He was a nobody, nothing, below the radar. So useless, they believed the only way he could get a woman was by being a novelty. Or paying her. *That's* how little his people thought of him.

So why was he taken? Why was he here? Was it government sanctioned? He looked around him, at the well-maintained shuttle and Fighters in matching uniforms. They certainly *seemed* like they could be government. But why would the government be after him?

He looked over at Jessie again, and he dismissed the question even before it fully formed in his head. They couldn't *possibly* be after her. She was an artist, beautiful and full of light. She was kind and seemed to inspire everyone to like her.

Except maybe his sister. But that wasn't Jessie's fault. Clearly, Tesa had her own problems, problems she needed to work out on her own.

So why were they here?

Before he could think it through more, something changed, his stomach shifting around as the shuttle started its descent. It was a quick descent and in mere moments, they landed, the shock suppressors shifting slightly as they came to a stop.

Suddenly, there was a wave of clicking and shuffling as the team stood and approached. One opened the bay door while others reached him and Jessie, removing their seatbelts and pulling them to their feet with strong hands on their arms.

"Move," they said, almost in unison.

He and Jessie were shoved forward, stumbling into the light of the not yet fully set sun. He blinked, his eyes watering slightly as they adjusted. They were in a dockyard filled with other identical shuttles. Each was sleek and black, with the emblem of the Wesan Fighters on it, the planetary government's own army and police.

Well, that answers one question… and begs many more.

<hr>

Jessie squawked as one of the men shoved her into a small room. She lost her balance, slamming down onto the hard floor on her hands and knees. "Thank God they already removed the cuffs."

She rubbed her fingers over her abraded palms and raw wrists, scanning her new surroundings as her knees throbbed beneath her.

It was a prison cell.

There was a small cot with a thin mattress and even thinner pillow. White sheets. The walls were the same material as the floor. There was no window. There was a toilet and sink in the corner.

And there was no doorknob on the inside of the door…

She sighed, standing gingerly to her feet. Her knees didn't want to completely straighten, so she suspected she'd scraped them raw as well.

But where was Delyn? They'd been guided out of the shuttle and into this building, a blocky cement-ish monstrosity that needed a serious session with an architect. The inside had been no better, just more blocky walls and lack of imagination.

She thought back, trying to recreate the map she'd been working on in her head when they'd guided her here. She'd counted out steps, noting placement of doorways and turns. Delyn and his guards had been behind her, and at some point, she'd realized that she was alone with her captors. Delyn wasn't behind her anymore. But where?

"Shit."

She started pacing and running her hand through her hair. "What do I do now?" There was no way she was escaping from this place. This room gave nothing away. No options, no hope. "What would Cass do?" Her sister wouldn't have to ask that. Her sister would probably be halfway to escaping by now.

Except… her sister would have never gotten herself into this mess in the first place. She was smart, careful, cunning. She didn't take risks if she could help it. Jessie laughed at herself, shaking her head. "Not me. I'm the ultimate risk taker."

She sighed again and sat down on the cot, slouching in defeat as she mouthed, "What would Cass do?" one more time.

Delyn was brought straight to an almost empty room, filled only with a table and two chairs. He was dumped into one of the chairs, his hands yanked behind him and locked in place with a click. He jerked at his restraints, but they held firm, keeping him trapped in his seat.

The men escorting him walked away, their footsteps receding before the door closed, sealing him in. He looked around, but there was nothing to see. There were no cameras, no windows, no mirrors. Nothing. It felt like somewhere you would be taken if they wanted you to disappear.

He gulped, suddenly realizing just how bad their situation was.

Why on Wesa would someone bring them here? Why treat them so roughly? It had to be a mistake.

That thought was like a light bulb turning on. Of course! Clearly, this was a mistake. Maybe a case of mistaken identity or a typo on a report. They had the wrong people. That had to be it.

He just needed to convince them of that.

CHAPTER NINETEEN

The Handler read through the file as he walked, barely noticing the plain gray walls around him. He'd been called in because of a breach. It was unusual, this breach. He'd been The Handler for over a decade, but he'd never encountered a breach on this level. Usually, it was someone stumbling onto the wrong files accidentally or jumping a fence they weren't supposed to. Occasionally, he'd have to deal with enemies or clients trying to uncover their secrets, to harm them or gain leverage, respectively.

This, however, made no sense. He had two suspects, neither of which made sense as culprits, and yet the digital evidence was clear. One or both of them had hacked the Archive Vault. He had logs recording the opening of files inside the vault, many files. Based on the timestamps, it seemed reasonable that the files were not only opened, but also read.

But why? That was the part that didn't make sense to him as he slowed to a stop in front of the interrogation room, where two guards stood at attention, one on each side of the door. He flipped to the personal profile of the woman first. He wouldn't be interrogating her yet, but her page came up first in the file. Nineteen Earth years old, shape-shifter, an artist on one of the Ateles' many colonies. He sneered, disgusted with the enemy race. They were like a plague across the stars, using their military prowess to get what they wanted.

Not that it mattered in this instance. The woman, Jessie Allen, had no obvious history beyond a few months ago. No record of habitation on any civilized planet, no credit history, no accounts. That might be suspicious under other circumstances, but as he continued to scan the page, which was largely empty, he could admit that, being from Earth, that wasn't terribly surprising, especially for one so young. Earth didn't share their records with the rest of the civilized universe, so any records from there would have been outside his reach. And because of her age, anything beyond about a year ago might have been under her guardians' names. She likely got her own habitation and accounts when she moved out of her guardians' home.

The other, a Pardus male named Delyn An, was, similarly, a mystery. Delyn was only exceptional in how unproductive he was in society. He'd been assigned Seeder, but had no offspring registered to his name. He had been granted a ship by the local council, but his file held little else other than family ties and where he originated.

The Handler shook his head, wondering what could have compelled either of them to do such a heinous act. Neither of them seemed likely to have the skills required for the crime, and he couldn't fathom a motive.

Still, he started formulating questions in his head. How did Jessie meet Delyn, and why was she with him? Did either of them have programming experience not in their files? Did Delyn hold resentment regarding his station in life or his failures?

Closing the file, he waved his hand to open the door. It obeyed quietly, exposing Delyn's back with his hands strapped to the supports of his chair by cuffs locking his wrists together. He stepped forward, making sure to make noise, taking advantage of that time when the suspect was most vulnerable, when he knew there was someone behind him but couldn't see who.

The reaction was often telling.

Delyn tensed, then whirled around, the cuffs cutting into his wrists as he strained to see. This was a man unused to this type of situation and nervous about the outcome. Fear of the unknown. Someone accustomed to interrogation likely wouldn't respond at all.

In a few strides, he passed the table and stood behind the remaining empty chair, resting his hands on the cold metal frame. "Delyn An," he said, nodding once before placing the file decisively on the table. The paper slapped against the metal surface, drawing the eye and ear. This was one of several reasons he preferred paper. It was so much more dramatic than a tablet.

Delyn took in a breath, likely to calm himself, then started to speak without prompting. "Listen. This is clearly a mistake. I don't know what this is about, but you obviously have the wrong person. I'm just a Seeder. Never done a thing wrong in my life other than being terrible at my role."

The Handler stared Delyn down, not moving from his spot. He watched, expecting a quick victory over the younger man in this lopsided battle of wills. He was right. Delyn quickly looked uncomfortable, then glanced away, squirming in his seat.

Satisfied, he pulled out his chair, letting the legs scrape against the floor before sitting. He watched for a moment more before leaning back, giving the suspect space to relax. He'd seen enough to know he would get better answers this way.

"Tell me how you met Jessie Allen."

<hr>

It was a relief when the interrogation was over. Delyn felt like he'd been wrung dry. The man, who never gave his name, asked him question after question. It was strange, and he had this impression that everything from the man's tone to his body language was carefully choreographed to get exactly what he wanted from Delyn.

And he probably got it.

Delyn couldn't deny he'd held nothing back. Whatever the man asked for, he gave it. He remembered thinking he should stop talking at times, but the words kept spilling out of his mouth like vomit after food poisoning. By the time he was dumped into a cell, he was relieved to escape. He still had no idea what this was all about, but right now, he didn't want to know. He just wanted to go home.

With a sigh, he collapsed onto the bed and leaned against the cold wall. The room was quiet, with only his own breathing and the sound of the sheets shifting under him breaking the silence. It was eerie, like the world had fallen away, leaving nothing behind but the space he could see. He could easily imagine the door opening to an endless blackness.

He shivered and hugged himself, rubbing his arms to get rid of the feeling, but it was pointless. It wasn't physical and ran straight to his heart. There was no hope left, only an unnamed icy emotion that chilled him to the bone.

The Handler sat in his temporary office just down the hall from the interrogation room. The room was almost as barren as the interrogation room had been. Plain desk, chair, a built-in computer. He had his papers spread out over the desk's surface. He would be contacted when Jessie was ready for him.

In the meantime, he was going over the transcript of the Delyn An interrogation. There wasn't much there. They'd spent a couple hours together, but the young man was completely oblivious. When given any latitude, he kept insisting this was a mistake, that he'd done nothing wrong. He couldn't deny the boy was probably right. Delyn had nothing to do with the breach. He was fairly certain of that.

But that still left the woman from Earth. She was a bit of a mystery, and he wondered how that interrogation would go. Would she be like Delyn, talkative and naïve? Or would there be something else there, something sinister?

He wondered about her past, her history. What wasn't written there? She was young, so he doubted she'd done much of interest yet, for good or ill, and he couldn't imagine she had many connections, but that didn't mean she *didn't* have them. He'd heard of child assassins who used their supposed innocence to get near their targets and thieves who used children to get into impossibly small spaces. A child was not necessarily innocent, and he was unfortunate enough to know that fact.

He hated not knowing what those nineteen years held. He shifted the pages around on the desk, putting her profile dead center. His finger tapped against it restlessly, the pages taunting him with what he didn't know.

Who was she?

And why did she do it?

Jessie jumped when the door to her cell opened. She been in the room for what felt like hours now, and after a while, it was easy to forget about the world around her. She'd been meditating and fantasizing about wooded wonderlands and painting, but now reality reared its ugly head.

"Get over here, woman," the man said, his face tense with anger.

She stood slowly, crossing the room at a leisurely pace, enjoying how his face nearly turned purple as she approached. There was no way she was hurrying for this bastard.

He grumbled something nasty under his breath as she approached, then grabbed her arm, jerked her around, and locked the cuffs on once more.

"Move it," he said as he shoved her into the hall.

She took it in stride, trying to remember the calm from her meditation. It was getting harder with every moment, though.

In the hall, they were met by another guard, who motioned her forward with a gun. They retraced the path they'd taken to get to her cell earlier, stopping around the place she'd theorized they'd left Delyn.

So, not a cell. Maybe an interrogation room? An office?

She got her answer soon enough. The one on her right opened the door, while the one on her left guided her inside. He was gentler and seemed less angry than the first, encouraging her to sit with a gentle hand before securing her with her hands behind her back.

He left without a word spoken.

Yup, definitely an interrogation room.

The room was bare except for a table and two chairs, one of which she was seated in. It was a classic setup from human cop shows, except it didn't have the two-way mirror. No cameras either, but she did spot what might be a microphone in one corner, barely larger than a bug, so the room *was* being recorded.

Jessie had never been in this situation before. She'd been a good kid back on Earth, never getting in trouble and trying not to be a pain to her sister, who was really trying to make things work. Even at a young age, when she couldn't quite grasp the reality of their parents abandonment, she'd seen her sister's struggles. She'd tried to help, keeping her things neat, feeding herself, doing her homework, trying to be quiet when her sister looked *really* tired.

Those first years had been hard. This was back when they lived in the apartment. Her sister had been working constantly and looking back, Jessie suspected that was when Cass started illegal hacking. She suspected they wouldn't have made ends meet otherwise. It got worse when Victoria moved in. Victoria had mental health problems, and their home was just too small for three people.

Things got a little better when they moved to the shifter caravan, but things didn't *truly* turn a corner until they got the *Trojan* and started living on it. Jessie finally had her own room and could express herself any way she wanted. Cass was no longer worrying about money, and the tension was finally gone. Jessie hadn't even realized the true depths of it until that ship took off for the first time. It was like a weight was finally lifted, and Jessie was euphoric. For a little while there, she suspected her ebullience had driven her sister nuts. She'd bounced all over the *Trojan*, exploring and expounding on its many virtues.

Her life experiences had taught her not to cause trouble for people, to be good, but also to be realistic. She could be optimistic, but she never lost sight of reality. And their reality had always been real simple… money = life. Piracy was just sort of a natural progression. Humans were largely looked down upon throughout the universe. Their friend, Ellie, had figured out how to use her diplomacy skills to become a cargo ship captain, but Cass didn't have those skills. She didn't tend to trust people and could be vulgar and crass.

Cass's primary skill of worth was programming, which she'd taught herself. But other species didn't use that programming language, so legit jobs were not an option. Jessie wished she could say that the two of them going into piracy was a shock, but it wasn't. She'd suspected for years that her sister was doing something illegal on the side to try to make ends meet. It was just too impossible to provide for the two of them in modern society.

And she'd seen the struggles her sister had worked through shortly after they'd taken off from Earth. She suspected her sister had wanted to go straight, had seen it as a new opportunity, but space could be just as unforgiving in its own right as America had been. If anything, it had felt like maybe they'd traded a good situation for a bad one.

In the early days, after the novelty had worn off for Jessie, she'd wondered why they'd left. Things had been good at the shifter caravan. They'd had plenty of food, shelter, and Jessie had never wanted for kids to play with or people to watch out for her. Her sister no longer had to work so many hours, and she didn't need to do anything sly on the side, either.

But at some point, Jessie had come to realize that Cass had never been truly comfortable there. It had felt too good to be true, and her sister just wasn't comfortable with good fortune unless she snatched it with her own two hands. And so, running low on resources, Cass had used the one thing she was truly good at and seized fortune for herself, starting their journey as pirates.

Jessie had seen it all as a grand adventure. It was rebellious and romantic to her. Meanwhile, her sister always insisted on protecting her, preventing her from participating. Cass had used her skills to create programs that were virtually impossible for aliens to guard against, seeing as they knew nothing of human programming languages.

And she'd had a code. She refused to hurt people. She tried to complete each job without a lick of violence, often putting people to sleep by manipulating the life support systems. It worked like a dream, and they'd entered a period of their life that was surprisingly comfortable. They went from job to job like ghosts, never detected and never caught.

Which she supposed was why this situation she found herself in was so foreign. She'd never had any experience with law enforcement or official agencies. Ellie contracted with the Ateles military, but that was the closest she'd ever been to anyone in an official capacity.

She looked behind her, wondering how long the interrogator was going to keep her waiting. There *had* to be an interrogator. This entire room had a very "you're about to be interrogated" feel to it. It was designed to be intimidating, to leave someone with no way out, physically or psychologically. Jessie smiled to herself.

Not for me, though.

For a sufficiently creative person, there was always a psychological escape. Some might look at these drab, plain walls and be unnerved or feel trapped. Her? She ran through in her mind what supplies she would need to get started with a mural. She thought about what to decorate the walls with. Something… local. Maybe local plantlife.

Her mind went to that field she'd been drawing and painting recently, and she could easily see herself covering every square inch of real estate in this room with that scenery. She imagined what brush strokes she would use, what colors would be best. What style would she use? Photorealistic or surreal? What about the mood? Bright and happy? Moody but promising a brighter future? Or maybe warm and comforting?

The door opened behind her, and she dragged herself out of her thoughts, turning in her seat as curiosity got the better of her. The man in the doorway was clearly Pardus, with the oddly shaped ears and unusually bright eyes. He was also clearly not like the people who brought her here. He didn't wear a uniform, but rather something reminiscent of a suit back on Earth. The style was different. It had a tunic-length shirt that reminded her of a suit jacket and pants to match, but didn't have a shirt underneath it. His shoes were shiny, polished to within an inch of their life. Every article of clothing was clean and looked pressed, like it was important that every seam and line was precisely in their designated place.

Even his hair was just so, long and in a perfect queue at the base of his skull. Each strand was smoothed in place, like they wouldn't even dare to disobey him. His appearance spoke of someone in complete control of himself. A flash of the Men in Black or those guys from Firefly that wore the blue gloves popped into her head and stuck.

This is a man of mystery, of secrets.

After several moments, he stepped forward, each movement controlled and precise. He crossed the room and stood behind the chair across from her, hands resting carefully on the backrest. A folder was held in one hand, and it struck her as significant that he was using paper and not a tablet.

It's all theater.

He slapped the folder on the table and took his seat, resting his hands over the folder as he settled in. "How did you meet Delyn An?" His voice was modulated, calm, focused. It was almost eerie in its tone.

"He placed an ad. Why do you want to know?" She tilted her head, trying to throw him off his game.

He didn't answer. "What was the ad for?"

"He's a Seeder. What do you think the ad was for?"

He paused, staring at her like he wasn't sure what to do with her. "Do you have any connections to the Ateles?"

Why would he ask that? She thought for a moment, but all she could remember was that the Ateles didn't like the Pardus very much. She couldn't remember why. "I have a friend that works for the Ateles military. My sister is in a relationship with an Ateles. Are you a member of the Pardus government? Are the Ateles your enemy?"

He paused even longer this time, telling her more than he realized. "Have you ever carried out any requests on the behalf of the Ateles?"

"No. And I'm thinking not a member of the government. That's too overt. You feel like a spy or something. I'm thinking more like a fixer. You keep the secrets, don't you? The things they don't want anyone to know?"

The Handler knew immediately that this interrogation was going to be different. From the very beginning, it was unlike any encounter he'd ever had. She wasn't nervous, but she also wasn't defensive, either. She was calm, sweet, curious, answering each question without giving anything away, rarely pausing to think.

But she also always tacked on a question after each answer. He didn't respond, but he felt like he might as well have. Each time, she seemed to know more and more.

How was she doing it?

And why couldn't he get a read on her? Usually, by now, he had a pretty good feel for a person, but she was this grand enigma. Within a few minutes, she knew more about him than any of the Fighters in this facility. It was like she absorbed it from the air or read his mind.

It unnerved him.

But after a while, he realized he was missing an entire dimension of their interactions. She was far smarter and more cunning than he gave her credit for. He started to see the battle of wills that had been going on all along without him noticing. She'd been playing with him, teasing information out of him while he got almost nothing in response.

He knew she knew people from Ateles, but not who or what their roles were. He knew she had a sister, but not anything about how she earned a living or who she associated with. He knew she'd answered an ad Delyn An had placed, but not what the nature of their relationship was now.

The Handler felt cornered. He'd tried working around the most important questions without giving anything away, but she was slippery as a fish. After an horo, he feared that short of asking her directly if she'd hacked the Archive Vault, he would never know.

And he couldn't do that. It would violate his directive to maintain the secret.

Trying to retain his composure, he stood and straightened his clothing, his hands brushing down the stiff material. "We'll speak again soon."

She gave him a sly smile. "I look forward to it."

He stared her down for a beat longer, starting to formulate a plan in his mind. He needed to reach out to some of his less "official" contacts and get more information on her.

She was definitely more than she seemed.

CHAPTER TWENTY

*D*elyn lay on the bed in his cell, staring at the ceiling and slowly going mad. The ceiling swirled with imaginary patterns as boredom, fear, and uncertainty got the better of him.

It was the silence that affected him the most. He could deal with the boredom. He'd spent more than his share of time alone and with little to entertain him. His father had ensured that Delyn would never be the center of attention. He could deal with the uncomfortable bed, which was so thin he could feel the frame digging into every soft spot on his body. The discomfort and pain were actually a useful distraction. He could even deal with the fear and uncertainty. Sort of.

What he couldn't deal with was the silence. On a ship, he had the noises of the engines, the life support systems, and various machines doing their jobs. In the community, he had people filling the void. Sometimes, they were small sounds, sighs heard through the walls or gentle footsteps going down the hallways. Other times, they were louder, more dramatic. People fought, yelled, laughed. People got angry and stomped off in a huff. People cursed when they hurt themselves or an endeavor didn't go according to plan.

Simply put, life was noisy, and he supposed that was why this place unnerved him so. It felt like death. There was no sound, and it made him feel like life had ended. The mind could play tricks on you after a while, especially in isolation like this.

So when the door opened after so long in silence, it was like a gun going off. Delyn jerked and fell off the bed, landing in a crouch, like he was expecting a threat.

The guard who'd entered his cell immediately tensed, reaching for his weapon. "Stand down," he growled, glaring at Delyn like he wanted him to try something.

Delyn relaxed, collapsing onto his butt on the floor. He didn't know why he'd reacted like that, and now cold fear lanced through him. He was on the floor, vulnerable, in too awkward a position to fight back if needed.

What did they want? Why were they here?

He slowly tried to get to his feet, cautious of the guard who still had his hand resting on the weapon at his hip. He reached for the edge of the bed, using it to stand up the rest of the way.

When he was upright, the guard approached, then motioned with a hand for Delyn to walk before him out of the cell. He hesitated. *What's going on?* The last two times he'd been outside this room, they'd cuffed him, but now they weren't? He didn't know if that was a good thing or a bad thing, but he stepped forward. Another guard waited in the hall and started moving as soon as he exited the room. They moved in a procession, with Delyn in the middle.

They traveled at a quick clip, the guards seemingly unconcerned with the man they were escorting. After multiple turns,

Delyn lost track of where they were. When they finally reached a door, the guard opened it, and sunlight spilled in, blinding Delyn momentarily.

"Move," someone said, and he did.

The sun was bright and low in the sky, telling him it was morning. The guards continued urging him forward. This was a different door than the one he'd entered through when he'd arrived. They followed a path, not a shuttle in sight, just half-dead plants, cement walkways, and blocky buildings. He could see now that there was more than one building here, though it was hard to tell how many. They all looked the same: simply, gray, and awkward. He could imagine Jessie painting them just to give them some life.

Jessie…

Suddenly, an urgency hit him, and he didn't want to leave. He wanted to speak up, ask where she was. Was she okay? But the guards remained silent, moving inexorably forward. Any time he started to slow down to ask a question, the one behind him barked, "Move," and he picked up speed again.

Finally, they stopped at a fence. It was plain and unassuming. Industrial and ugly, just like the buildings. It could keep people out or in, with more than a few deterrents against climbing visible even to his own untrained eye.

The front guard spoke a few mumbled words into his comm, and the gate before them buzzed and clicked. He pushed, and it swung open. Then he turned to face Delyn, motioning with an arm for him to get lost.

Delyn paused for only a moment before rushing through. He turned back, again to ask about Jessie, but the gate was already closing in his face.

Now what?

The Handler frowned down at his tablet, looking at the updated reports about his prisoner, Jessie Allen. Even with calling in favors, there wasn't much. He had more information on her associates than he did her.

Cassandra "Cass" Allen was a privateer for Inia Intergalactic. She'd had several run-ins with Diehli Corporation and seemed to be a less than savory character. She owned her own spaceship, a human-manufactured ship called the *Trojan*. Jessie was her only family. She had one significant other, an Ateles male named Kou. Her species designation was listed as Earth Shape-Shifter.

Eleanor aka "Ellie," unknown last name, was a cargo ship captain, currently contracted with Ateles military command through Jerunt Axt. She owned an identical ship, though he couldn't find any registration for it, probably because of the military connection. She had two family members, parents Emma and Beeyun, both diplomats. Mother was an Earth Shape-Shifter. Father was Danaus. She had one significant other, an Ateles male named Zee.

Victoria Chan had no known occupation. She had one run-in with the Diehli. She owned an identical ship called the *Discovery*. No known family members. She had one significant other, owner of Inia Intergalactic, Inia Surg. Her species designation was listed as Earth Shape-Shifter.

He placed the tablet down gently on the surface of the desk. He had no information on Jessie before she arrived on that Ateles colony. She was a mystery, and he didn't like mysteries.

Leaning back in his chair, he let out a deep breath, trying to think. He had two suspects, one he'd already released. He *knew* Jessie was the culprit. There was no doubt, but nothing added up. He had no evidence that she had the experience or skills to pull off the hack. She had some contact with people associated with the Ateles and Inia Intergalactic, both of which could be potential clients for this type of information, but no indication that she'd had contact with either since leaving her sister's ship.

So why did she do it?

Usually, in situations like this, that was the easy question. It often took very little to find a motive. A little background research, maybe a few carefully worded and timed questions in interrogation. That was generally all it took to get the answers he needed, but not this time.

His comm buzzed, and he looked down. *Of course.* "Connect." He leaned back once more.

"How close are you to answers?"

"Hello to you, too, Magistrate."

"Handler, this is serious," he snapped.

He could practically envision the Magistrate's face going red with indignation. "Of course, it's serious. What makes you think I'm not taking this seriously? It's my job to take this seriously." His voice never changed in tone or volume, just as calm and assured as ever. He might not feel in control, but the Magistrate didn't need to know that.

"We need this done. We can't have any loose ends."

"Of course."

That was the problem. For the first time in his career, he couldn't be sure if there *were* loose ends.

It had taken horos for Delyn to find any semblance of civilization. As it turned out, the facility where he'd been held wasn't far from the outskirts of the capital city, Westra… unless you were walking. He had no means of communication or transport, so walking had been his only option.

And the moment he'd seen the tall, elegant spires of the capital, he'd been dismayed. His home was on the other side of the planet. How the hell was he going to get back?

But more importantly, how was he going to help Jessie? Why was he the only one released? What was going on?

Delyn pushed those thoughts aside. For now. He had to. He needed to move forward. He needed to act. After they'd released him, he'd been forced to make a choice. He could have easily obsessed over what was happening to Jessie, just stand outside the gates and worry about her until something terrible happened. But no matter what, reality would have asserted itself. He couldn't escape it. He was just one person. Alone, he had no hope of helping Jessie. He wasn't a Fighter and even a solitary Fighter couldn't go up against that type of security and expect any sort of victory. He needed a plan, and the first part of that plan was getting to people who would help him.

His community.

His friends.

His family.

Once closer to the city, he managed to get a ride from a kind soul willing to take him to a transport depot. He was a smaller man, much like himself, and had a constant smile on his face, even when worry framed his eyes. But even though the other man could clearly see something was wrong, he didn't ask. He kept his mouth shut.

It wasn't until Delyn looked into one of the mirrors of the transport that he realized just *why* the man had looked so concerned. He hadn't bathed since before his capture, his hair was in disarray from laying on that bed for so long in that cell, and his trek from the facility had done a number on him. He had sweat soaking parts of his shirt, and his pants and shoes were marred from contact with dirt and greenery. No wonder the man looked worried.

"Do you need money?" the driver asked as they finally stopped at his destination.

"No, I have money in my account." Wesa, and much of the known galaxies, used accounts that could be accessed biometrically, so someone was never without their currency.

He nodded. "Good luck and safe journey."

"Thank you. And thank you for stopping."

"It looked like you needed it."

Delyn laughed for the first time since being captured. "That I did."

"Where are you going?"

"Home."

He nodded. "It's always nice to go home."

Delyn wasn't sure he could entirely agree, but this time, it was certainly necessary.

He took a deep breath and stepped out of the vehicle and into the afternoon sunlight. The transport depot was an odd place, seemingly both organized and a mess at the same time. Vehicles for rent or hire ran in neat rows in front of him, with larger shuttles and spaceships waiting in the distance behind a building that was at once impressive and aging around the edges.

He walked between the aisles of vehicles. None of them were new, some of them having seen previous damage from careless drivers, but each, he knew, would be in good repair. Transport depot companies prided themselves on keeping safe vehicles for their customers.

As he approached the building, its features became more obvious. The front was a wall of windows that had an almost rainbow hue to them in the current lighting. They were framed with silvery metal that had dark spots he suspected refused to come clean anymore. Growing closer, he could see that the once pristine glass had small nicks and fine scratches on them, a result of many years of service.

Stepping inside, he was greeted immediately by a friendly salesperson. "Do you need assistance?"

"I need to get home to Valana."

"Of course, of course," the salesman said with a smile, pointing at a map in the center of the room. "If you show me where it is, I can make a few recommendations for transport."

The map was more of a wall, stretching nearly half the length of the room. He immediately picked out his home, tapping it on the map's enameled surface.

"Hm, that's quite a distance. I would recommend a shuttle. We have both private and public shuttles." He pulled a tiny tablet from his pocket and started entering data and scrolling content. "Let's see. We have two private shuttles ready for hiring and the next public shuttle to that area leaves in six hours. It'll have you arriving at your destination tomorrow, late morning?"

Delyn frowned. Ordinarily, he would just go with the public shuttle. They were drastically cheaper and what was a few extra hours when you were traveling, right? But his mind drifted back to Jessie. Jessie, who was still trapped in that place.

What was happening to her? Was she okay? What would happen to her if he delayed because of money?

He didn't want to know. He didn't want to have to find out. "Private."

"Excellent choice, sir. We can have you in the air within the horo and back home by late evening."

"Thank you."

"Waiting area is right through there."

He led Delyn over to a small, cushy waiting area away from the main room. When the door closed behind him, he realized the room was sound dampened as well. A gentle, soothing music played through overhead speakers, and he sat down, but couldn't relax.

There was too much to do. And he could feel the time ticking away.

<hr>

The shuttle was a luxury Delyn had never experienced in his life. He'd been on a public shuttle a time or two, but they were always large, crowded affairs with everyone touching everyone else and not a window in sight. The seats were often poorly padded and only large enough for a child to sit in.

Conversely, this shuttle was a small one. It could seat maybe a dozen people with large windows showing off the views below. The seats were big and luxurious, with rich purple fabrics. An attendant offered refreshments, pillows, and blankets to make him more comfortable.

He was too anxious to accept any of it.

Instead, he practically bit through his lip as he looked out the window, watching the distance fly by, hoping for something he recognized. He could feel time slipping away, and with every moment, his concern for Jessie grew.

What were they doing to her? Would she be okay until he could come up with a plan? What type of plan would that be?

He shook his head. "What am I thinking?" He'd always been a failure, never managing to be good enough in anyone's eyes. Why would he expect any different now?

Because she *sees me that way.*

A little of the stress slipped away, and he smiled. There was something inherently hopeful and bright about Jessie. He got the feeling that it wouldn't matter how much he failed, she would just keep encouraging him to try something else until something stuck. He couldn't deny there was something refreshing about her, something that made him see himself and the world just a little differently.

The seat creaked a little as he leaned back, some tensed part of him finally releasing.

"I just have to save her," he whispered under his breath. It didn't matter how much of a screw up he was. Jessie needed him, and he was going to do everything in his power to help her. No matter what.

"We'll be landing in a few minutes. Please make sure all items are secured. Thank you for flying with us."

Delyn looked up as the intercom activated with the announcement. It had been quiet for hours. He looked out the window, realizing he recognized their location. They really were close.

As they started to descend, he could see people in the community moving. They looked like ants, but he could imagine them pointing up, wondering who was visiting.

The touchdown was almost unfelt, then the pilot spoke again over the intercom. "We've now landed, and you're free to depart. Thank you again for flying with us."

He nodded, even though the pilot couldn't see him, and stood. The attendant smiled at him, a woman who looked like she enjoyed the luxuries of this shuttle just as much as the clients did.

"Right this way, sir," she said as she followed him out.

The shuttle had a ramp at the back for departing, and he stepped out into the setting sun a short distance away from his own ship. "Thank you," he said, turning to nod at the attendant.

"It's been a pleasure, sir."

"Delyn," a voice squealed, so distorted he couldn't immediately place it. He turned and his sister came out of nowhere, tackling him in a flying hug. "Oh, Delyn, I was so worried." She pulled back. "Are you all right?"

He took a steadying breath. "Yes."

She didn't look convinced, instead looking behind him at the open ramp of the shuttle. "Where's Jessie?"

"They… didn't release her."

"Release her? What's going on?" She rubbed his shoulders, her gaze filling with concern. "Is she going to be okay?" Her voice got brittle with that last question.

"I don't know."

Her eyes welled with tears. "I'm so sorry."

"Tesa?"

"This is all my fault. I shouldn't have…"

"Shouldn't have what?"

She took in a shaky breath and shook her head. "I shouldn't have gone off on Jessie like that." She dropped her arms and stepped back, turning away from him. "I… I was getting angry at her for no good reason. When I saw you guys get taken….

"I chased her away. She… she wouldn't have even been out there if it wasn't for me."

"Hey," he said, grabbing her gently by the shoulders and forcing her to face him. "It's not your fault. Those guys were professionals. They knew what they were doing. People like that… they *make* opportunities when they can't find them. There's nothing you could have done."

She sniffed, stray tears spilling from her eyelids. "You're right," she whispered as she visibly tried to pull herself back together. With a final wiping of the tears from her cheeks, she said, "Do you want to go inside? Are you hungry? Tired?" Her voice was still thick with the tears she'd shed. "Sorry." She shook her head. "I'm just keeping you out here, and you probably don't want to be."

He squeezed her shoulders again lightly. "It's fine. I get it. And yeah, we can go inside if you want. I think there's a lot to talk about."

"Like getting Jessie back."

"Exactly."

They were quiet as they walked back to the Farmers' house.

"Delyn!" someone shouted, and suddenly they were surrounded. It seemed like the entire community was outside waiting for him. It felt overwhelming, like he would be crushed by the surge of bodies. The noise was intense, unrecognizable as words, as each person fought to speak at once.

"Enough!" Tesa yelled, her high-pitched voice somehow booming over the others. "Give him space," she continued as the crowd quieted. "Better."

"What happened? Where were you? We were worried," Mother Mae said. Her steel gray hair was in disarray and her usually stern demeanor was absent, her emotions pushing creases into the skin on her face.

"We were taken by Fighters. Held and interrogated," Delyn said, trying to keep his mind from seeing those events again. He needed to keep his head on straight, focus on getting Jessie back. She was still out there, still in their hands. That was unacceptable.

Several people gasped.

"Do you know what they wanted?" Mak asked as he pushed to the front to be closer to his friend.

"Not really. But I don't think it was me they were after."

"Jessie," Tesa said.

He nodded. "They still have her."

"Then we'll get her back," Tesa said, gripping his arm in solidarity.

"We will," Mak said, nodding.

"Thanks."

"Well, don't just stand there," Faelee's said in her most authoritative tone, clapping her hands once to get everyone's attention. "This boy needs a few moments peace, a little comfort, and a good meal to settle him. Move it!"

Everyone scattered except Delyn, Mak, and Tesa. They each looked at each other, and Delyn knew they had his back. They would help him get Jessie back.

"So, what did they ask you? Maybe that'll help us figure out what they wanted and help us get her back," Tesa said as she led the three of them to the Farmer's house.

"Will it? Or will it just get us in more trouble?" Delyn followed behind, feeling both helplessly clueless on what to do next and grateful for the support of those closest to him.

"I don't know, but knowing what they want could give us leverage." Mak looked over at Delyn meaningfully as they reached the front door. "I think we need that right now. I think we need every advantage we can get."

They settled in the front room. It was a little surreal to him after spending time in that cell and interrogation room, where a hard cot and an even harder chair were the only comforts. The cushions of the couch seemed to swallow him up, making him want to swim out of them. He didn't, largely because the way they hugged him also felt comforting, like a friend offering solace during trying times.

"Why don't you start at the beginning?" Mak said as he sat down on the edge of his seat cushion.

Tesa stood next to him, annoyed, as she looked down at him. "I already asked him to talk about the interrogation. We need to know what they want."

"And what about their resources? What are they capable of? We need that more than knowing what they want."

Tesa frowned, crossing her arms and plopping on the couch with a huff. She didn't look at Mak as silence settled over the trio.

Since it seemed Mak had won that confrontation, Delyn started at the beginning. "It was a team of Fighters, definitely Pardus, well-organized and wearing identical uniforms. The shuttles had the Wesan Fighters insignia on them."

"That covers a lot of ground. They could be armed forces."

"Possibly. They had a shuttle, took us to a facility outside the capital. There were a lot of shuttles parked outside."

"That's bad," Mak said as he fidgeted in his seat.

"We went into a plain, nondescript building. There were at least one interrogation room and two cells, though I believe there were probably a lot more. It seemed like a big facility. It had tall fences, locked electronically, with climbing deterrents."

"Anything else?" Mak leaned forward.

He shook his head. "I don't know. I didn't see much."

"Well then, what about the interrogation? What did they ask?" Tesa said, leaning forward, elbows on her knees.

"Um, it was pretty generic at first. Asking how I'd met Jessie, I think. I don't really remember."

"Well, what *do* you remember?"

Delyn racked his brain. He remembered the feeling of being interrogated more than anything else. A feeling of helplessness, isolation, and feeling like if he only told them what they wanted to know, everything would go back to normal. His cheeks blazed with heat as he realized he'd done exactly what they'd wanted him to do. He couldn't imagine anyone being easier to interrogate, and it bruised his ego a little.

No wonder my father thinks so poorly of me.

He shook himself mentally.

No, stop it. That type of thinking wasn't helping anyone, let alone Jessie. He needed to focus, so he closed his eyes, taking deep breaths. What did they want? What was the feel of the questions? Was there a theme? How did it flow?

Why did they want us?

Delyn remembered a lot of background questions, things he now suspected were supposed to lull him into cooperation. He remembered that each time there was a topic change, it seemed the most natural thing in the world.

Information. It was all about what he knew. The man asked about computer skills. "Computers," he blurted out suddenly after a prolonged silence.

"What?" Mak and Tesa said in unison.

"He was asking about computer skills. I remember that. He came back to that multiple times."

Tesa nodded. "Probably trying to catch you in a lie, see if the details matched up."

"What?" A lie?

"Yeah, I've read that's a technique used in police investigations. Also psychological profiles. You ask very similar questions spread throughout the session and if the information doesn't mesh, it can be indicative of lying."

"Oh. I wasn't lying."

"I don't think you were, but if he was asking those types of questions multiple times, then he probably wanted an accurate answer. That's significant." Tesa leaned back and bit her lip as she thought. "You know, I caught Jessie on the computer one time. She slammed her computer shut immediately. Maybe…"

"She didn't do anything wrong."

Tesa pointed an annoyed finger at him. "First, you don't know that. How long have you known her?"

Delyn colored with embarrassment. He really hadn't known her long, not long at all. Certainly, he hadn't known her long enough to be positive she'd done nothing wrong. You could know a person your entire life and still be surprised by their misdeeds.

Still, he just had such a hard time believing Jessie was guilty of any wrongdoing. She was sunshine. He couldn't imagine any real darkness in her, no matter how hard he tried.

"Second," Tesa continued, "she could have done nothing wrong or thought she'd done nothing wrong, and still be the impetus behind this. I mean, I've watched enough thriller videos and law enforcement procedurals to know sometimes good guys get into bad situations."

Delyn smiled. He'd forgotten his sister's obsession with those types of videos. Growing up, she'd dragged him onto the couch in the evenings to spend *horos* watching her videos. Her eyes would light up as the mysteries unfolded, and she would grab onto his sleeve when especially harrowing events happened on-screen. She was an addict, but it was sort of adorable.

"Wait here," Tesa said, standing up. "I'm gonna go get her computer." She dashed out of the room, her steps pounding up the stairs.

Meanwhile, a girl he didn't really recognize walked into the room with a tray of food. "I hope you're... doing good. Welcome back," she said, ducking her head as she placed the tray on the table between the couches.

"Thanks," Delyn said as he reached for a sandwich. The food smelled heavenly as he lifted it to his mouth. He could smell the fresh bread and the spices used on the meat.

He'd barely taken two bites when Tesa stormed back into the room, computer in hand. She dropped back into her seat triumphantly, settling the computer before her and opening the lid. "Oh," she said, looking disappointed.

"What is it?" he said after swallowing his latest bite.

"I don't recognize the characters on the screen."

Delyn leaned forward, but couldn't see. "What do you mean?"

Tesa turned the screen to face him. It had a white background with colored edging and black foreign characters in neat horizontal lines going across. "Well, that's unfortunate."

"At least it doesn't look like it's locked. Let me see." Mak waved his fingers at Tesa, reaching for the computer.

"What do you have in mind?"

"Well, if she did something computer-related that the Pardus government is concerned about, it's probably going to be on her computer, and it's probably going to be in Wesan. She might have needed to use a translator, but the original should still be here.

"Of course, this all relies on the idea that the whole situation started because of something on this computer."

"Makes sense," Tesa said as she leaned back to see over Mak's shoulder. "How are you doing that?"

Delyn wondered what Mak was doing as he took another bite and washed it down with a glass of juice.

"Icons. There's a lot of icons in this operating system. Some of the symbology is easy. Others, I'm not sure I understand. But... this looks like a browser. And look at this menu. See how the symbol next to each entry is identical? I think that's multiple pages on the same website, so I think that's a browsing history." Mak stared intensely at the screen, even leaning slightly forward as he concentrated on his task. "Let's check this one out," he mumbled under his breath.

Then his eyes widened, and he jerked backward.

"That's the government symbol. This is a government website," Tesa said as she hovered over Mak's shoulder.

"No, no it's not. I've been to the government website. This isn't laid out right," Mak said.

"But it's in another language. Couldn't it be just formatted weird?" Tesa shrugged.

"I don't think so. I think this is definitely government, but I don't think we're supposed to be seeing it."

She pointed at the screen. "So, how do we get it in our language, because this is useless?"

"Random button mashing?" Delyn volunteered, trying to be helpful.

Tesa looked like she wanted to throw something at him. "This is not a video game, Delyn."

"He's right, though. There just might be a button somewhere on here that she used to translate the page. If we can find it, maybe we can translate it back."

Time moved very slowly that evening. Delyn nearly fell asleep as Mak played around with Jessie's computer, trying to get the page to translate. People came and went, asking how he was doing or if he needed anything. He offered each of them a few polite words and pretended to be busy.

But really, he wasn't busy. He was the opposite of busy. He *needed* to be rescuing Jessie, but he was doing nothing. Time was slipping away from him, and he still hadn't left this couch. Was she okay? He had to believe she could take care of herself. She'd seemed so strong when they were first taken.

She'd reassured him, trying to give him moral support when they'd been strapped into those seats on the shuttle. He had to believe she could keep it together until they planned out how to get her out.

His gaze roamed around the room, landing on little tchotchkes of small animals, windows that had been cleaned to within an inch of their lives, flowing curtains that almost reached the floor, and an empty fireplace waiting to be lit. It was all so ordinary, like there was nothing wrong, like nothing bad had ever happened in the history of the world.

"Gah!" he said, throwing himself to his feet.

"Delyn?" Tesa said, dragging her eyes away from the computer screen.

"We need to do something," he said as he started pacing.

"We are. We're trying to get answers. We're trying to figure out what we're up against."

"Are we? Are we really? Because I don't think we need this. I think we have enough information already to go there and get her out. We're stalling."

Tesa stood and approached him. "We're not. I know you're frustrated. I get it. Honestly, I am too. I feel like this is all my fault. I let my own issues and insecurities get the better of me, and she's paying the price for it. I *do* want to get her back, but none of us are hardened Fighters. Even if we got the best Fighters in the community backing us, we would probably still be at a disadvantage. This facility sounds well equipped, and that is a government website. You said yourself that that place was just outside the capital, meaning probably global govern-ment. The Wesan Fighters insignia on the shuttles pretty much confirms that. They probably have first pick of the best Fighters on the *planet*. We don't want to go into that uninformed. Do you want to risk people getting hurt? Getting killed?"

"Of course not."

Tesa nodded. "Me neither. So, we have to play this smart."

"Got it," Mak said, his fist jerking into the air in triumph.

They both spun around to face him. "What is it?"

"Hold on. Just got the site untranslated." He frowned, his fingers running over the trackpad below the keyboard. "It seems to be an archive vault of some sort. Historical data, but…" He shook his head. "I don't recognize any of this. I'm just touching on the surface here so far, but this stuff isn't in the history lessons." He turned to Tesa and Delyn. "How could I have not heard of this?"

"What is it?" Tesa snapped.

"It starts with talking about the time before the war." Mak continued scrolling, his gaze rapidly running over the text on-screen as his fingers hovered over the trackpad. Time ticked by while Tesa paced, and Delyn hovered in anticipation.

He realized this must have been where Jessie had learned about pair bonds. She'd said she'd found a source telling how things were before. Clearly, this was it. Somewhere in that document, it told how the social strata were before the war. But why hide it? He could see how it might have fallen out of favor during the war, could even understand how people might not have bothered to try to bring it back when there were more pressing concerns like rebuilding, but why keep it a secret? It didn't make sense to him.

He was brought out of his thoughts when Mak suddenly stopped and said, "Great skies above." He looked up. "We've been lied to." Mak looked down at the screen, then back up again, looking a little lost, but slowly a determined expression entered his eyes, and he pressed the computer closed with a click of its latch. "We need to get everyone together." He stood and walked out of the room.

"What was that about?" Tesa said, watching Mak leave.

"Nothing good."

———

Tesa was shocked and torn. They'd translated the site, figured out why both Delyn and Jessie had been taken, but it certainly didn't help them any. In fact, the more she thought about it, the more it sent chills through her blood. She shivered, wrapping her arms around her for a little comfort and warmth.

Did we screw up?

Was Delyn right?

Were we just wasting time?

She thought of Jessie, wondering if they'd made a terrible mistake. What if she was hurt or even killed because of their reckless curiosity? She'd already made so many mistakes. She couldn't bear to make another, one with a potential for such devastating consequences.

Around them, people had started amassing. They didn't have a clue, and they wouldn't. She, Delyn, and Mak had decided not to tell them yet. It wouldn't help them get Jessie back and would only complicate the issue. But hiding this left a bad taste in her mouth, like she was just as bad as the government that had lied to them and twisted their fates in unnatural ways. Who was she to hide the truth from them, even if only for a few hours or days?

"It's gonna be okay," Mak said, reaching over and rubbing her shoulder.

"Maybe." She wasn't so confident. She could see the few Fighters from Valana gathering, just as clueless as the rest of them. They had to suspect this was about Jessie and Delyn's capture, but no one had any idea of the full bombshell that loomed over all their heads.

This is about Jessie. We can handle the rest later.

They had a plan for that, too. After this meeting, they would hopefully have a cadre of people preparing to storm the facility. Meanwhile, Delyn would reach out to Jessie's family using her computer. Her family needed to know, but they also needed help with their second problem. None of them knew anything about circumventing a massive government conspiracy spanning centuries. They were in over their heads, and Jessie's sister was a pirate and hacker, according to Delyn. Maybe she would be able to help somehow.

"Thank you all for coming," Delyn said, his voice filling the parush.

The chaotic din of the crowd dampened. Tesa and Mak stood a little straighter as they backed up Delyn.

"As you know, me and Jessie were recently taken. I was let go, but she was not. I know you don't know her well. She only recently arrived here, but she's a good person, kind. I intend to get her back. I'm asking that you help. Please."

"You're kidding, right?" their father sneered, pushing through the crowd with his bulk. "We heard the stories when Tesa came running back here. An organized group of Fighters, well trained, and they took you without much of a fight. And you expect us to go up against that? For a stranger?" He shook his head. "I always knew you were weak. Hopeless. A drain on society. I'd kinda hoped that, as a Seeder, maybe you could provide *something* to the community, but you can't even get *that* right. Now you want to risk our people, our families, for a stranger? Are you nuts?"

"Enough!"

Tesa jerked as a loud voice silenced the crowd. She didn't recognize it, and she watched as everyone seemed to jerk their heads in the same direction.

Toward Delyn.

Tesa was shocked. All his life, Delyn had let their father walk all over him, treating him like garbage. It had made her feel sorry for her brother and had been part of the reason they'd become so close. She had other brothers and sisters, but none she was as close to as Delyn. The more their father tried to hurt him, the more she'd wanted to boost him up, offer him her strength and support. She couldn't believe he'd finally stood up to him. She'd started to believe he never would, that he would let the older man walk all over him for the rest of his life.

Tesa took half a step closer to her brother, wanting to support him even more as he continued to speak.

"You have every right to your opinion. You can say what you want about me, but don't speak for the others. And certainly don't speak for me." He turned, addressing the crowd once more. "As I said, I know you don't know Jessie very well. But she's a good person, and she unknowingly stumbled upon something very rotten here on Wesa, something I have every intention of addressing, though I don't know how at the moment. Right now, our focus needs to be on her. It's the clearest course of action I can think of, and the most immediate threat."

A voice called out from the crowd. "What did she discover?"

"I would rather not say until we get back. I don't want our heads to be filled with this revelation when there's a life on the line."

Tesa stepped up. "May I?" She touched his arm, smiling at him proudly, before turning to the crowd. "I know you have questions. Honestly, the three of us are all reeling from what we found out. It's huge, shocking, and life changing. Like Delyn said, none of us are really sure what to do with that information right now, but something will need to be done. All of us would be happy to tell you once Jessie's safe, but telling you now is just going to make rescuing her more dangerous. As it is, the three of us are all shaken to the core by this news. When we get back, we'll tell you, and I guarantee it'll shake you, too. We can't afford that if we're going to save her, though.

"So, let's focus on one problem at a time. Let's bring back our friend."

Upraised hands and a roar of indecipherable voices filled the space, and she knew they would get the support they needed.

After the meeting in the center of Valana, Delyn retreated back inside while Tesa and Mak tore off to prepare his ship for the rescue. He had other things he needed to do.

Like reach out to Jessie's family.

He only knew a little about Jessie's sister, Cass, from stories she'd told him. He knew she was a pirate. Well, actually, she was a privateer working for Inia Intergalactic.

Which means she might have some pretty impressive contacts, maybe even impressive enough to solve our other problem.

Jessie's computer was still resting on the table in the living room. He stared at it from the doorway, feeling like he was on a precipice. It was weird, like he physically didn't want to enter the room. He could feel it like a pressure in his body holding him back.

He pushed forward, sitting down on the couch. A part of him wanted to get up and move, unsatisfied with sitting when there was so much to do. But still, he pulled the cool laptop onto his legs and opened it. Like before, the device was in a language he couldn't hope to understand. He searched the keyboard, hoping for symbols he might recognize. Maybe not all of them were her native alphabet. Maybe some of them were symbolic in nature.

"What I could really use is some voice controls," he said as he scanned the top row of symbols, which seemed to be comprised of a surprisingly large number of geometric shapes, four with combinations of triangles and lines.

"Wesan identified," a strangely accented voice said from the speakers. "Would you like voice controls set up in Wesan?"

He froze, momentarily surprised by the sudden voice breaking the silence. "Yes," he said in a rush.

"Vera well. Voice controls activated. Please speak a command."

"Place a call to Cass."

"Placing a call to Cassandra Allen."

Delyn held his breath as a comm screen opened up on the device. It was black with flashing characters in the center.

Moments later, the call connected, and a woman who looked strikingly like Jessie, only with purple hair and a far different demeanor, stared back at him.

"You're not Jess," she said, leaning forward aggressively. "Where's my sister, and what are you doing with her computer?"

"Easy." He held up a hand to calm her. "I'm not the bad guy. My name is Delyn. I'm a Pardus."

"What?!" a deeper voice roared in the background.

Chills ran up Delyn's spine, and he gulped. The voice conjured up an image of a man who could lift a single fist and pummel him into the ground. When the man filled the screen behind Cass, the ominous vision was confirmed. On the computer, he looked like the largest Ateles he'd ever seen, not that he'd seen a whole lot of them. The Pardus tended to avoid the Ateles, even when traveling the stars.

Still, even by Ateles standards, a warrior race unparalleled in the universe, this man sent uncommon dread through him. He was big, angry, and half covered in metal.

"Down, boy," Cass said, stretching a hand back to pat the beast on the chest. Turning around, she refocused on the screen. "Now, tell me what I want to know."

"As I said, I'm a friend."

"That's yet to be seen."

He gulped again. Cass was equally as daunting as her partner. "I'm a friend of Jessie's. A few days ago, we were both taken by forces unknown. Today, I was released. Jessie wasn't. I'm organizing people to go get her. I wanted to let you know of the situation, but also, I was hoping you could help me with something else. I don't think it's safe to talk about it here, but she could really use all her friends and family after her ordeal, if you get what I mean."

Cass finally leaned back on-screen, eying him critically. "I think I do. We'll be there shortly… for moral support," she said with a smirk.

Delyn sighed in relief. "I also think you should have her personal effects. In case something went wrong." He patted the computer intentionally. The camera was aimed in such a way that Cass should have been able to see the gesture.

Jessie's sister looked thoughtful for a moment before speaking. "Of course. She would want me to have all the art on her tablet and computer. And it would definitely be a comfort. In case things went wrong," she said, emphasizing the last sentence.

Delyn nodded and ended the call.

She understood.

<hr>

Jessie paced her cell, feeling a little incompetent.

Cass would have figured a way out of this by now.

"Stop it," she said, interrupting her restless movement. While it was true her sister was formidable, she wasn't a magician, and this was the equivalent of a locked room mystery.

How do you get out of a locked room with no windows, no doorknob, and no tools?

The answer was you didn't. You got someone to let you out. She looked around her, at the desolate walls and nearly non-existent furnishings, and knew that was the answer. She wasn't sure how she was going to get away from the guards, but she knew she needed to somehow. Jesse wasn't the strongest person in the world, nor was she much of a fighter, but she had other things going for her. She was smart, creative, and a shifter…

But how could she use her shifter abilities to her best advantage? She was fairly small, and no amount of shifting could change her mass. Mass was mass. It didn't change just because you wished really hard, so she couldn't make herself strong enough to overpower these guys.

Besides, they had weapons. She didn't.

Then again, maybe she could *make* herself some weapons.

As she had that thought, she heard the door opening.

She turned and smirked as the guard entered. "I'm being summoned?"

"You know the drill," he said, lifting the cuffs into the air.

She offered her wrists, palms lazily facing the sky like she didn't have a care in the world. The cuffs were cold and hard as they locked in place, but not tight, which was something at least. And the guards made no moves to strong-arm her down the hallway, which was promising as well. If they expected her cooperation, they wouldn't be as prepared when she made a run for it.

She only half paid attention as they walked to the interrogation room, noting they were following the same path as last time and the time before. She let them guide her into the room and lock her to the chair, calm as you please. The room was the same as before, but it felt different, maybe because *she* was different. She didn't have a fully formed plan, but it was blooming, developing the first blushes of promise. If she used her time wisely, she could escape when they tried to take her back to her cell.

When the door opened again, she didn't bother looking. She knew who it would be. He was much like he'd been last time, a carefully curated persona that she suspected usually got results. "Good day."

"I had a few more questions for you," he said as he took his seat.

"I would expect nothing less." He was probably going to try to ease into things like he did last time. He didn't seem like the type to ambush people with questions. That should give her some time to think while he was getting her nice and complacent.

Think, think, think. She couldn't change her mass, but she could form natural weaponry and defenses. Natural weapons. Claws, fangs, spikes, horns and antlers, venoms and poisons. She didn't know enough about biology to make venoms or poisons, not to mention it might not work. Claws would probably be good. Adapting fingernails to claws was a pretty basic process. Almost any shifter could do it once they knew how to shift.

"Tell me. What is your interest in Wesa?"

"None. Lovely planet, though." Still, no claw was gonna get through those cuffs. That was a first priority. She would be at a distinct disadvantage if she couldn't get her hands free.

"So you've done nothing to look into the Pardus or Wesa since first getting in touch with Delyn An?"

"Little here and there. Wanted to know what I was getting into." She shrugged, her mind elsewhere.

The cuffs were pretty basic, just a simple ratcheting lock mechanism to fit any size wrist. As long as no one was touching the cuffs, all she had to do was reduce the size of her hands. The cuffs should slip right off. Maybe she could do that while she was shifting her nails into claws?

"Could you expand on that?"

"Well, I had volunteered to be a surrogate," she said absent-mindedly.

And what was she going to do about *their* weapons? She couldn't outrun a gun blast... but she did remember about an animal whose scales were used for crude bulletproofing. They were just made of keratin. That was a very common protein in the body.

Doable.

"What did you research? Did it help you make a decision?"

"I don't know."

"You don't know. You don't know what you researched? Or you don't know if it helped you make a decision?"

"Both?" She was having a hard time keeping up the two thought streams. "I decided not to do it. Was a little too intimate for me."

"You were at first willing to carry another's offspring in your body, but then some part of it was too intimate for you?"

She shook her head. "I didn't know how it was done. I thought it would be a clinical process. Turns out it required sex. That was one step too far for me."

"Why is that?"

"Because sex should be personal. It should be intimate, an expression of mutual affection." She thought of all her sister's many brief liaisons before meeting Kou and shuddered. Never. She just couldn't do it.

"I see. And what do you think of the Pardus reproductive process in general?"

"It's a travesty," she blurted, not even realizing what she'd said. For a moment there, she'd been so caught up in her own feelings, remembering all the times some random stranger had slinked out of her sister's room, that she hadn't been thinking.

Realizing what she'd said, she jerked her head up, and fear chilled her as she looked her interrogator in the face. There was the subtlest grin on his lips and satisfaction in his eyes. He'd caught her, tricked her.

He knew.

"Fine," she said, lifting her chin in defiance. "I *know*. I know what the government did. You destroyed *everything*. Everyone's lives, everyone's hopes and dreams. Their chances at happiness. You turned your entire species into a commodity to be bought and sold like slaves. Only they don't know they're slaves. They don't know their choices have been taken away from them. It's despicable."

She leaned back, wishing she could cross her arms to complete the picture, and started frantically running her mind through the last details of her plan.

How do I get past the doors?

What if they're locked?

How do I outrun my pursuers?

What path do I take to freedom?

Jessie needed to figure it all out now, because she wasn't going to get another shot. She was almost certain she'd given the man everything he needed in this last session, and there was no fucking way she was waiting around for the consequences.

She was escaping… today.

CHAPTER TWENTY-ONE

*D*elyn sat in the cockpit of his ship with his sister at his side. The ship was small, so there wasn't much space, but they managed to fit a good dozen people semi-safely in its confines.

The sensors registered the other vehicles they'd managed to scrounge together for this enterprise. It wasn't much, and some were more crammed than this one, but everyone had managed to come on this rescue mission. Even his father had begrudgingly come along, muttering something about it not mattering if everyone was going to be idiots about it.

He still couldn't believe he'd stood up to the man. As his hands hovered over the controls, preparing to land in the next few diceros, he couldn't believe his own audacity. It felt shocking and freeing and terrifying at once. He half expected his father to retaliate in some small way, just like he had with the brawl days ago, and it made him realize for the first time how very small the older man was. He got off on lording over others and drew personal esteem from the accomplishments and perceived strengths of his offspring. It was an ego trip for him, and when a child didn't rise to the expectations required of said ego, he didn't handle it well.

The more he thought about it, the less the man appeared in his mind until he wondered why he'd ever let him push him around.

"You ready?" Tesa asked as she leaned over his shoulder.

He looked at her, then out at the trees below them. The plan was to land in a few clearings near the facility and walk in. Close, but not too close. The facility was close enough to the capital that he hoped they could land somewhere without notice and within reasonable walking distance. He *hoped* the presence of a few vehicles flying nearby wouldn't raise any suspicions. There was bound to be lots of traffic near the capital, right?

But that was also why they were now splitting off in different directions. He continued forward as the others moved off slightly to the right or left. It would be another five diceros or so before they reached their designated landing points, which were spread out strategically. They didn't want it to appear as if they were moving in formation.

"Delyn?"

He shook his head. "Sorry. Got lost in my head a little there." He smiled, focusing on his sister in earnest now.

"It's okay. It's been an eventful day."

"More than one."

"True." She turned away, looking distant.

"It's not your fault, you know."

Tesa nodded, but didn't look at him. She cleared her throat before speaking again. "I know. It's just... I... This whole thing has made me see myself in a new light. I'm not sure I like it."

"I know what you mean."

She gave him a pointed look. "You are actually better for everything that's happened. I can see it. You would have never spoken up to our dad like that before. Not in a million years. I don't know what's gotten into you, but I like it." She smiled. "Keep up the good work."

He smiled too, shaking his head. "Keep up the good work, huh?"

"Is it Jessie? Is that the difference?"

Delyn looked away, pretending to focus on flying once more, but the ship's autopilot did most of the work. Tesa probably knew that, too.

Was it Jessie? He suspected the answer was yes. Jessie encouraged him, encouraged him to expand his horizons and try new things. She was earnest and passionate, creative and strong. She stood up for herself and had no trouble speaking her mind. He found he envied those things in her.

"Could she be your mate?" Tesa continued.

"What?" He jerked his head around, staring at Tesa in bewilderment. It hadn't occurred to him that she knew about mates yet.

"From the archive. It mentioned mates." She looked uncomfortable, squirming in her seat and struggling to maintain eye contact. "I only really glanced at it, but it sounded really nice. A partner, someone who would be your constant companion. It kind of sounded like something that would just happen, like two people were drawn to each other and the more they got to know each other, the stronger the bond got. Eventually, the two would become inseparable."

Delyn looked away again, uncomfortable with the topic change. He and Jessie had both been thinking along the same lines. It was weird the way he and Jessie had come together. And yet he loved being around her. He felt better when they were together. Even on the shuttle, when they were captive and on the way to the facility, surrounded by enemies, he'd taken some strange comfort from her being there. Comfort, but also dread. He'd wanted nothing more than for her to be safe, but being with her had made it easier, too.

"There. That's our landing site," he said, changing the subject.

"Fine. Don't answer. You're lucky, you know? I would so like to have a mate. Honestly, I don't even care if it's sexual. It's easy enough to get sex from the Seeders."

"What in Wesa, Tesa! I don't need to hear that!" he shouted in outrage.

She laughed. "Oh my, you're such a prude."

"I am not."

"It's perfectly natural, Delyn." She snorted. "And if you string the Seeders along, you can get quite a bit of foreplay out of it."

"Please stop." He tried to focus on the opening in the trees, wishing he could land *now* so he could escape this conversation.

"Have you done it with Jessie? I mean, she did come here as a potential surrogate, right?"

I'm not hearing this. I'm not hearing this.

The trees approached, the opening in their canopy growing larger. The engines whined slightly as they started their descent.

"I bet she's a screamer. I could see her being a screamer."

Not hearing this.

The gap in the trees was large enough for the ship, but it was still a bit of a tight squeeze, which made him nervous. He monitored the autopilot for errors, watching the sensors and cameras as the trees grew uncomfortably close.

"She strikes me as the adventurous sort. Passionate, you know?"

The ship landed with a loud thud, the entire compartment jerking. He disengaged the harness and practically ran from the conversation.

"Coward!" his sister yelled as he rushed down the hallway toward the rear exit.

Yes, he was, because there was nothing he wanted to discuss with his sister less than their respective sex lives.

Delyn passed people in each room. There weren't enough secure seats, so some were standing, bracing against whatever they could find. He nodded at them as he passed.

When he reached the rear of the ship, he turned around, suddenly really nervous. They were all ready, each carrying whatever weapons they'd been able to come up with, but only a few wearing any sort of protective clothing. In a small community like Valana, there were few Fighters, and body armor was a low priority, resource-wise. Most of the Fighters only had a single suit for emergencies. They wore them now.

Tesa was near the back, smirking at him, but keeping her mouth shut.

He took a deep breath. "Is everyone ready?"

"As ready as we'll ever be," someone said sardonically.

A few other people laughed at the statement, and he smiled.

Delyn nodded. "Okay. You know the drill. Stay safe. Don't do anything stupid. The Fighters and I will enter the facility. The rest of you will create a distraction. Keep it simple.

"Good luck."

He activated the ramp and darkness greeted them. With a steadying breath, he walked out into the night.

<hr>

Jessie was patient as the interrogation ended. The guard helped her from the chair and guided her into the hallway. The interrogator was already gone. Just the three of them stood in the otherwise empty hall.

With an outstretched arm, one of them encouraged her to move back toward her cell. With a tingling and crawling feeling along her wrists and hands, she started shifting. She could feel as the cuffs grew looser, but she obliged her captors for the moment. The cuffs started to slip down against her thumbs. She continued walking at a sedate pace, even though it was in the wrong direction. The cuffs slipped past her thumbs, slipping right off her hands. For a breathless moment, they were airborne, before impacting the floor with a show-stopping clang and clatter.

The guards stopped in their places, shocked and staring down at the two circlets lying unoccupied on the ground.

"Game time," she muttered.

With breathtaking speed, she finished her shift. Her fingers had shortened, her nails now transformed into deadly claws. Her limbs and feet changed, adapting themselves to running on all fours. As she dropped down closer to the ground, ready to run, her skin broke out in keratinous scales, protecting her fragile skin.

Jessie ran.

The men shouted, but she ignored them, focusing on the path she remembered from when she'd first arrived. Jessie pushed herself to top speed, pushing herself further and shifting her lungs and circulatory system on the fly when she got winded. She took the first corner at max speed as gunfire sounded behind her. She ignored it. They would either hit her or they wouldn't. She couldn't do anything about that. Hopefully, the scales would work as armor, protect her some from a hit, but if it didn't, it didn't.

The once quiet facility grew loud as her nails scraped and dug into the floor with each step and the pursuers chased after her, firing off shots, and presumably recruiting others. She didn't slow, though, keeping her mind focused on remembering the way out.

A few more turns and the outer door was in sight. She nearly slammed up against it as she tried to screech to a halt. She pulled herself up on two legs and opened the door. Darkness blanketed the dockyard outside, moonlight glinting off the reflective metal.

Jessie dropped down on all fours once more and fell into another run. Her muscles were starting to burn from the exertion, and she could feel hunger gnawing at her insides, a warning that she was overdoing it. But she didn't let that stop her, pushing herself harder and harder as she careened around landing gear and under fuselages.

Gunshots continued to serenade her, and then finally, a siren split the air. But she could see the fence now. It was nothing special, but it didn't need to be. It looked similar to chain-link fences back home with some nasty barbs at the top.

Shit.

She couldn't climb it, that was for damned certain.

I need another option.

And that was when she saw Delyn. He was crossing the clearing beyond the fence, looking like a conquering hero, with a handful of people in body armor backing him up. She slowed as she approached the barrier between them, feeling a profound sense of relief at seeing him.

He'd come for her. Somehow, he'd escaped or been let go, and he'd come back for her. She smiled, but her shifted form didn't lend well to the expression.

With renewed focus, she eyed the fence, wondering if she could cut through it with her claws. She swatted at the material. It rang and groaned, but held firm.

On the other side, Delyn and his team reached the fence. She looked behind her, looking for threats, wondering how much time they had left.

"Jessie?" he asked.

She turned around, sitting on her butt. "In the flesh."

"You look different."

She shrugged. "Sometimes you have to get creative."

"You're always creative," he said with a smile.

She pointed at the fence. "Got anything for that?"

One of the Fighters lifted a tool. "Yup, we planned for this."

"Brilliant. Let's go then."

CHAPTER TWENTY-TWO

The ride back was surprisingly uneventful. The entire time, she kept expecting them to get chased or shot down. She expected to get caught again.

But nothing happened.

Instead, Jessie alternated between taking trips to the kitchen to eat whatever was left over from their trip to Wesa and listening as Delyn and his sister chatted awkwardly up front. There was something in the air between them, some unspoken secret she couldn't lay a finger on, and she wasn't inclined to ask what it might be. Better to let sleeping dogs lie.

When they landed, everyone seemed to race out of the vehicles, eager to celebrate their victory, a victory that seemed just a little too easy for her tastes.

In no time, there was food, music, and dancing, and everyone was outside. Jessie sat at the periphery of the merrymaking, enjoying the ambiance. On a normal day, she would have been right in the center of all that mess, but she was tired. Too much stress. Too much shifting. Too much running.

She'd got lucky. Looking back, she couldn't believe she hadn't been shot or out-powered. One of the guards could have easily grabbed her right after she'd shifted and stopped her escape before it even started. It was probably a testament to the tactical advantage of the element of surprise that she managed to escape at all.

Hours had passed slowly as the party continued to rage on, but recently, some people had finally started wandering off to their beds. It was well into the deepest, darkest parts of the night, the sky like a blackout curtain above them, when a roar carried over the music, causing her to look up. She smiled, recognizing that ship design in a heartbeat.

Delyn walked up to her with a plate of food. "Looks like she's here."

"She?"

"Your sister."

"You called Cass?"

"Yeah. Was that okay?"

She shook her head, the smile on her face growing. "Of course. She's my sister. She's always welcome." Jessie smirked. "Were you hoping for her to come to the rescue?"

He sat down next to her. "Actually, I was hoping she might be able to help us figure out what to do with that info you uncovered."

She paled slightly, suddenly wishing she'd spoken up sooner. *Secrets always come back to bite you, after all.* "I was meaning to tell you." *Eventually.* She couldn't kid herself, though. That "eventually" was probably a long way in the future. She wasn't a coward, necessarily, but she also wasn't inclined to invite trouble, especially a trouble she didn't know how to handle.

And yet trouble keeps finding you, now doesn't it?

"It's okay. It's not exactly the simplest thing to bring up in a conversation." He shrugged, a gentle smile gracing his lips.

"No, I suppose not. Not that that was my reason." She looked away, feeling that familiar guilt taunting her.

I don't deserve him.

"What was?"

"I'm selfish?" She looked over at him, feeling like a fool. She should have known better. After last time with the blue rock, she should have definitely known better. When you ended up with something, information or otherwise, that you weren't supposed to have, you couldn't just pretend you didn't see it. It was a turning point, a point of no return. You had to deal with your new reality as best you could. She'd convinced herself that it wasn't her problem, and on some level, it wasn't, but she'd forgotten the most basic aspect of these types of situations.

People had a tendency of *making* it your problem.

"How so?" Delyn asked, nudging her with his shoulder.

"I convinced myself that it wasn't my problem, that I didn't have to do anything about it. Hell, I convinced myself that I *couldn't* do anything about it. But I was just lying to myself. I think the truth is I didn't *want* to do anything about it. I wanted to forget it existed. I wanted to put it behind me and move on."

"Well, it *is* really big."

She nodded. "And, like I said, I'm selfish."

"Well, then, I think most people are. It's not a bad thing to be selfish, I don't think. It's just normal. People focus on their own lives, get stuck in a rut, never look to see what's going on around them. They can completely miss a lot of things that way."

"I suppose. I guess I just find it hard to believe that other people could see something like that and just ignore it."

"Well, you were right. What could you have done? I've been thinking about it myself, and I don't have any answers, either."

Jessie scratched her head. Her hair was greasy and knotted from however long she'd been in captivity, and she pulled her hand back, suddenly craving a shower. She sighed. The shower would have to wait, though. She'd had a lot of time to think while in captivity, and now her mind wouldn't let her stand on the sidelines. She just couldn't be selfish anymore. Jessie bit the bullet and said, "You might not have answers, but maybe I do."

"Like what?"

"Like us," Cass said, startling them both.

"Cass!" Jessie said, jumping up to her feet and throwing herself into her sister's arms.

"Hey, Jess. Glad you're okay."

Her sister was wearing her body armor, and she could feel a weapon digging into her flank, but she didn't care. "I've missed you."

Cass chuckled. "I've missed you, too." Cass pulled back, looking down at Delyn. "I guess we missed the action?"

He shrugged. "There wasn't much action to speak of. Jessie did most of the work."

"Really?" her sister said, looking at her thoughtfully.

Jessie shrugged. "I shifted." She wiggled her fingers. "Needed to get out of the cuffs."

Cass punched her shoulder with a smile. "*That's* my girl."

Jessie shook her head. "Plus claws, running on all fours, and keratin scales."

"Ooh," Cass said, looking thoughtful. "I like. I haven't tried that one before."

"Probably decent body armor in a pinch."

Cass nodded. "Probably. Now, back to what you guys were talking about. I might have an idea."

<hr>

The Handler waited outside the Magistrate's rooms. It was the middle of the night, and everyone was probably asleep, but this type of news didn't wait. The drive from the facility was a short one, and unfortunately, a journey he'd made more times than he could count. It took constant effort to keep a secret on this scale, so he was a busy man.

The hall was empty and dimly lit. From the other side of the door, he could hear movement, someone shuffling to answer, most like. The door opened to a groggy man in elegant garments, most likely a robe thrown on in a rush from the state of it.

"I have bad news. We should speak inside," he said softly, showing no emotion at the failure. And it *was* his failure. *He'd* let her escape. *He'd* underestimated her. While they'd only had a couple sessions, he should have known. He should have paid more attention. She was a sly one, and his research had already identified her as a shifter. Even a modicum of research might have told him everything one of her kind was capable of. Even a little effort could have set some precautions in place, like mild starvation. Earth was stingy with their information, but that was a detail he'd managed to pick up after the fact. Shifters couldn't shift when starving.

He'd gotten sloppy, made a mistake. It wasn't like him, and now they had a mess to clean up.

The Magistrate nodded and stepped aside, ushering him in. The room was large and filled with muted tones and elegant fabrics. Statuary and plants decorated the floor and many flat surfaces. The Handler settled himself in a well-cushioned chair while the Magistrate resituated his robe before seating himself. "Well, speak."

"We've had an escape at the facility."

"Explain." His eyes drooped, looking like he was only half awake.

"A prisoner, a shifter from Earth who hacked our Archive Vault, escaped tonight. The men were able to track her and her accomplices back to a community here," the Handler said, pulling out his tablet and loading a map of the location. "I had just confirmed her knowledge of the vault right before she escaped. I would say she is an active threat to the stability of our government and the secret that keeps it operating."

"Indeed. And do we know everyone she's been in contact with since discovering the secret?"

"It should only be the people of this community, to my knowledge. There have been no outbound signals coming from the community of Valana while she was staying there."

The Magistrate nodded. "Good. Then this can be contained."

The Handler stilled, picking up on what the Magistrate was suggesting they do. "Are you sure, sir?"

"Yes. Take the entire place out. Do it quietly. Ensure there are no survivors or witnesses."

"It'll be done."

<hr>

It was approaching the wee hours of the morning. In the hours that had followed, more of Jessie's friends had shown up. Victoria had arrived with Surg in the *Discovery*. Shortly after that, Taln, Eirse, and her crew showed up in the *Areon*. Jessie didn't recognize any of the other people that disembarked, but she was surprised to see Eirse. The last time she'd seen her, she was defecting from the Diehli, supposedly under at least a little duress.

Now, she and Taln seemed almost chummy. There was a tension between them, but she couldn't say for sure if it was a good or bad thing. Eirse was more relaxed to Taln's stick-up-your-butt intensity, but it seemed to be working for them.

Right now, they were off in a corner, chatting with the rest of the group about strategies for getting the word out. Jessie sat on the stoop with Victoria at her side, feeling a little left out.

"So, you did it," Victoria said.

Jessie turned to her. Victoria had a small smile on her face. Her eyes glowed slightly in the dim lighting. Almost everyone else had gone to bed long ago, and the air was eerily quiet, with just the occasional insect breaking the silence in her little corner. She could just barely hear the murmuring of voices, but it was easy to ignore. "What do you mean?"

"You left. I remember at your birthday party. You were talking about needing to leave. I'm glad you did. It can be really easy to fall into a rut, and then even if you're miserable, it's easier to stay in that rut than make a change." She leaned in, bumping Jessie's shoulder. "Am I right?"

"Yeah. You are." Jessie shook her head. "I probably should have left the moment I turned eighteen. Cass wouldn't have objected. She would have probably done exactly what she did, *regardless* of when I left."

"What did she do?"

"Basically, insist that I contact her constantly."

"Oh, that would drive me nuts."

"I know. Better me than you, right?"

Victoria laughed. "I don't think that's how the phrase goes."

"But that's what works for us, isn't it? That's the important part."

"I suppose." Victoria paused, staring off at the group who were essentially trying to decide the fate of this planet. "So, did you find what you were looking for?"

Jessie stopped breathing for a moment. Did she find what she was looking for? What *was* she looking for? What did she tell Victoria back then?

That's right. I wanted to find myself.

Jessie laughed. Victoria could be adorably literal at times. At the time, she'd asked Jessie if she was lost. And yet, the answer was yes. Her true self, the one that would make her most happy, was lost somewhere inside, somewhere she couldn't reach without spreading her wings, testing her boundaries. The ship had started feeling confining, like she couldn't breathe, couldn't move. She loved her sister, but she had come to realize that she would never figure out who she was supposed to be, let alone who she was meant to be with, if she didn't leave the nest.

For a while there, she'd done nothing but what she'd always done. She drew, painted, enjoyed her surroundings, met new people. It was exciting and new, and that was great for a spell. It didn't help her find herself, though. She was still doing the same old things. She'd gone somewhere new, but she hadn't really spread her wings.

Not until she met Delyn. There was something about him that made her want to help right from the start. Maybe it was risky, seeing as he was a bit of a work in progress, but weren't they all? No one was perfect, and there was just something about him that made her want to help him be the best he could be. Not fix him, necessarily, but just build him up. If nothing else, she liked being around him, especially once they no longer had that surrogacy contract hanging over their heads.

And she'd fallen in love with his community nearly as much as she had him. So many of them were unbelievably welcoming, and while Tesa was one of the least welcoming of the batch, she really liked her. Tesa kind of reminded her of her sister, a bit abrasive, and not always easy to get along with, but worth the trouble. She was so protective of her brother, and Jessie could certainly respect that. She was also open with her affection when she'd opened up to that person. Jessie remembered first meeting Tesa, with the other woman practically jumping at Delyn to hug him. It reminded her of how she acted with her own sister.

She looked around her, seeing a place that, in its own way, continued to remind her of the shifter caravan she used to live in for so short a spell. It looked nothing like it, really, but it reminded her of it all the same. The people helped each other out. They gathered together in times of strife. And they were willing to risk their lives to rescue her. She still couldn't believe they'd done that. She wasn't one of them. They'd only just met her, but it didn't matter. They still came, putting themselves in danger for her. It made her feel like she belonged.

And it was all because of Delyn. Delyn, who loved to learn and research. Delyn, who came to her rescue when he was let go and she wasn't. Delyn, who looked like a really hot elf and didn't know a thing about sex.

Jessie smiled, shaking her head at him not knowing what masturbation was. There was so much out there that she'd never experienced, and he'd never dreamed of. She looked forward to teaching him and experimenting together.

Jessie wanted to be with him, even if their relationship went up in flames some day, she wanted to give it a shot. She wanted hot, passionate interludes in bed and relaxing evenings on the couch as they watched the sun set. She wanted times when they couldn't keep their hands off each other, and times when they shared private jokes between them as family looked on in befuddlement. She wanted what Cass and Kou had.

Suddenly, her sister's romance didn't bother her so much. It felt like something to aspire to, rather than something to run from. When had that happened? What had changed?

I love him, that's what.

It wasn't really a surprise when the thought popped into her head. It was almost like the culmination of a long journey. You knew it was coming, you were heading straight for it, but it was still pleasantly breathtaking when you reached it. "Yes, I did," she said, responding to Victoria's earlier question.

Yes, she'd found what she was looking for.

"Good. I'm glad."

"He makes me want to be a better person." She shook her head. "Even earlier tonight, I told him I was selfish, but I'm not sure I am anymore. And I'm not sure when that changed."

"What *did* change?"

She looked over at Victoria, her gaze intense. "I've known about what the government did here for quite a while, before we landed, in fact. I didn't say anything. Figured it wasn't my business."

"That doesn't sound like you."

"Doesn't it?" Jessie thought it sounded exactly like her, though she wanted to change. She didn't want to be selfish anymore. She wanted to help. She wanted to be part of something.

"It's not the whole story, though, is it?"

Jessie started to say that yes, it was, but stopped herself. "No, I guess it isn't. I wanted to tell Delyn right from the very start. I just didn't know how or if it was the right thing to do." She shook her head and looked away.

"But now you're doing something about it. Sometimes, I think, we do things that seem selfish or wrong not because we're bad people, but because we don't know how to do the right thing, so we do nothing. It's easier to do nothing. Doing the right thing is hard. Doing it when there's opposition is even harder.

"When I was sixteen, staying with my parents would have been the easy thing. It required no work, no effort except the effort needed to survive. Standing up for myself was hard. Making that change, fixing what was wrong, was hard. But it was worth it."

"I know. I'm glad you did. It's been really nice knowing you, even when you're being antisocial."

"Hey," she said, putting her hands up in the air. "Antisocial is my thing. It's what I do. I've got Surg for the social crap."

Jessie laughed as another engine roared overhead.

"Another one of my ships," Victoria said, looking up at the sky as a shadow passed overhead. "Must be Ellie and her crew."

"How could you tell?"

"I'd recognize those engines anywhere. Come on. Let's go greet them." Victoria stood, offering Jessie a hand.

Victoria's hand was slightly clammy in the early morning air, but Jessie took it and rose to her feet. They looped around the buildings, the structures little more than dim outlines in the dark, and walked to where the ships were parked.

Dust was puffing up into the air as the duo approached and the ship touched down. The soft hum of the engines cut off shortly after, and they waited. Minutes ticked by before the ramp lowered and backlit bodies paraded out. "Jessie! Victoria! It's been so long," a woman called out, rushing up to greet them. It was Ellie, and the moonlight illuminated her purple skin and dark hair, a far cry from the "costume" she used to wear. Back in the day, before she met Zee, Ellie had suffered from body image issues. She'd always been treated as "other" on Earth because, as a shifter with an alien father, her natal form wasn't human. As a reaction, she'd often shifted into the form of a leggy redhead with pale skin. It was her way of protecting herself from the cruelty of the world, and she'd rarely taken it off before meeting Zee.

Zee, a dark-skinned Ateles with a spattering of silver scars from his life as a soldier, was right behind her, full of grins as they made this rare visit. He, along with the people behind him, were Ateles special forces, and they were often on missions. It was a rare moment indeed when they managed to get the entire gang together, and Jessie was glad.

"It's good to see you, too," Jessie said, giving Ellie a big hug.

Zee sidled up beside them, stretched out his arms, and engulfed all three of them, squeezing the air out of them in his exuberance.

"Zee, 'nuff," Jessie said, struggling for breath.

Victoria was nearly apoplectic. Jessie knew she often didn't like touching.

"Sorry. It's been a while." He scratched his neck, looking a little embarrassed.

Meanwhile, one of the other soldiers stepped up, cutting into the reunion. "So, I assume we're here because of the forces amassing around the town."

"What?!" Victoria and Jessie shrieked in unison.

CHAPTER TWENTY-THREE

There was only one room in Ellie's ship that could house their entire group. Delyn stood off to the side with Jessie, watching as a comms officer with the Ateles military, a group he'd been told from birth was the enemy, detailed the information he'd collected as they were landing. The wall display in the neat bedroom showed an overhead view of the entire area, including a variety of heat signatures in the trees. He pointed out some of the heat signatures, smaller ones that were people, as well as the larger forms of ships.

It was surreal. His mind couldn't seem to process it.

At his side, Jessie squeezed his hand encouragingly as she, too, stared at the screen, intent on the presentation. She was quite possibly the only person keeping him together right now.

Our government turned against us.

It was a constant refrain in his head. At one point, he could have forgiven the kidnapping. That could have just been a mistake. The secrets, he could have possibly forgiven, too. They must have had their reasons. He might not agree with those decisions, and he thought they should change their policies, but he didn't know entirely why they did it or why they maintained those secrets. You couldn't really judge someone fully without knowing their motives.

But this… this was not the government he thought he knew. This was a nightmare. This wasn't a small group kidnapping a couple people to keep government secrets. This was too big, too much.

"Any questions?"

Jessie raised her hand. "How can just a handful of people go up against a force like that? I just… it doesn't seem possible."

"If we wanted to win, it probably would be. I don't think we have to win. I think we just have to buy time."

"And that's where we come in," Victoria said. "With a little bit of technomagic, we can possibly take the fight out of the enemy."

"So, we're still going through with it? Telling the world."

"I think they've forced our hand," Cass said. "There's no way out but through."

Jessie nodded.

"So, what can we do?" Delyn said. "I get the general idea. But what do I do?"

"First, gather everyone, arm them if possible. Prepare them for the inevitable. Then you and Jessie meet back here. This ship has the most advanced communications equipment available to us at the moment."

Delyn nodded and walked with Jessie out of the ship. The morning was quiet and a small crowd followed them off the ship, knocking on doors, rousing people from sleep even as the first rays of morning touched the sky. He and Jessie waited for everyone to walk outside.

It was an agonizing series of minutes as the sky grew brighter, degree by degree, and people stumbled out of their homes, rubbing their eyes and groaning at the early horo.

When everyone was outside, Delyn started speaking. "I have some unfortunate news for you. There is a force amassing outside the town. We're not sure about their numbers or what they're capable of, but it's very likely they're going to attack."

People started arguing in a chaotic din.

"Please, quiet! I know you may have questions or may be scared. We're going to do what we can. And that means we need you, all of you, to help."

"Why are they here?" someone asked.

"I don't know, but the timing is suspicious."

"It's because of the rescue," another person said.

"We should give her back."

"We should apologize. Maybe we can ask for forgiveness."

"Enough!" Taln said.

Delyn jumped and turned to her. He hadn't even noticed the unfamiliar woman standing next to them. She was intimidating, to say the least, and it was no surprise when the crowd quieted instantly.

"Better," she said to the cowed audience. "This isn't like an argument between friends. You can't just apologize or beg forgiveness. And it's too late to be turning anyone over, though the very idea is sickening. They're here for a reason. If they just wanted her back, they wouldn't send an army. They wouldn't need to. They're here for *you*. They're at *your* doorstep. You can't simply ignore that or expect it to go away without fighting back.

"Now, we have a plan. We are going to fight back in the only way we can. Jessie and Delyn here are essential to that plan. But in order for it to work, we need your help. We need *time*. We need to delay those forces until we can implement the plan. Now, I don't know when they'll attack, but they *will* attack, and nothing you do will stop that. So, will you help us?"

The community was unusually quiet and still. No one was arguing or complaining, but no one was offering suggestions, either. Slowly, people started nodding their heads or stepping forward. Some rose their arms in assent.

"Thank you," Taln said, bowing her head in acknowledgment.

Now, they just needed to tell the world.

Jessie felt a little guilty. And not just because she was the instigator of all this mess. No, she felt guilty because while other people would be risking their lives when the government decided to strike, she would be in here, in this ship, in relative safety.

But that was the way of things. Everyone had their role to play. Some roles were more dangerous than others, and you never knew which one you would get. She'd lived through situations where her role was dangerous. Today, her role was important, vital, and maybe the most important thing someone would do on this planet for generations.

And she didn't feel ready *or* worthy.

She waited with Delyn at her side while the others worked out the technical parts of the plan. Cass was working on a virus that could infect the communications systems of Wesa. Surg and Victoria were in another part of the ship, working to prepare the ship's hardware for the monumental task ahead. Everyone else was outside, armed and waiting for the inevitable.

And if we fuck up here, they could all die.

Jessie's stomach was churning with anxiety as time ticked by relentlessly. She squeezed Delyn's hand harder, feeling like she could fly apart at any moment.

The engines kicked on, and she jumped, yelping a little. She looked around, embarrassed.

"Relax," Cass said, not even moving a muscle as she continued her work. "It's part of the plan. With the engines running, we can divert additional power to communications and boost the signal."

Right. She knew that.

She started going over the plan in her head, just to ease her anxiety. They were going to record a live broadcast of her and Delyn explaining what had happened and attach the files she'd found. The communications system would reach out to the satellites that allowed global communication, and Cass's virus would force the message to be sent to every comms device on the planet. Within the hour, there wouldn't be a single person on Wesa who *didn't* know the truth.

"Okay, that's it," Cass said, pushing back from the desk. "Angus, how are Victoria and Surg doing?"

"One moment." Silence filled the room as they waited.

"All done," Victoria said, startling all three of them as she entered the room.

"You guys ready?" Surg said from behind her, looking intently at the two of them.

Jessie looked over at Delyn and said, "Yes." There was something in his expression, in his eyes, that helped. She couldn't say what it was. There was a softness to it, relaxed, but also sharp, intense. It made her feel like everything would be fine, like they could do anything they set their minds to. She felt a moment of confidence, but she feared it wouldn't last. "Let's do this."

Before she lost her nerve.

They stepped into position. Cass nodded when she was ready.

"People of Wesa. My name is Jessie Allen. I am a shifter from Earth, and I have something you are going to need to hear."

Taln waited on the edge of town, idly playing with her weapons, Eirse at her side. The teal-colored woman was similarly engaged, checking the charge on her guns, tightening holsters, adjusting her clothing to ensure full range of motion.

It was a good thing Eirse wasn't paying attention, because Taln was absolutely checking the other woman out. There was just something about the Tursiops female that had drawn her from that very first moment they'd met at Diehli headquarters. Of course, the woman's easy confidence had been an instant turn on. She'd always been a sucker for a confident being.

But she'd also loved her magnificent thighs and that hint of danger that seemed to always hang around the woman. She'd come to love her teal skin, easy smile, and voice like a song. She could listen to Eirse for horos.

And Eirse didn't have a clue.

Taln sighed and stared off into the distance, wondering when the battle would start. She could certainly use a distraction from her unrequited lust with her subordinate.

And that was possibly the worst part. Eirse was a subordinate, placed in her care after she'd defected from the Diehli. She was Taln's responsibility, so no matter how much she might have wanted to lick her from head to toe, she just didn't feel comfortable acting on it. Inia Intergalactic didn't have any specific rules *against* fraternizing with subordinates, but it still made her uncomfortable, like she would be taking advantage, like it would put Eirse in an awkward position.

Taln shook her head. She needed to get her head in the game. She stood and slowly scanned her surroundings. They weren't in a very defensible position. The village was a small circle of buildings. No walls and most of the buildings were made of materials like wood. None of it would hold up to sustained fire. Most of the villagers were on the roofs. Some were armed with long-range weapons, but some were just up there because it was the safest place in this fight. There was nowhere else to put them.

Those that had fighting experience were on the ground. There weren't a lot of fighters from the village, so most of the people down here consisted of her small crew, Cass's Kou, and the special forces team the Earthling Ellie had brought. It wasn't much. It wasn't nearly enough.

It was going to have to be.

"When do you think they'll strike?" Eirse asked as she settled her rifle on her lap.

"Well, if it were me, I would have struck in the middle of the night. Though, the sun is coming up in that direction," she said, pointing her finger at the lightening sky behind the woods in the distance. "If they strike with the sun at their back, it'll be hard to hit them. At this point, I think that's the most likely scenario."

Eirse nodded. "Yeah, that's true. Shouldn't be long, then." She stood, looping the rifle's strap over her shoulder. "We should have placed sensors in the field."

Taln shook her head. "We didn't have any. We weren't expecting to play a defensive role here. Just maybe rescue."

"True."

Someone yelled something, and they all tensed. Eirse's rifle immediately flipped into her hands, aiming at the field before them.

Taln couldn't see anything, but that didn't mean there wasn't something there. The crops ahead were tall, nearly as tall as she was, and they could easily hide a person. In addition, the sun had just peeked over the horizon, causing her to squint as its gilded rays tinted the vista. "Ready," she said calmly.

Eirse moved a step closer, her legs staggered and toes spread out to increase stability. Taln stepped into a shooting stance as well, nearly shoulder to shoulder with Eirse. The plants moved, but she couldn't tell if it was troop advancements or the wind.

Then a shot cracked through the air. Her finger twitched against the trigger guard. She took a single steadying breath in and out and raised her gun to aim, scanning the scene before her. Then she saw it, a shape moving through the field. She fired, and moments later, the air was filled with the sounds of battle.

People shouted, guns fired, and she spotted the occasional fighter drop out of sight in the tall vegetation. She and Eirse moved in unison, advancing but trying to keep within relative cover. The enemy was closer than she would have liked, already almost to the edge of the village.

When the first combatant stepped out of the field within arm's reach of their hiding place, she threw her rifle over her shoulder, switching to close contact fighting. She advanced, Eirse at her back, and had him in a hold before he even knew she was there. She twisted, and he dropped to the ground, limp.

Gunshots continued around them, but here, the environment worked slightly in their favor. They were between two buildings, but the buildings had been updated over the years, making little additions that jutted out from the smooth walls. There were also small outbuildings and supplies strewn about. It gave cover. Not much, and certainly not enough to protect them from being shot, but it was enough to keep them out of direct line of sight and allow for the element of surprise in close combat.

Before long, surprise was no longer an option. The enemy was everywhere. Every person on the ground was fighting close up. Fists and knives were flying, and she and Eirse were fighting back to back. Taln was both excited and terrified. They were surrounded, outnumbered, and possibly out-skilled, but they were holding on. She took a blow to the flank and grunted as she bent over, breathing through the pain before straightening, a knife already in her right hand. The blade sank deep under the poor bastard's ribcage.

"Look out," Eirse said. She held a retractable staff, her rifle abandoned on a strap against her back, swinging it out to Taln's unprotected right side as another fighter tried to take advantage. She jerked her knife out as her opponent dropped to the ground. Her hand was sticky, covered in blood, making her grip a little precarious, but she moved to the right. Eirse swung again with her staff, keeping her opponent occupied as Taln sliced into his ribs, ending the fight. Blood welled on his tan uniform, and he collapsed, weakened by blood loss.

Time disappeared, replaced with the pounding of her heart. Her arms moved in steady motion, her legs sliding in graceful arcs across the hard-packed dirt. She could feel exhaustion weighing down on her as the battle dragged on, threatening to pull her under. Each kick, each swing, each thrust felt like it took more effort than the last. Her senses had narrowed down to tracking movement and feeling the heat of Eirse's body at her back.

Then it all stopped.

Taln breathed heavily into the silence, her mind unable to process the sudden change. She looked around herself, seeing fighters, both friend and foe, stopped and staring at their wrists. A profound relief washed over her, and she leaned into Eirse's back with a sigh.

It was over.

It was a bloody battle. Remarkably so, actually. She could see her fellow Fighters falling. They'd been told it would be an easy mission. They'd been told this community was working against the government, that they'd been convicted of treason.

It was surprising. She'd never heard of an entire community being convicted like that, but she didn't question it. That wasn't her job.

She'd expected an easy win. They were to slip into the community at first light, before anyone would be awake. The tan uniforms would make their approach practically invisible with the sun at their backs.

And yet, when they got there, the community was ready… and armed. The first shots were fired before they even reached the buildings. And it only grew worse from there.

So when her comm went off in the middle of the bloodbath, it was beyond surprising. It was like snapping her out of a nightmare. Everyone had stopped, frozen in place.

It wasn't possible. The comms didn't work like that. When they started a mission, their comms were set on a combat hold. They would only receive comms from their team, allowing them to communicate with each other without distraction. But on-mission comms didn't have notifications. The comms just came through, a sometimes constant stream of voices keeping them organized and working as a team.

The notification sound had a visceral effect on all of them. It was the emergency klaxon. It was supposed to only be used by the government, and only in cases of disaster. Even so, it shouldn't have sounded mid-mission.

What type of emergency could necessitate bypassing a combat hold? It could literally get someone killed.

She looked down, trepidation causing her hands to tremble slightly. The battlefield was eerily silent as she tried to activate the display, but it didn't immediately respond because it was still on the combat hold.

She deactivated the hold.

There was a single message waiting, a video. She tapped to watch it, and it started playing on her heads-up display.

After that, nothing was ever the same.

CHAPTER TWENTY-FOUR

"Deep in thought?" Delyn said.

Jessie turned around and smiled. The battle had ended hours ago, and she'd spent the last little while watching the sun continue to rise in the sky. In the parush before her window, she could see people milling around, the relief palpable. They didn't celebrate the way they had after rescuing her. She suspected the shock of the revelation had been too great.

Even so, there was an odd feel to the scene, like a new beginning now that the secret was out. People seemed curious, looking at each other differently than they had before, and certain people, like Delyn's father, looked anxious, like they didn't know what they would do now. After all, the Seeder role was an invention of the drone mating system. If true mating was to be encouraged, it wouldn't be necessary.

Her smile grew as Delyn crossed the room, reaching for her hand when he got close enough. He hadn't changed a bit, and he didn't seem even the slightest bit worried, even though he was a Seeder himself. "So, what'll you do now?" she asked.

He smiled at her. "I don't know. It's kind of exciting, isn't it?" He laughed.

"Well, I mean, you weren't any good at being a Seeder."

"No, I wasn't. And I'm okay with that."

Jessie leaned in and hugged him around his waist, resting her chin against his chest to look up at his face. "Me too."

"So, what do you plan to do?" he asked in turn, his fingers running lightly over her back as he wrapped his arms around her.

"I think I want to stay."

"Yeah?"

She nodded. "I like it here. I like the idea of being part of a community. I never had that before, not really." She changed positions, resting her cheek against his chest now, and sighed. "It was just always me and my sister. We had friends, but we never really had anything that felt like a home."

"Hey," Delyn said, tipping her head up with a couple fingers under her chin. "You've always had a home. You have people who love you, who will do anything for you. At the drop of a hat, they came here to help you, to protect you or rescue you. That's something I've never had." His fingers shifted, caressing her cheek now.

Jessie wanted to say that he had Mak and Tesa and Faelee and Mae, but she was suddenly breathless, and speech was impossible. There was something in his eyes she couldn't quite read, but she was dying to find out what it was.

"I love you, Jessie. I think you're my mate. There's just been something about you from the moment we met. I've been drawn to you, and every moment we've been together has only made it feel stronger. Being away from you, not knowing if you were okay, was brutal. Every moment I wasn't trying to save you felt like an eternity."

"Oh, Delyn," she said as she leaned up to kiss him. Her lips quivered as they touched his, and she moved her hands, reaching up to feed her fingers into his hair. The kiss was perfect and sweet, matching the moment. She pulled back for a breath. "Oh, God, Delyn, I love you, too. I don't have any idea why. Everything just feels right with you. You're home to me." She brushed the hair from his temple, loving the soft feel of it and the shining brightness of his eyes looking at her as she admitted her feelings.

"Jessie?"

"Yes," she said on a breath.

"I'm going to kiss you now."

"God, yes."

He leaned down, and this time, when his lips touched hers, it was not sweet. He devoured her, expressing his passion in a way that left her brain practically oozing out of her ears.

"Yes," she said as they came up for air and stumbled toward the couch. She pulled at his hair, feeling desperate to have his lips touch hers once more.

His hands roamed, the gentle touches like a tease, leaving her gasping for more.

"Please," she said into his mouth.

Then he was touching skin and shivers ran up and down her body.

"More," she said as she, too, moved her hands, reaching to touch him. Frustrated with his clothing in the way, she growled. Her nails shifted to claws with barely a thought, and she tore his shirt from his body. She smiled with a breathless chuckle, pulling back from the kiss to appreciate what she'd revealed. There was something about him hovering over her with his shirt shredded and hanging around his shoulders that turned her into a bit of an animal.

She pushed him over, straddling his waist, and ripped her own shirt up over her head.

"You are so beautiful."

She leaned down and licked his lips playfully. "So are you." Next, she nipped his lips, trailing her hands down his well-muscled torso. He wasn't bodybuilder strong, but he was still firm enough that she could have touched him forever.

She started working her way down his body, her hands leading and her mouth following.

"Jessie," Delyn said as her hand touched his waistband.

She took her time undoing his pants, kissing each patch of warm flesh she exposed. He lifted his hips to help her, and she pulled back when his erection popped out to greet her.

Satisfied with his progress, she stood up with a grin and started running her hands down her own body, slowly teasing him as she worked her pants and underwear down her legs.

Delyn's bright eyes were alive with the fire of his passion, waiting on her every movement like a starving animal stalking prey.

"Comere," he said, grabbing her and dragging her atop him when she kicked her pants away.

She settled against his hard phallus and couldn't resist arching and rubbing against him like a cat demanding attention. Little sparks of pleasure shot out from her clit where she was rubbing it against him.

"Yes, Jessie, yes," Delyn begged, gripping her hips and encouraging her to continue.

This continued, her head falling back and her breaths getting ragged as the pleasure grew, but then she stopped. It wasn't enough.

"No," Delyn moaned in complaint, dragging out the syllable.

Jessie leaned down, hands on his shoulders, and kissed his eyelids. "Relax. I just want more."

"More?" he said, sounding confused.

"I want you inside me."

"But…"

"Shh. It's okay." She stroked his cheek. "It doesn't always have to be for implantation. It can be for fun or pleasure or affection. And don't forget, you already blew your load recently, so no drones for you." She waggled her finger at him with a grin.

"What about the other way? I know you don't want kids yet."

She leaned back. "Well, first," she counted off on her fingers, "we don't even know if that's possible. And second, shifters can control their fertility, so it's a nonissue. Nobody's getting pregnant today." And suddenly, she wasn't worried about whether she could have kids some day. She had Delyn, and he was enough. If they wanted kids in the future, there were so many options. They would figure out a way.

She looked down at him with affection and caressed his cheek. "Do you want to do this?"

He nodded. "I think so."

"Are you sure?"

"With you? Always."

"Okay." She leaned down and kissed him as she lifted herself to line them up. Her muscles quivered as she felt his tip brushing against her. When he was right there, she pressed down, feeling her body stretch around him, accommodating him. They went slow, his hands resting on her hips as she controlled their speed. She took deep breaths as her heart pounded away in her chest. It was weird but nice as she took him into her for the first time. There was a fullness to it that she liked, and she reached down, rubbing her clit because she couldn't help herself. Her body clenched and released around him and then suddenly, they were one.

Jessie dropped her hands to his chest. She'd known he was big, but he felt bigger than she'd expected, and it almost felt like he was touching her belly button from the inside. She rocked against him experimentally and gasped, feeling something come to life inside her.

He groaned, gripping her hips harder. "Whatever that was, you liked it."

She nodded her head and did it again. She groaned herself, her head falling back, hair brushing against her lower back teasingly.

"Let me move, Jessie. Please let me move."

She nodded quickly and eagerly. He lifted her, and she helped, resting on her knees. He slipped out slowly, and she wanted to push back downward, welcoming him back. Instead, he pulled out almost to the tip, then slapped his hips upward, connecting them once more with a crack of sound that filled the room.

She whimpered, digging her nails into his shoulders.

He did it once more, nice and slow, and she wanted to yell at him, to demand he get on with it. Instead, she bit her lip, her muscles trembling with everything she was feeling.

"I have a better idea," he said, hips still flexed upward.

He pulled her down, sat up, then flipped them around. Now, she was below him, and he was kneeling next to the couch. She looked up at him, her butt hanging off the cushions, and nodded in encouragement. He began a steady rhythm. They stared into each other's eyes and before long, Jessie was lost, lost in sensation, lost in his gaze. She wanted to stay here forever. She could feel the pleasure building, knew it would soon come to an end, but she didn't care. She tried to hold it off, tried to hold on to this moment for as long as possible, but it was inevitable. She came with a high-pitched sound she refused to call a scream.

While she was still coming down from her own high, her brain too fried to process much of anything, Delyn collapsed against her. Only then did she notice how sweaty they both were, how the room was a little too cool.

Or how the door was currently open to her left.

She started laughing.

"What is it?" He leaned up off her.

"We left the door open."

He looked over. "Well, at least nobody came in."

Which was, of course, when her sister stepped into the doorway.

Jessie shrieked in surprise, reaching to drag Delyn closer to cover herself. Her first instinct was to bury her head against his chest, but then she paused. Memories of all the times she'd caught Cass in flagrante delicto flashed through her head. She stared at him for a moment, not looking him in the eyes, then realized how childish she was acting. Was it embarrassing to get caught like this by her sister? Yes. She wouldn't be surprised if every inch of skin right now was flaming red with it, but as her brain started to process more than just the shock of the situation, she realized that Cass wasn't reacting as Jessie always had. She looked over and caught her sister smirking at her silently. Feeling challenged, she looked her sister right in the eyes and wrapped her arms and legs slowly around Delyn. She stared Cass down, as if daring her to comment. Her heart raced a little in her chest, but she didn't relent.

Cass laughed, clutching her belly and throwing her head back. When she recovered, she shook her head as she wiped the tears from her eyes. "I suppose I deserved that." She nodded at Delyn, then looked back at Jessie. "So, I'm guessing you're staying."

"Yeah."

"Good. This place fits you, I think. Especially him," she said, her smirk giving away the double entendre.

"I would throw something at you right now if I could," she snapped at her sister in irritation. And yet surprisingly, her embarrassment didn't rise up again at the comment. For years, she'd caught her sister in the act and had hated being exposed to her sister's sexual exploits, but now, she almost didn't care. She'd done the same sort of thing Cass always did, and she was okay with it. The world wouldn't end just because her sister had caught her naked with a guy. Sure, there was that moment of shock, that instinctive reaction to cover up, but nothing bad had happened. It was actually sort of freeing.

Cass laughed again as she walked away.

"Sorry about that," Delyn said, his cheeks tinged an aggressive shade of red.

"Not your fault. I feel like I started this."

"Did you?"

She smirked. "If we put some clothes on, we could go upstairs and I could let you start the next round."

"Deal," he said, pushing away and offering her a hand.

"Race you?" she asked as she started putting her pants on.

"Let's just try not to flash anyone else, shall we?"

Jessie pulled on her shirt. "That's not a no."

"Jessie…"

She grinned as she tugged her shirt in place, then took off at a dead run as her laughter filled the house.

———————

We did it.

A week had passed, and Jessie still couldn't believe it. She couldn't believe it had actually worked. The entire time, she'd been expecting everyone to die. The entire time she was recording that video, the same thought kept going through her head.

I'm killing them.

But no one on their side died. People had been hurt, some badly enough to be sent off for emergency treatment, but nobody died. With Surg's people and the Ateles special forces, the attacking Fighters were, for the most part, out-skilled, even if they weren't outnumbered. Her friends, family, and allies had managed to hold them off long enough to get the message out.

The message had hit like a bomb.

As she stared out the windows at the crops behind the house, her mind ran through those moments after the message had sent. She and Delyn had stood there shoulder to shoulder, their hands pressed together in a death grip. The wait had been unbearable as the moments dragged on.

Had it worked?

Had the fighting stopped?

Did the message get out?

Did people believe it?

She couldn't stop the ping-pong thoughts from bouncing all around her head as she'd tried to hold herself together. It had felt like her hand in Delyn's was the only thing keeping her from completely falling apart.

Then Angus's voice had filled the room. "The fight's ended."

With a breath of relief, the tension had faded from the room. They'd left the ship, moving to the center of town. There were people cheering on the rooftops and people in tan uniforms standing around in shock. Taln had proudly walked up to them and told them they'd been successful, that as soon as the message went out, the fighting stopped.

In the days that followed, they'd received reports from all over the planet. The people were outraged. The response was immediate and violent. People had flooded their government centers in anger while those more shocked than angry watched on through broadcasts. Meanwhile, reporters and talk show hosts voiced their own outrage or speculated on how this would affect their world.

The government was in turmoil. They lost control of every-thing, including their own military. No one would listen to them. No one could trust them.

It was relatively safe in small, out of the way places like Valana. Life sort of returned to normal for a spell. After all, there were chores to do. But it didn't stop people from sharing updates. Every activity seemed to be filled with information sharing and speculation. Worrying about what would happen if the planet were invaded right now. Sharing when the command structure of the Wesan Fighters had promised it would protect their planet, even if they refused to follow government orders. Speculating on what would happen if the global government fell. Would they return to the same governing structure they had before the war?

Even during all this upheaval and speculation, there was another, more subtle change happening. People started seeing each other in different lights. She wasn't sure Delyn noticed, but she and the rest of the guests in Valana probably did. There was this nascent curiosity growing in the community. At night, curled up next to Delyn in bed, when the house quieted and she could hear every sound as if it echoed off the walls, the stifled groans of people experimenting reached her ears. There was a sexual liberation going on, and it made her smile.

Still, surprisingly quickly, the worst of the upheaval started to die down. The protests and riots in the capital city dwindled, and a practice of total and brutal honesty developed in the government. Magistrates at the global level, fearing for their jobs and lives, put themselves on live broadcasts sharing details of both their professional and personal lives in a way that engendered a fledgling amount of trust. Sometimes out of sheer selfishness, they desperately worked to unearth the truth, and it became clear that the secret had been especially well kept, even from their own government officials. Reporters shared stories of members of the government fleeing in the night, and speculation rose as to whether those people had known the truth. Those that remained were left with an angry populace that weren't willing to be placated with empty words.

The people demanded change, and quite quickly, some Magistrates took center stage with their comparable outrage. A select few spoke up, promising change. They vowed to end the practices of encouraging drone mating and hiring out their Fighters as mercenaries. They vowed that they would attempt to make peace with the Ateles, pointing out that members of the Ateles race were involved in uncovering this terrible conspiracy.

Jessie didn't know if it was all empty words, but at the moment, it didn't matter. The secret was out, and it would transform the world. She suspected that was enough.

"Jessie?" Tesa said meekly from behind her.

She spun around at the intrusion, surprised to see Tesa standing there awkwardly in the doorway. "Yes?"

Delyn's sister seemed to stretch her spine and step forward. "I wanted to apologize."

"Tesa, it's fine." She shook her head. "We can't always control our emotions. I don't blame you. I don't know what you were going through, but clearly it was something you needed to get off your chest."

Tesa wouldn't look her in the eye. "I shouldn't have gone off on you like that. And then you got kidnapped because of that."

Jessie rushed forward, pulling the woman into a hug. "Tesa, no. No, that's not your fault."

"It feels like my fault," she said, her voice thickening with emotion.

"They would have got us, eventually. I mean, they were friggin' soldiers, for crying out loud."

Tesa laughed. "That's what Delyn said."

"Well, your brother is pretty smart."

Tesa looked up. Her face was red, unshed tears sparkling at the edges of her eyes. "I'm glad he found you."

Jessie smiled. "Me too."

Tesa sniffed, then pulled out of Jessie's hold. She allowed it, letting the other woman pull herself together.

"I should also apologize for how I treated you since you first came here."

"Well, Delyn *did* say you were slow to warm up to people."

Tesa shook her head. "Yeah, but not like that." She cleared her throat. "I didn't have any idea at the time, but apparently I had some issues to work through with how our society handles trans people."

"Oh?"

"Yeah, I didn't even realize it until you came here. When everything's a monolith, you can't see the contrast. I envied you, I realize, looking back. I envied the fact that you didn't need to go through surgery to be accepted. At first, I told myself that you weren't serious about being trans, that you could detransition at any time because you were a shifter, and *that* was the problem. But after a while, I realized that wasn't true. I started remembering things that I'd never really noticed before." She paused, looking up at Jessie, her gaze intense. "I didn't have a choice. There was all this undercurrent of social pressure to either fully transition or recant. Looking back, I wish I could have just gone through it without all that pressure."

"Oh, Tesa," Jessie said, stepping forward again and wrapping her in a tight hug. "This is the only pressure you should have to worry about." She hugged her even tighter for emphasis.

Tesa laughed. "True."

Jessie stepped back, a smile on her face. "Better?"

"Yeah."

"I'm glad." She changed holds, looping an arm around Tesa's shoulder. "Now, come on. My sister's supposed to be heading out today. We should see her off."

Tesa nodded as they walked out to the *Trojan*. Most everyone else had already left. Ellie and her crew had left first, the Ateles soldiers uncomfortable with being here during a potential civil war. Next had been the *Discovery* and *Areon*. Victoria was uncomfortable with being around people for that long, so Surg had indulged her.

Now, it was Cass and Kou's turn. Jessie disengaged from Tesa as they reached the ship.

Cass rushed out, dust puffing up around her feet as she stepped off the ramp. "Come here and wish your sister good luck," she said, opening her arms wide.

Jessie smirked and lunged at her, nearly knocking her over.

Cass laughed. "You're a bit big for that, Jess."

Jessie dropped her feet to the ground, continuing the hug on a more relaxed basis as she looked up at Cass. "Didn't want you to forget I'll always be your little sister."

"Oh, I could never forget. God, I still remember when you were like two." Cass's expression grew strained.

Jessie worried that her sister was thinking about when their parents had abandoned them. "Well, things are better now. I mean, you have Kou," she said as the big Ateles softie started walking down the ramp.

Cass looked over her shoulder. "That I do." She looked back at Jessie. "And you have Delyn. Think it's gonna last?"

"Well, I'm hopeful. After all, who would have thought *you* would ever settle for one guy?"

Cass laughed as Kou wrapped an arm around her waist.

"You take care of her, Kou."

He looked at Cass, probably feeling like he'd walked into some sort of trap.

Jessie laughed. "Relax. I don't expect the impossible."

He smiled, then reached over and hugged her, Cass stepping back to let him. "Stay safe, Jessie."

"You, too."

They broke apart, and the couple walked onto the ship, waving constantly until the ramp made it impossible to see. Jessie grabbed Tesa's arm and led them farther away, giving the ship space to launch.

"You going to miss her?" Tesa asked as the engines came to life.

"Every day," Jessie said, watching as the ship lifted off the ground, then flew out of sight.

EPILOGUE

It had been months now since the world had completely changed in a moment. Jessie and Delyn were now living in a building dedicated to tradespeople in Valana. She missed staying in the Farmers' house, but it was nice having a proper place, a place that was theirs, and not feeling like a guest.

They still went there often for meals.

Delyn was running a popular website where he wrote articles unraveling the former administration's secrets, both regarding their history and biology. In no time, it was sponsored by the government. She remembered a broadcast where they'd encouraged people to check it out, stating they wanted to practice a policy of transparency with their people from then on.

Meanwhile, Jessie was working to rebuild her career here on Wesa. It was a different culture, and she wasn't exactly sure how her artistic talents would be best served here, but she was excited to figure it out. Currently, she was painting a mural on the back of the Farmers' house. Faelee had asked her to, saying she wanted something nice to look at while they were in the fields.

Roles around Valana had also become more fluid and flexible. A few people had wanted a change, petitioning for a reassignment, and the Seeder role was all but eradicated. Some still held that role, but it had dwindled significantly, with most people flirting around with the idea of finding a significant other. Carers were still a thing, but Jessie suspected the role would become more like a daycare than a parent in the future. People were showing even more interest in the children, some even talking about how other species raised their own, though no one had really suggested yet that they wanted to do that themselves.

Outside of Valana, a lot had changed as well. The world government had made a lot of promises, and some of them had even come to fruition already. The practice of sending out their Fighters as mercenaries had ended. There was a lot of talk about how that might affect the people. After all, the mercenary business had been a big earner for the government. Would taxes increase? Would services decrease? So far, it was yet to be seen.

They'd also launched a marketing campaign encouraging people to end the drone system. It glossed over the fact that drones grew up faster, a major argument for keeping the practice as it allowed people to be productive members of society faster, and focused on how increased genetic diversity would only benefit the Pardus people as a species.

Every time they saw one of those broadcasts, Delyn would break into a monologue on the benefits of sexual reproduction, making her smile. She loved seeing him so passionate, and she often shut him up with a make-out session on the couch.

Stepping into their room after a long day working on the mural, she smiled at how the room had become their own. Delyn had printouts of research stuck to the wall above his computer desk. Jessie had painted the rest of the walls with murals. Her easel stood in one corner, her drawing tablet and laptop on the bedside table. She'd dropped her pajamas on the floor this morning before heading out.

Jessie sat down on the bed, reaching for the laptop, suddenly having the urge to contact Kaea and thank her. She'd never really become the friend Jessie had initially hoped for, but she couldn't deny the woman had helped change her life for the better. She opened her computer and started writing a message, letting her know how things had gone.

Thank you, Kaea, for hiding me that day. You have no idea how much I appreciate it. I wanted you to know that I'm doing fantastic. I found a great home, a community, and a man who loves me. I couldn't be happier…

Taln stood taller, straightening her uniform as she paused outside Inia Surg's office. It was always a little unnerving to be called into the big boss's office, even more so now that he often wasn't here. After meeting Victoria, he'd let his brother take over much of the operations, allowing him time to be with her.

So nerves and curiosity surged through her as she reached forward to knock on the door to the normally unoccupied office.

"Enter," he said after she'd rapped on it three times.

She opened the door, entering into an opulent space that was clearly intended to impress. She tried to ignore the high end art or fancy furnishings, keeping her chin level to the ground as her steps ate up the distance on the plush carpeting. "Sir," she said as she stopped in front of the guest chairs stationed at his desk, taking a pose with her hands clasped behind her back and her feet shoulder width apart.

"At ease, please," he said with a hand gesture.

She paused for a moment, feeling uncomfortable about relaxing in his presence. She stood that way as much out of nerves as out of respect, and now she wasn't sure how to hold herself.

"I have a new assignment for you, if you're interested. You don't have to take it."

"I'm listening."

"I've been contacted by the Pardus government. They're asking for our assistance with an issue that sprouted up after their recent upheaval. With their global military still not back to normal, they're not in an adequate position to handle it themselves."

"Yes, sir?"

"It seems the Pardus government has broken all ties with the Diehli, and they're concerned about retaliation, especially considering the current state of their military."

Taln froze. She'd helped protect a small community on Wesa just months before. "They were working with the Diehli?"

"Yes, it seems the Diehli was their largest client. They've broken ties mostly because they've shut down their mercenary services. But it also seems the Diehli may have had a pivotal role in choices the Pardus government made after their civil war."

"You're kidding, right?" She'd always known the Diehli was a great, big trash heap of a company, but this seemed insane, even for them. They'd actually played a part in changing the governing policies of an entire planet and species. How was that even possible? That level of power and influence for a mere company was just crazy.

"I'm afraid I'm not. I reassured them that we had a common motivation where the Diehli were concerned, and that we would be willing to help."

"Help what?" she said, the outburst completely out of character. "We've been going at the Diehli for years. We've never made *any* progress."

Surg leaned forward. "I think it's time we changed tactics." He folded his hands together in front of him. "How would you like to help take down the Diehli for good?"

READY FOR MORE?

This series will continue with Taln and Eirse in Shifting Shadows.

Taln and Eirse have been tasked with helping stop the Diehli for good. They arrive at a Diehli research facility, only to find it abandoned… or is it?

Now Available for Pre-Order

DID YOU ENJOY THE BOOK?

Danielle

ALSO BY DANIELLE FORREST

THE DARKEST DAY SERIES

Mila's Flight

Mila's Shift

Tristan's Choice

Terra's Fate

The Darkest Day Collection

A SHIFT IN SPACE SERIES

Shifting Sides

Shifting Cargo

Shifting Loot

Shifting Paradigms

Shifting Tides

Shifting Shadows